No More Parades

No More Parades
Ford Madox Ford

MINT EDITIONS

No More Parades was first published in 1925.

This edition published by Mint Editions 2021.

ISBN 9781513290782 | E-ISBN 9781513293639

Published by Mint Editions®

MINT
EDITIONS

minteditionbooks.com

Publishing Director: Jennifer Newens
Design & Production: Rachel Lopez Metzger
Project Manager: Micaela Clark
Typesetting: Westchester Publishing Services

Contents

PART I

I

When you came in the space was desultory, rectangular, warm after the drip of the winter night, and transfused with a brown-orange dust that was light. It was shaped like the house a child draws. Three groups of brown limbs spotted with brass took dim high-lights from shafts that came from a bucket pierced with holes, filled with incandescent coke, and covered in with a sheet of iron in the shape of a tunnel. Two men, as if hierarchically smaller, crouched on the floor beside the brazier; four, two at each end of the hut, drooped over tables in attitudes of extreme indifference. From the eaves above the parallelogram of black that was the doorway fell intermittent drippings of collected moisture, persistent, with glass-like intervals of musical sound. The two men squatting on their heels over the brazier—they had been miners—began to talk in a low sing-song of dialect, hardly audible. It went on and on, monotonously, without animation. It was as if one told the other long, long stories to which his companion manifested his comprehension or sympathy with animal grunts. . .

An immense tea-tray, august, its voice filling the black circle of the horizon, thundered to the ground. Numerous pieces of sheet-iron said, "Pack. Pack. Pack." In a minute the clay floor of the hut shook, the drums of ears were pressed inwards, solid noise showered about the universe, enormous echoes pushed these men—to the right, to the left, or down towards the tables, and crackling like that of flames among vast underwood became the settled condition of the night. Catching the light from the brazier as the head leaned over, the lips of one of the two men on the floor were incredibly red and full and went on talking and talking. . .

The two men on the floor were Welsh miners, of whom the one came from the Rhondda Valley and was unmarried; the other, from Pontardulais, had a wife who kept a laundry, he having given up going underground just before the war. The two men a the table to the right of the door were sergeants-major; the one came from Suffolk and was a time-serving man of sixteen years' seniority as a sergeant in a line regiment. The other was Canadian of English origin. The two officers at the other end of the hut were captains, the one a young regular officer born in Scotland but educated at Oxford; the other, nearly middle-aged and heavy, came from Yorkshire, and was in a militia battalion. The one runner on the floor was filled with a passionate rage because the elder officer had refused him leave to go home and see why his wife, who had sold their laundry, had not yet received the purchase money from the buyer; the other was thinking about a cow. His girl, who worked on a mountainy farm above Caerphilly, had written to him about a queer cow: a black-and-white Holstein— surely to goodness a queer cow. The English sergeant-major was almost tearfully worried about the enforced lateness of the draft. It would be twelve midnight before they could march them off. It was not right to keep men hanging about like that. The men did not like to be kept waiting, hanging about. It made them discontented. They did not like it. He could not see why the depot quarter-master could not keep up his stock of candles for the hooded lamps. The men had no call to be kept waiting, hanging about. Soon they would have to be having some supper. Quarter would not like that. He would grumble fair. Having to indent for suppers. Put his account out, fair, it would. Two thousand nine hundred and ninety-four suppers at a penny half-penny. But it was not right to keep the men hanging about till midnight and no suppers. It made them discontented and them going up the line for the first time, poor devils.

The Canadian sergeant-major was worried about a pigskin leather pocket-book. He had bought it at the ordnance depot in the town. He imagined himself bringing it out on parade, to read out some return or other to the adjutant. Very smart it would look on parade, himself standing up straight and tall. But he could not remember whether he had put it in his kitbag. On himself it was not. He felt in his right and left breast pockets, his right and left skirt pockets, in all the pockets of his overcoat that hung from a nail within reach of his chair. He did not feel at all certain that the man who acted as his batman had packed that pocket-book with his kit, though he declared he had. It was very annoying. His present wallet, bought in Ontario, was bulging and split. He did not like to bring it out when Imperial officers asked for something out of a return. It gave them a false idea of Canadian troops. Very annoying. He was an auctioneer. He agreed that at this rate it would be half-past one before they had the draft down to the station and entrained. But it was very annoying to be uncertain whether that pocket-book was packed or not. He had imagined himself making a good impression on parade, standing up straight and tall, taking out that pocket-book when the adjutant asked for a figure from one return or the other. He understood their adjutants were to be Imperial officers now they were in France. It was very annoying.

An enormous crashing sound said things of an intolerable intimacy to each of those men, and to all of them as a body. After its mortal vomiting all the other sounds appeared a rushing silence, painful to ears in which the blood audibly coursed. The young officer stood violently up on his feet and caught at the complications of his belt hung from a nail. The elder, across the table, lounging sideways, stretched out one hand with a downward movement. He was aware that the younger man, who was the senior officer, was just upon out of his mind. The younger man, intolerably fatigued, spoke sharp, injurious, inaudible words to his companion. The elder spoke sharp, short words, inaudible too, and continued to motion downwards with his hand over the table. The old English sergeant-major said to his junior that Captain Mackenzie had one of his mad fits again, but what he said was inaudible and he knew it. He felt arising in his motherly heart that yearned at the moment over his two thousand nine hundred and thirty-four nurslings a necessity, like a fatigue, to extend the motherliness of his functions to the orfcer. He said to the Canadian that Captain Mackenzie there going temporary off his nut was the best orfcer in His Majesty's army. And going to make a bleedin' fool of hisself. The best orfcer in His Majesty's army. Not a better. Careful, smart, brave as a 'ero. And considerate of his men in the line. You wouldn't believe. . . He felt vaguely that it was a fatigue to have to mother an officer. To a lance-corporal, or a young sergeant, beginning to go wrong you could mutter wheezy suggestions through your moustache. But to an officer you had to say things slantways. Difficult it was. Thank God they had a trustworthy cool hand in the other captain. Old and good, the proverb said.

Dead silence fell.

"Lost the ——," they "aye," the runner from the Rhondda made his voice startlingly heard. Brilliant illuminations flickered on hut-gables visible through the doorway.

"No reason," his mate from Pontardulais rather whined in his native sing-song, "why the bleedin" searchlights, surely to goodness, should light us up for all the —— "Un planes to see. I want to see my bleedin' little 'ut on the bleedin' Mumbles again, if they don't."

"Not so much swear words, 0 Nine Morgan," the sergeant-major said.

"Now, Dai Morgan, I'm telling you," 09 Morgan's mate continued. "A queer cow it must have been whatever. Black-and-white Holstein it wass. . .

It was as if the younger captain gave up listening to the conversation. He leant both hands on the blanket that covered the table. He exclaimed:

"Who the hell are you to give me orders? I'm your senior. Who the hell. . . Oh, by God, who the hell. . . Nobody gives me orders. . ." His voice collapsed weakly in his chest. He felt his nostrils to be inordinately dilated so that the air pouring into them was cold. He felt that there was an entangled conspiracy against him, and all round him. He exclaimed: "You and your —— pimp of a general. . . !" He desired to cut certain throats with a sharp trench-knife that he had. That would take the weight off his chest. The "Sit down" of the heavy figure lumping opposite him paralysed his limbs. He felt an unbelievable hatred. If he could move his hand to get at his trench-knife. . .

09 Morgan said: "The ——'s name who's bought my bleedin' laundry is Williams. . . If I thought it was Evans Williams of Castell Goch, I'd desert."

"Took a hatred for it cawve," the Rhondda man said. "And look you, before you could say. . ." The conversation of orfcers was a thing to which they neither listened. Officers talked of things that had no interest. Whatever could possess a cow to take a hatred of its calf? Up behind Caerphilly on the mountains? On an autumny morning the whole hillside was covered with spider-webs. They shone down the sun like spun glass. Overlooked the cow must be.

The young captain leaning over the table began a long argument as to relative seniority. He argued with himself, taking both sides in an extraordinarily rapid gabble. He himself had been gazetted after Gheluvelt. The other not till a year later. It was true the other was in permanent command of that depot, and he himself attached to the unit only for rations and discipline. But that did not include orders to sit down. What the hell, he wanted to know, did the other mean by it? He began to talk, faster than ever, about a circle. When its circumference came whole by the disintegration of the atom the world would some to an end. In the millennium there would be no giving or taking orders. Of course he obeyed orders till then.

To the elder officer, burdened with the command of a unit of unreasonable size, with a scratch headquarters of useless subalterns who were continually being changed, with N.C.O.'s all unwilling to work, with rank and file nearly all colonials and unused to doing without things, and with a depot to draw on that, being old established, felt that it belonged exclusively to a regular British unit and resented his drawing anything at all, the practical difficulties of his everyday life were already sufficient, and he had troublesome private affairs. He was lately out of hospital; the sackcloth hut in which he lived, borrowed from the Depot medical officer who had gone to England on leave, was suffocatingly hot with the paraffin heater going, and intolerably cold and damp without it; the batman whom the M.O. had left in charge of the hut appeared to be half-witted. These German air-raids had lately become continuous. The Base was packed with men, tighter than sardines. Down in the town you could not move in the streets. Draft-finding units were commanded to keep their men out of sight as much as possible. Drafts were to be sent off only at night. But how could you send off a draft at night when every ten minutes you had two hours of lights out for an air-raid? Every man had nine sets of papers and tags that had to be signed by an officer. It was quite proper that the poor devils should be properly documented. But how was it to be done? He had two thousand nine hundred and ninety-four men to send off that night and nine times two thousand nine hundred and ninety-four is twenty-six thousand nine hundred and forty-six. They would not or could not let him have a disc-punching machine of his own, but how was the Depot armourer to be expected to punch five thousand nine hundred and eighty-eight extra identity discs in addition to his regular jobs?

The other captain rambled on in front of him. Tietjens did not like his talk of the circle and the millennium. You get alarmed, if you have any sense, when you hear that. It may prove the beginnings of definite, dangerous lunacy. . . But he knew nothing about the fellow. He was too dark and good-looking, too passionate, probably, to be a good regular officer on the face of him. But he *must* be a good officer: he had the D.S.O. with a clasp, the M.C., and some foreign ribbon up. And the general said he was: with the additional odd piece of information that he was a Vice-Chancellor's Latin Prize man. . . He wondered if General Campion knew what a Vice-Chancellor's Latin Prize man was. Probably he did not, but had just stuck the piece of information into his note as a barbaric ornament is used by a savage chief. Wanted to show that he, General Lord Edward Campion, was a man of culture. There was no knowing where vanity would not break out.

So this fellow was too dark and good-looking to be a good officer: yet he was a good officer. That explained it. The repressions of the passionate drive them mad. He must have been being sober, disciplined, patient, absolutely repressed ever since 1914—against a background of hell-fire, row, blood, mud, old tins. . . And indeed the elder officer had a vision of the younger as if in a design for a full-length portrait— for some reason with his legs astride, against a background of tapestry scarlet with fire and more scarlet with blood. . . He sighed a little; that was the life of all those several millions. . .

He seemed to see his draft: two thousand nine hundred and ninety-four men he had had command of for over a couple of months—a long space of time as that life went—men he and Sergeant-Major Cowley had looked after with a great deal of tenderness, superintending their morale; their morals, their feet, their digestions, their impatiences, their desires for women. . . He seemed to see them winding away over a great stretch of country, the head slowly settling down, as in the Zoo you will see an enormous serpent slowly sliding into its water-tank. . . Settling down out there, a long way away, up against that impassable barrier that stretched from the depths of the ground to the peak of heaven. . .

Intense dejection: endless muddles: endless follies: endless villainies. All these men given into the hands of the most cynically care-free intriguers in long corridors who made plots that harrowed the hearts of the world. All these men toys: all these agonies mere occasions for picturesque phrases to be put into politicians' speeches without heart or even intelligence. Hundreds of thousands of men tossed here and there in that sordid and gigantic mud-brownness of mid-winter. . . By God, exactly as if they were nuts wilfully picked up and thrown over the shoulder by magpies. . . But men. Not just populations. Men you worried over there. Each man a man with a backbone, knees, breeches, braces, a rifle, a home, passions, fornications, drunks, pals, some scheme of the universe, corns, inherited diseases, a greengrocer's business, a milk walk, a paper stall, brats, a slut of a wife. . . The Men: the Other Ranks! And the poor —— little officers. God help them. Vice-Chancellor's Latin Prize men. . .

This particular poor —— Prize man seemed to object to noise. They ought to keep the place quiet for him. . .

By God, he was perfectly right. That place was meant for the quiet and orderly preparation of meat for the shambles. Drafts! A Base is a place where you meditate: perhaps you should pray: a place where in peace the Tommies should write their last letters home and describe 'ow the guns are 'owling 'orribly.

But to pack a million and a half of men into and round that small town was like baiting a trap for rats with a great chunk of rotten meat. The Hun planes could smell them from a hundred miles away. They could do more harm there than if they bombed a quarter of London to pieces. And the air defences there were a joke: a mad joke. They popped off, thousands of rounds, from any sort of pieces of ordnance, like schoolboys bombarding swimming rats with stones. Obviously your best-trained air-defence men would be round your metropolis. But this was no joke for the sufferers.

Heavy depression settled down more heavily upon him. The distrust of the home Cabinet, felt by then by the greater part of that army, became like physical pain. These immense sacrifices, this ocean of mental sufferings, were all undergone to further the private vanities of men who amidst these hugenesses of landscapes and forces appeared pygmies! It was the worries of all these wet millions in mud-brown that worried him. They could die, they could be massacred, by the quarter million, in shambles. But that they should be massacred without jauntiness, without confidence, with depressed brows: without parade. . .

He knew really nothing about the officer in front of him. Apparently the fellow had stopped for an answer to some question. What question? Tietjens had no idea. He had not been listening. Heavy silence settled down on the hut. They just waited. The fellow said with an intonation of hatred:

"Well, what about it? That's what I want to know!"

Tietjens went on reflecting. . . There were a great many kinds of madness. What kind was this? The fellow was not drunk. He talked like a drunkard, but he was not drunk. In ordering him to sit down Tietjens had just chanced it. There are madmen whose momentarily subconscious selves will respond to a military command as if it were magic. Tietjens remembered having barked: "About. . . turn," to a poor little lunatic fellow in some camp at home and the fellow who had been galloping hotfoot past his tent, waving a naked bayonet with his pursuers fifty yards behind, had stopped dead and faced about with a military stamp like a guardsman. He had tried it on this lunatic for want of any better expedient. It had apparently functioned intermittently. He risked saying:

"What about what?"

The man said as if ironically:

"It seems as if I were not worth listening to by your high and mightiness. I said: 'What about my foul squit of an uncle?' Your filthy, best friend."

Tietjens said:

"The general's your uncle? General Campion? What's he done to you?"

The general had sent this fellow down to him with a note asking him, Tietjens, to keep an eye in his unit on a very good fellow and an admirable officer. The chit was in the general's own writing, and contained the additional information as to Captain Mackenzie's scholastic prowess. . . It had struck Tietjens as queer that the general should take so much trouble about a casual infantry company commander. How could the fellow have been brought markedly to his notice? Of course, Campion was good-natured, like another man. If a fellow, half dotty, whose record showed that he was a very good man, was brought to his notice Campion would do what he could for him. And Tietjens knew that the general regarded himself, Tietjens, as a heavy, bookish fellow, able reliably to look after one of his protégés. . . Probably Campion imagined that they had no work to do in that unit: they might become an acting lunatic ward. But if Mackenzie was Campion's nephew the thing was explained.

The lunatic exclaimed:

"Campion, *my* uncle? Why, he's *yours!*"

Tietjens said:

"Oh no, he isn't." The general was not even a connection of his, but he did happen to be Tietjens' godfather and his father's oldest friend.

The other fellow answered:

"Then it's damn funny. *Damn* suspicious. . . Why should he be so interested in you if he's not your filthy uncle? You're no soldier. . . You're no sort of a soldier. . . A meal sack, that's what you look like. . ." He paused and then went on very quickly: "They say up at H.Q. that your wife has got hold of the disgusting general. I didn't believe it was true. I didn't believe you were that sort of fellow. I've heard a lot about you!"

Tietjens laughed at this madness. Then, in the dark brownness, an intolerable pang went all through his heavy frame—the intolerable pang of home news to these desperately occupied men, the pain caused by disasters happening in the darkness and at a distance. You could do nothing to mitigate them! . . . The extraordinary beauty of the wife from whom he was separated—for she was extraordinarily beautiful!—

might well have caused scandals about her to have penetrated to the general's headquarters, which was a sort of family party! Hitherto there had, by the grace of God, been no scandals. Sylvia Tietjens had been excruciatingly unfaithful, in the most painful manner. He could not be certain that the child he adored was his own. . . That was not unusual with extraordinarily beautiful—and cruel!—women. But she had been haughtily circumspect.

Nevertheless, three months ago, they had parted. . . Or he thought they had parted. Almost complete blankness had descended upon his home life. She appeared before him so extraordinarily bright and clear in the brown darkness that he shuddered: very tall, very fair, extraordinarily fit and clean even. Thoroughbred! In a sheath gown of gold tissue, all illuminated, and her mass of hair, like gold tissue too, coiled round and round in plaits over her ears. The features very clean-cut and thinnish; the teeth white and small; the breasts small; the arms thin, long and at attention at her sides. . . His eyes, when they were tired, had that trick of reproducing images on their retinas with that extreme clearness, images sometimes of things he thought of, sometimes of things merely at the back of the mind. Well, tonight his eyes were very tired! She was looking straight before her, with a little inimical disturbance of the corners of her lips. She had just thought of a way to hurt terribly his silent personality. . . The semi-clearness became a luminous blue, like a tiny gothic arch, and passed out of his vision to the right. . .

He knew nothing of where Sylvia was. He had given up looking at the illustrated papers. She had said she was going into a convent at Birkenhead—but twice he had seen photographs of her. The first showed her merely with Lady Fiona Grant, daughter of the Earl and Countess of Ulleswater—and a Lord Swindon, talked of as next minister for International Finance—a new Business Peer. . . All three walking straight into the camera in the courtyard of Lord Swindon's castle. . . all three smiling! . . . It announced Mrs. Christopher Tietjens as, having a husband at the front.

The sting had, however, been in the second picture—in the description of it supplied by the journal! It showed Sylvia standing in front of a bench in the park. On the bench in profile there extended himself in a guffaw of laughter, a young man in a top hat jammed well on to his head, which was thrown back, his prognathous jaw pointing upwards. The description stated that the picture showed Mrs. Christopher Tietjens, whose husband was in hospital at the Front, telling a good story to the son and heir of Lord Birgham! Another of these pestilential, crooked newspaper-owning financial peers. . .

It had struck him for a painful moment whilst looking at the picture in a dilapidated mess anteroom after he had come out of hospital—that, considering the description, the journal had got its knife into Sylvia. . . But the illustrated papers do not get their knives into society beauties. They are too precious to the photographers. . . Then Sylvia must have supplied the information; she desired to cause comment by the contrast of her hilarious companions and the statement that her husband was in hospital at the Front. . . It had occurred to him that she was on the warpath. But he had put it out of his mind. . . Nevertheless, brilliant mixture as she was, of the perfectly straight, perfectly fearless, perfectly reckless, of the generous, the kind even—and the atrociously cruel, nothing might suit her better than positively to show contempt—no, no contempt! cynical hatred—for her husband, for the war, for public opinion. . . even for the interest of their child! Yet, it came to him, the image of her that he had just seen had been the image of Sylvia, standing at attention, her mouth working a little, whilst she read out the figures beside the bright filament of mercury in a thermometer. . . The child had had, with measles, a temperature that, even then, he did not dare think of. And—it was at his sister's in Yorkshire, and the local doctor hadn't cared to take the responsibility—he could still feel the warmth of the little mummy-like body; he had covered the head and face with a flannel, for he didn't care for the sight, and lowered the warm, terrible, fragile weight into a shining surface of crushed ice in water. . . She had stood at attention, the corners of her mouth moving a little: the thermometer going down as you watched it. . . So that she mightn't want, in damaging the father, atrociously to damage the child. . . For there could not be anything worse for a child than to have a mother known as a whore. . .

Sergeant-Major Cowley was standing beside the table. He said:

"Wouldn't it be a good thing, sir, to send a runner to the depot sergeant cook and tell him we're going to indent for suppers for the draft? We could send the other with the 128's to Quarter. They're neither wanted here for the moment."

The other captain went on incessantly talking—but about his fabulous uncle, not about Sylvia. It was difficult for Tietjens to get what he wanted said. He wanted the second runner sent to the depot quartermaster with a message to the effect that if G.S. candles for hooded lamps were not provided for the use of his orderly room by return of bearer he, Captain Tietjens, commanding Number XVI Casual Battalion, would bring the whole matter of supplies for his battalion that same night before Base Headquarters. They were all three talking at once: heavy fatalism overwhelmed Tietjens at the thought of the stubbornness showed by the depot quartermaster. The big unit beside his camp was a weary obstinacy of obstruction. You would have thought they would have displayed some eagerness to get his men up into the line. Let alone that the men were urgently needed, the more of his men went the more of *them* stayed behind. Yet they tried to stop his meat, his groceries, his braces, his identification discs, his soldiers' small books. . . Every imaginable hindrance, and not even self-interested common sense! . . . He managed also to convey to Sergeant-Major Cowley that, as everything seemed to have quieted down, the Canadian sergeant-major had better go and see if everything was ready for falling his draft in. . . If things remained quiet for another ten minutes, the "All Clear" might then be expected. . . He knew that Sergeant-Major Cowley wanted to get the Other Ranks out of the hut with that captain carrying on like that, and he did not see why the old N.C.O. should not have what he wanted.

It was as if a tender and masculine butler withdrew himself. Cowley's grey walrus moustache and scarlet cheeks showed for a moment beside the brazier, whispering at the ears of the runners, a hand kindly on each of their shoulders. The runners went; the Canadian went. Sergeant-Major Cowley, his form blocking the doorway, surveyed the stars. He found it difficult to realize that the same pinpricks of light through black manifolding paper as he looked at, looked down also on his villa and his elderly wife at Isleworth beside the Thames above London. He knew it to be the fact, yet it was difficult to realize. He imagined the trams going along the High Street, his missus in one of them with her supper in a string bag on her stout knees. The trams lit up and shining. He imagined her having kippers for supper: ten to one it would be kippers. Her favourites. His daughter was in the W.A.A.C.'s by now. She had been cashier to Parks's, the big butchers in Brent-ford, and pretty she had used to look in the glass case. Like as if it might have been the British Museum where they had Pharaohs and others in glass cases. . . There were threshing machines droning away all over the night. He always said they were like threshing machines. . . Crikey, if only they were! . . . But they might be our own planes, of course. A good welsh rarebit he had had for tea.

In the hut, the light from the brazier having fewer limbs on which to fall, a sort of intimacy seemed to descend, and Tietjens felt himself gain in ability to deal with his mad friend. Captain Mackenzie—Tietjens was not sure that the name was Mackenzie: it had looked something like it in the general's hand—Captain Mackenzie was going on about the wrongs he had suffered at the hands of some fabulous uncle. Apparently at some important juncture the uncle had refused to acknowledge acquaintanceship with the nephew. From that all the misfortunes of the nephew had arisen. . . Suddenly Tietjens said:

"Look here, pull yourself together. Are you mad? Stark, staring? . . . Or only just play-acting?"

The man suddenly sank down on to the bully-beef case that served for a chair. He stammered a question as to what—what—what Tietjens meant.

"If you let yourself go," Tietjens said, "you may let yourself go a tidy sight farther than you want to."

"You're not a mad doctor," the other said. "It's no good your trying to come it over me. I know all about you. I've got an uncle who's done the dirty on me—the dirtiest dirty ever was done on a man. If it hadn't been for him I shouldn't be here now."

"You talk as if the fellow had sold you into slavery," Tietjens said.

"He's your closest friend," Mackenzie seemed to advance as a motive for revenge on Tietjens. "He's a friend of the general's, too. Of your wife's as well. He's in with every one."

A few desultory, pleasurable "pop-op-ops" sounded from far overhead to the left.

"They imagine they've found the Hun again," Tietjens said. "That's all right; you concentrate on your uncle. Only don't exaggerate his importance to the world. I assure you you are mistaken if you call him a friend of mine. I have not got a friend in the world." He added: "Are you going to mind the noise? If it is going to get on your nerves you can walk in a dignified manner to a dugout, now, before it gets bad. . ." He called out to Cowley to go and tell the Canadian sergeant-major to get his men back into their shelters if they had come out. Until the "All Clear" went.

Captain Mackenzie sat himself gloomily down at table.

"Damn it all," he said, "don't think I'm afraid of a little shrapnel. I've had two periods solid of fourteen and nine months in the line. I could have got out on to the rotten staff. . . It's damn it: it's the beastly row. . . Why isn't one a beastly girl and privileged to shriek? By God, I'll get even with some of them one of these days. . ."

"Why not shriek?" Tietjens asked. "You can, for me. No one's going to doubt your courage here."

Loud drops of rain spattered down all round the hut; there was a familiar thud on the ground a yard or so away, a sharp tearing sound above, a sharper knock on the table between them. Mackenzie took the shrapnel bullet that had fallen and turned it round and round between finger and thumb.

"You think you caught me on the hop just now," he said injuriously. "You're damn clever."

Two stories down below someone let two hundred-pound dumb-bells drop on the drawing-room carpet; all the windows of the house slammed in a race to get it over; the "pop-op-ops" of the shrapnel went in wafts all over the air. There was again sudden silence that was painful, after you had braced yourself up to bear noise. The runner from the Rhondda came in with a light step bearing two fat candles. He took the hooded lamps from Tietjens and began to press the candles up against the inner springs, snorting sedulously through his nostrils. . .

"Nearly got me, one of those candlesticks did," he said. "Touched my foot as it fell, it did. I did run. Surely to goodness I did run, cahptn."

Inside the shrapnel shell was an iron bar with a flattened, broad nose. When the shell burst in the air this iron object fell to the ground and, since it came often from a great height, its fall was dangerous. The men called these candlesticks, which they much resembled.

A little ring of light now existed on the puce colour of the blanket-covered table. Tietjens showed, silver-headed, fresh-coloured, and bulky; Mackenzie, dark, revengeful eyes above a prognathous jaw. A very thin man, thirtyish.

"You can go into the shelter with the Colonial troops, if you like," Tietjens said to the runner. The man answered after a pause, being very slow thinking, that he preferred to wait for his mate, 09 Morgan whatever.

"They ought to let my orderly room have tin hats," Tietjens said to Mackenzie. "I'm damned if they didn't take these fellows' tin hats into store again when they attached to me for service, and I'm equally damned if they did not tell me that, if I wanted tin hats for my own headquarters, I had to write to H.Q. Canadians, Aldershot, or some such place in order to get the issue sanctioned."

"Our headquarters are full of Huns doing the Huns' work," Mackenzie said hatefully. "I'd like to get among them one of these days."

Tietjens looked with some attention at that young man with the Rembrandt shadows over his dark face. He said: "Do you believe that tripe?"

The young man said:

"No. . . I don't know that I do. . . I don't know what to think. . . The world's rotten. . .

"Oh, the world's pretty rotten, all right," Tietjens answered. And, in his fatigue of mind caused by having to attend to innumerable concrete facts like the providing of households for a thousand men every few days, arranging parades states for an extraordinarily mixed set of troops of all arms with very mixed drills, and fighting the Assistant Provost Marshal to keep his own men out of the clutches of the beastly Garrison Military Police who had got a down on all Canadians, he felt he had not any curiosity at all left. . . Yet he felt vaguely that, at the back of his mind, there was some reason for trying to cure this young member of the lower middle classes.

He repeated:

"Yes, the world's certainly pretty rotten. But that's not its particular line of rottenness as far as we are concerned. . . We're tangled up, not because we've got Huns in our orderly rooms, but just because we've got English. That's the bat in our belfry. . . That Hun plane is presumably coming back. Half a dozen of them. . ."

The young man, his mind eased by having got off his chest a confounded lot of semi-nonsensical ravings, considered the return of the Hun planes with gloomy indifference. His problem really was: could he stand the —— noise that would probably accompany their return? He had to get really into his head that this was an open space to all intents and purposes. There would not be splinters of stone flying about. He was ready to be hit by iron, steel, lead, copper, or brass shell rims, but not by beastly splinters of stone knocked off house fronts. That consideration had come to him during his beastly, his beastly, his infernal, damnable leave in London, when just such a filthy row had been going on. . . Divorce leave! . . . Captain McKechnie second attached ninth Glamorganshires is granted leave from the 14/11 to the 29/11 for the purpose of obtaining a divorce. . . The memory seemed to burst inside him with the noise of one of those beastly enormous tin-pot crashes—and it always came when guns made that particular kind of tin-pot crash: the two came together, the internal one and the crash outside. He felt that chimney-pots were going to crash on to his head. You protected yourself by shouting at damned infernal idiots; if you could out-shout the row you were safe. . . That was not sensible but you got ease that way! . . .

"In matters of Information they're not a patch on us." Tietjens tried the speech on cautiously and concluded: "We know what the Enemy rulers read in the sealed envelopes beside their breakfast bacon-and-egg plates."

It had occurred to him that it was a military duty to bother himself about the mental equilibrium of this member of the lower classes. So he talked. . . *any* old talk, wearisomely, to keep his mind employed! Captain Mackenzie was an officer of His Majesty the King: the property, body and soul, of His Majesty and His Majesty's War Office. It was Tietjens' duty to preserve this fellow as it was his duty to prevent deterioration in any other piece of the King's property. That was implicit in the oath of allegiance. He went on talking:

The curse of the army, as far as the organization is concerned, was our imbecile national belief that the game is more than the player. That was our ruin, mentally, as a nation. We were taught that cricket is more than clearness of mind, so the blasted quarter-master, O.C. Depot Ordnance Stores next door, thought he had taken a wicket if he refused to serve out tin hats to their crowd. That's the Game! And if any of his, Tietjens', men were killed, he grinned and said the game was more than the players of the game. . . And of course if he got his bowling average down low enough he got promotion. There was a quartermaster in a west country cathedral city who'd got more D.S.O.'s and combatant medals than anyone on active service in France, from the sea to Peronne, or wherever our lines ended. His achievement was to have robbed almost every wretched Tommie in the Western Command of several weeks' separation allowance. . . for the good of the taxpayer, of course. The poor —— Tommies' kids went without proper food and clothing, and the Tommies themselves had been in a state of exasperation and resentment. And nothing in the world was worse for discipline and the army as a fighting machine. But there that quartermaster sat in his office, playing the romantic game over his A.F.B.'s till the broad buff sheets fairly glowed in the light of the incandescent gas. "And," Tietjens concluded, "for every quarter of a million sterling for which he bowls out the wretched fighting men he gets a new clasp on his fourth D.S.O. ribbon. . . The game, in short, is more than the players of the game."

"Oh, damn it!" Captain Mackenzie said. "That's what's made us what we are, isn't it?"

"It is," Tietjens answered. "It's got us into the hole and it keeps us there."

Mackenzie remained dispiritedly looking down at his fingers.

"You may be wrong or you may be right," he said. "It's contrary to everything that I ever heard. But I see what you mean."

"At the beginning of the war," Tietjens said, "I had to look in on the War Office, and in a room I found a fellow. . . What do you think he was doing. . . what the hell do you think he was doing? He was devising the ceremonial for the disbanding of a Kitchener battalion. You can't say we were not prepared in one matter at least. . . Well, the end of the show was to be: the adjutant would stand the battalion at ease: the band would play *Land of Hope and Glory*, and then the adjutant would say: *There will be no more parades*. . . Don't you see how symbolical it was: the band playing *Land of Hope and Glory*, and then the adjutant saying *There will be no more parades*? . . . For there won't. There won't, there damn well won't. . . No more Hope, no more Glory, no more parades for you and me any more. Nor for the country. . . Nor for the world, I dare say. . . None. . . Gone. . . Na poo, finny! No. . . more. . . parades!"

"I dare say you're right," the other said slowly. "But, all the same, what am I doing in this show? I hate soldiering. I hate this whole beastly business. . ."

"Then why didn't you go on the gaudy Staff?" Tietjens asked. The gaudy Staff apparently was yearning to have you. I bet God intended you for Intelligence: not for the footslogging department."

The other said wearily:

"I don't know. I was with the battalion. I wanted to stop with the battalion. I was intended for the Foreign Office. My miserable uncle got me hoofed out of that. I was with the battalion. The C.O. wasn't up to much. *Someone* had to stay with the battalion. I was not going to do the dirty on it, taking any soft job. . ."

"I suppose you speak seven languages and all?" Tietjens asked.

"Five," the other said patiently, "and read two more. And Latin and Greek, of course."

A man, brown, stiff, with a haughty parade step, burst into the light. He said with a high wooden voice:

"Ere's another bloomin' casualty." In the shadow he appeared to have draped half his face and the right side of his breast with crape. He gave a high, rattling laugh. He bent, as if in a stiff bow, woodenly at his thighs. He pitched, still bent, on to the iron sheet that covered the brazier, rolled off that and lay on his back across the legs of the other runner, who had been crouched beside the brazier. In the bright light it was as if a whole pail of scarlet paint had been dashed across the man's face on the left and his chest. It glistened in the firelight—just like fresh paint, moving! The runner from the Rhondda, pinned down by the body across his knees, sat with his jaw fallen, resembling one girl that should be combing the hair of another recumbent before her. The red viscousness welled across the floor; you sometimes so see fresh water bubbling up in sand. It astonished Tietjens to see that a human body could be so lavish of blood. He was thinking it was a queer mania that that fellow should have, that his uncle was a friend of his, Tietjens. He had no friend in trade, uncle of a fellow who in ordinary times would probably bring you pairs of boots on approval. . . He felt as he did when you patch up a horse that has been badly hurt. He remembered a horse from a cut on whose chest the blood had streamed down over the off foreleg like a stocking. A girl had lent him her petticoat to bandage it. Nevertheless his legs moved slowly and heavily across the floor.

The heat from the brazier was overpowering on his bent face. He hoped he would not get his hands all over blood, because blood is very sticky. It makes your fingers stick together impotently. But there might not be any blood in the darkness under the fellow's back where he was putting his hand. There was, however: it was very wet.

The voice of Sergeant-Major Cowley said from outside:

"Bugler, call two sanitary lance-corporals and four men. Two sanitary corporals and four men." A prolonged wailing with interruptions transfused the night, mournful, resigned, and prolonged.

Tietjens thought that, thank God, someone would come and relieve him of that job. It was a breathless affair holding up the corpse with the fire burning his face. He said to the other runner:

"Get out from under him, damn you! Are you hurt?" Mackenzie could not get at the body from the other side because of the brazier. The runner from under the corpse moved with short sitting shuffles as if he were getting his legs out from under a sofa. He was saying:

"Poor —— 0 Nine Morgan! Surely to goodness I did not recognice the pore ——. Surely to goodness I did not recognice the pore ——"

Tietjens let the trunk of the body sink slowly to the floor. He was more gentle than if the man had been alive. All hell in the way of noise burst about the world. Tietjens' thoughts seemed to have to shout to him between earthquake shocks. He was thinking it was absurd of that fellow Mackenzie to imagine that he could know any uncle of his. He saw very vividly also the face of his girl who was a pacifist. It worried him not to know what expression her face would have if she heard of his occupation, now. Disgust? . . . He was standing with his greasy, sticky hands held out from the flaps of his tunic. . . Perhaps disgust! . . . It was impossible to think in this row. . . His very thick soles moved gluily and came up after suction. . . He remembered he had not sent a runner along to I.B.D. Orderly Room to see how many of his crowd would be wanted for garrison fatigue next day, and this annoyed him acutely. He would have no end of a job warning the officers he detailed. They would all be in brothels down in the town by now. . . He could not work out what the girl's expression would be. He was never to see her again, so what the hell did it matter? . . . Disgust, probably! . . . He remembered that he had not looked to see how Mackenzie was getting on in the noise. He did not want to see Mackenzie. He was a bore. . . How would her face express disgust? He had never seen her express disgust. She had a perfectly undistinguished face. Fair. . . 0 God, how suddenly his bowels turned over! . . . Thinking of the girl. . . The face below him grinned at the roof—the half face! The nose was there, half the mouth with the teeth showing in the firelight. . . It was extraordinary how defined the peaked nose and the serrated teeth were in that mess. . . The eye looked jauntily at the peak of the canvas hut-roof. . . Gone with a grin. Singular the fellow should have spoken! After he was dead. He must have been dead when he spoke. It had been done with the last air automatically going out of the lungs. A reflex action, probably, in the dead. . . If he, Tietjens, had given the fellow the leave he wanted would be alive now!

Well, he was quite right not to have given the poor devil his leave. He was, anyhow, better where he was. And so was he, Tietjens. He had not had a single letter from home since he had been out this time! Not a single letter. Not even gossip. Not a bill. Some circulars of old furniture dealers. They never neglected him! They had got beyond the sentimental stage at home. Obviously so. . . He wondered if his bowels would turn over again if he thought of the girl. He was gratified that they had. It showed that he had strong feelings. . . He thought about her deliberately. Hard. Nothing happened. He thought of her fair, undistinguished, fresh face that made your heart miss a beat when you thought about it. His heart missed a beat. Obedient heart! Like the first primrose. Not any primrose. The first primrose. Under a bank with the hounds breaking through the underwood. . . It was sentimental to say Du bist wie eine Blume Damn the German language! But that fellow was a Jew. . . One should not say that one's young woman was like a flower, any flower. Not even to oneself. That was sentimental. But one might say one special flower. A man could say that. A man's job. She smelt like a primrose when you kissed her. But, damn it, he had never kissed her. So how did he know how she smelt! She was a little tranquil, golden spot. He himself must be a—eunuch. By temperament. That dead fellow down there must be one, physically. It was probably indecent to think of a corpse as impotent. But he was, very likely. That would be why his wife had taken up with the prize-fighter Red Evans Williams of Castell Goch. If he had given the fellow leave the prize-fighter would have smashed him to bits. The police of Pontardulais had asked that he should not be let come home—because of the prize-fighter. So he was better dead. Or perhaps not. Is death better than discovering that your wife is a whore and being done in by her cully? *Gwell angau na gwillth*, their own regimental badge bore the words. "*Death is better than dishonour*" . . . No, not death, *angau* means pain. Anguish! Anguish is better than dishonour. The devil it is! Well, that fellow would have got both. Anguish and dishonour. Dishonour from his wife and anguish when the prize-fighter hit him That was no doubt why his half-face grinned at the roof. The gory side of it had turned brown. Already! Like a mummy of a Pharaoh, *that* half looked. . . He was born to be a blooming casualty. Either by shell-fire or by the fist of the prize-fighter. . . Pontardulais I Somewhere in Mid-Wales. He had been through it once in a car, on duty. A long, dull village. Why should anyone want to go back to it? . . .

A tender butler's voice said beside him: "This isn't your job, sir. Sorry you had to do it. . . Lucky it wasn't you, sir. . . This was what done it, I should say."

Sergeant-Major Cowley was standing beside him holding a bit of metal that was heavy in his hand and like a candlestick. He was aware that a moment before he had seen the fellow, Mackenzie, bending over the brazier, putting the sheet of iron back. Careful officer, Mackenzie. The Huns must not be allowed to see the light from the brazier. The edge of the sheet had gone down on the dead man's tunic, nipping a bit by the shoulder. The face had disappeared in shadow. There were several men's faces in the doorway.

Tietjens said: "No: I don't believe that did it. Something bigger. . . Say a prize-fighter's fist. . ."

Sergeant-Major Cowley said:

"No, no prize-fighter's fist would have done that, sir." And then he added, "Oh, I take your meaning, sir. Nine Morgan's wife, sir. . ."

Tietjens moved, his feet sticking, towards the sergeant-major's table. The other runner had placed a tin basin with water in it. There was a hooded candle there now, alight; the water shone innocently, a half-moon of translucence wavering over the white bottom of the basin. The runner from Pontardulais said:

"Wash your hands first, sir!"

He said:

"Move a little out of it, cahptn." He had a rag in his black hands. Tietjens moved out of the blood that had run in a thin stream under the table. The man was on his knees, his hands rubbing Tietjens' boot welts heavily, with the rags. Tietjens placed his hands in the innocent water and watched light purple-scarlet mist diffuse itself over the pale half-moon. The man below him breathed heavily, sniffing. Tietjens said:

"Thomas, 0 Nine Morgan was your mate?"

The man's face, wrinkled, dark and ape-like, looked up. "He was a good pal, pore old ——," he said. "You would not like, surely to goodness, to go to mess with your shoes all bloody."

"If I had given him leave," Tietjens said, "he would not be dead now."

"No, surely not," One Seven Thomas answered. "But it is all one. Evans of Castell Goch would surely to goodness have killed him."

"So you knew, too, about his wife!" Tietjens said.

"We thocht it wass that," One Seven Thomas answered, "or you would have given him leave, cahptn. You are a good cahptn."

A sudden sense of the publicity that that life was came over Tietjens.

"You knew that," he said. "I wonder what the hell you fellows don't know and all!" he thought. "If anything went wrong with one it would be all over the command in two days. Thank God, Sylvia can't get here!"

The man had risen to his feet. He fetched a towel of the sergeant-major's, very white with a red border.

"We know," he said, "that your honour is a very goot cahptn. And Captain McKechnie is a fery goot cahptn, and Captain Prentiss, and Le'tennat Jonce of Merthyr."

Tietjens said:

"That'll do. Tell the sergeant-major to give you a pass to go with your mate to the hospital. Get someone to wash this floor."

Two men were carrying the remains of 0 Nine Morgan, the trunk wrapped in a ground sheet. They carried him in a bandy chair out of the hut. His arms over his shoulders waved a jocular farewell. There would be an ambulance stretcher on bicycle wheels outside.

II

The "All Clear" went at once after that. Its suddenness was something surprising, the mournful-cheerful, long notes dying regretfully on a night that had only just gone quiet after the perfectly astonishing row. The moon had taken it into its head to rise; begumboiled, jocular and grotesque, it came from behind the shoulder of one of the hut-covered hills and sent down the lines of Tietjens' huts long, sentimental rays that converted the place into a slumbering, pastoral settlement. There was no sound that did not contribute to the silence, little dim lights shone through the celluloid casements. Of Sergeant-Major Cowley, his numerals gilded by the moon in the lines of A Company, Tietjens, who was easing his lungs of coke vapours for a minute, asked in a voice that hushed itself in tribute to the moonlight and the now keen frost:

"Where the deuce is the draft?"

The sergeant-major looked poetically down a ribbon of whitewashed stones that descended the black down-side. Over the next shoulder of hill was the blur of a hidden conflagration.

"There's a Hun plane burning down there. In Twenty-Seven's parade ground. The draft's round that, sir," he said. Tietjens said:

"Good God!" in a voice of caustic tolerance. He added, "I did think we had drilled some discipline into these blighters in the seven weeks we have had them. . . You remember the first time when we had them on parade and that acting lance-corporal left the ranks to heave a rock at a sea-gull. . . And called you 'OP' Hunkey! . . . Conduct prejudicial to good order and military discipline? Where's that Canadian sergeant-major? Where's the officer in charge of the draft?"

Sergeant-Major Cowley said:

"Sergeant-Major Ledoux said it was like a cattle-stampede on the. . . some river where they come from. You *couldn't* stop them, sir. It was their first German plane. . . And they going up the line tonight, sir."

"Tonight!" Tietjens exclaimed. "Next Christmas!" The sergeant-major said:

"Poor boys!" and continued to gaze into the distance. "I heard another good one, sir," he said. "The answer to the one about the King saluting a private soldier and he not taking any notice is: when he's dead. . . But if you marched a company into a field through a gateway and you wanted to get it out again but you did not know any command in the drill book for change of direction, what would you do, sir? . . . You have to get that company out, but you must not use About Turn, or Right or Left Wheel. . . There's another one, too, about saluting. . . The officer in charge of draft is Second-Lieutenant Hotchkiss. . . But he's an A.S.C. officer and turned of sixty. A farrier he is, sir in civil life. An A.S.C. major was asking me, sir, very civil, if you could not detail someone else. He says he doubts if Second Lieutenant Hitchcock. . . Hotchkiss could walk as far as the station, let alone march the men, him not knowing anything but cavalry words of command, if he knows them. He's only been in the army a fortnight. . ."

Tietjens turned from the idyllic scene with the words:

"I suppose the Canadian sergeant-major and Lieutenant Hotchkiss are doing what they can to get their men come back."

He re-entered the hut.

Captain Mackenzie in the light of a fantastically brilliant hurricane lamp appeared to be bathing dejectedly in a surf of coiling papers spread on the table before him.

"There's all this bumph," he said, "just come from all the headquarters in the bally world."

Tietjens said cheerfully:

"What's it all about?" There were, the other answered, Garrison Headquarter orders, Divisional orders, Lines of Communication orders, half a dozen A.F.W.B. two four two's. A terrific strafe from First Army forwarded from Garrison H.Q. about the draft's not having reached Hazebrouck the day before yesterday. Tietjens said:

"Answer them politely to the effect that we had orders not to send off the draft without its complement of four hundred Canadian Railway Service men—the fellows in furred hoods. They only reached us from Etaples at five this afternoon without blankets or ring papers. Or any other papers for the matter of that."

Mackenzie was studying with increased gloom a small buff memorandum slip:

"This appears to be meant for you privately," he said.

"I can't make head or tail of it otherwise. It isn't marked private."

He tossed the buff slip across the table.

Tietjens sank down bulkily on to his bully-beef case. He read on the buff at first the initials of the signature, "E.C. Genl.", and then: "For God's sake keep your wife off me. I *will* not have skirts round my

H.Q. You are more trouble to me than all the rest of my command put together."

Tietjens groaned and sank more deeply on to his beef case. It was as if an unseen and unsuspected wild beast had jumped on his neck from an over-hanging branch. The sergeant-major at his side said in his most admirable butler manner:

"Colour-Sergeant Morgan and Lance-Corporal Trench are obliging us by coming from depot orderly room to help with the draft's papers. Why don't you and the other officer go and get a bit of dinner, sir? The colonel and the padre have only just come in to mess, and I've warned the mess orderlies to keep your food 'ot. . . Both good men with papers, Morgan and Trench. We can send the soldiers' small books to you at table to sign. . ."

His feminine solicitude enraged and overwhelmed Tietjens with blackness. He told the sergeant-major that he was to go to hell, for he himself was not going to leave that hut till the draft was moved off. Captain Mackenzie could do as he pleased. The sergeant-major told Captain Mackenzie that Captain Tietjens took as much trouble with his rag-time detachments as if he had been the Coldstream adjutant at Chelsea sending off a draft of Guards. Captain Mackenzie said that that was why they damn well got their details off four days faster than any other I.B.D. in that camp. He would say that much, he added grudgingly and dropped his head over his papers again. The hut was moving slowly up and down before the eyes of Tietjens. He might have just been kicked in the stomach. That was how shocks took him. He said to himself that by God he must take himself in hand. He grabbed with his heavy hands at a piece of buff paper and wrote on it a column of fat, wet letters

a
b
b
a
a
b
b
a and so on.

He said opprobriously to Captain Mackenzie:

"Do you know what a sonnet is? Give me the rhymes for a sonnet. That's the plan of it."

Mackenzie grumbled:

"Of course I know what a sonnet is. What's your game?" Tietjens said:

"Give me the fourteen end-rhymes of a sonnet and I'll write the lines. In under two minutes and a half."

Mackenzie said injuriously:

"If you do I'll turn, it into Latin hexameters in three. In *under* three minutes."

They were like men uttering deadly insults the one to the other. To Tietjens it was as if an immense cat were parading, fascinated and fatal, round that hut. He had imagined himself parted from his wife. He had not heard from his wife since her four-in-the-morning departure from their flat, months and eternities ago, with the dawn just showing up the chimney-pots of the Georgian roof-trees opposite. In the complete stillness of dawn he had heard her voice say very clearly "Paddington" to the chauffeur, and then all the sparrows in the inn waking up in chorus. . . Suddenly and appallingly it came into his head that it might not have been his wife's voice that had said "Paddington", but her maid's. . . He was a man who lived very much by rules of conduct. He had a rule: *Never think on the subject of a shock at a moment of shock.* The mind was then too sensitized. Subjects of shock require to be thought all round. If your mind thinks when it is too sensitized its then conclusions will be too strong. So he exclaimed to Mackenzie:

"Haven't you got your rhymes yet? Damn it all!" Mackenzie grumbled offensively:

"No, I haven't. It's more difficult to get rhymes than to write sonnets. . . death, moil, coil, breath. . ." He paused.

"Heath, soil, toil, staggereth," Tietjens said contemptuously. "That's your sort of Oxford young woman's rhyme. . . Go on. . . *What is it?*"

An extremely age-faded and military officer was beside the blanketed table. Tietjens regretted having spoken to him with ferocity. He had a grotesquely thin white beard. Positively, white whiskers! He must have gone through as much of the army as he had gone through with those whiskers, because no superior officer—not even a fieldmarshal—would have the heart to tell him to take them off! It was the measure of his pathos. This ghost-like object was apologizing for not having been able to keep the draft in hand: he was requesting his superior to observe that these Colonial troops were without any instincts of discipline. None at all. Tietjens observed that he had a blue cross on his right arm where the vaccination marks are as a rule. He imagined the Canadians talking to this hero. . . The hero began to talk of Major Cornwallis of the R. A. S. C.

Tietjens said apropos of nothing:

"Is there a Major Cornwallis in the A.S.C.? Good God!"

The hero protested faintly:

"The *R*.A.S.C."

Tietjens said kindly:

"Yes. Yes. The *Royal* Army. Service Corps."

Obviously his mind until now had regarded his wife's "*Paddington*" as the definite farewell between his life and hers. . . He had imagined her, like Eurydice, tall, but faint and pale, sinking back into the shades. . . "*Che faro senz' Eurydice?* . . ." he hummed. Absurd! And of course it might have been only the maid that had spoken. . . She too had a remarkably clear voice. So that the mystic word "Paddington" might perfectly well be no symbol at all, and Mrs. Sylvia Tietjens, far from being faint and pale, might perfectly well be playing the very devil with half the general officers commanding in chief from Whitehall to Alaska.

Mackenzie—he *was* like a damned clerk—was transferring the rhymes that he had no doubt at last found, on to another sheet of paper. Probably he had a round, copybook hand. Positively, his tongue followed his pen round, inside his lips. These were what His Majesty's regular officers of today were. Good God! A damned intelligent, dark-looking fellow. Of the type that is starved in its youth and takes all the scholarships that the board schools have to offer. Eyes too big and black. Like a Malay's. . . Any blasted member of any subject race.

The A.S.C. fellow had been talking positively about horses. He had offered his services in order to study the variation of pink-eye that was decimating all the service horses in the lines. He had been a professor—positively a professor—in some farriery college or other. Tietjens said that, in that case, he ought to be in the A.V.C.—the Royal Army Veterinary Corps perhaps it was. The old man said he didn't know. He imagined that the R.A.S.C. had wanted his service for their own horses. . .

Tietjens said:

"I'll tell you what to do, Lieutenant Hitchcock. . . For, damn it, you're a stout fellow. . ." The poor old fellow, pushing out at that age from the cloisters of some provincial university. . . He certainly did not look a horsy sportsman. . .

The old lietutenant said:

"Hotchkiss. . ." And Tietjens exclaimed:

"Of course it's Hotchkiss. . . I've seen your name signing a testimonial to Pigg's Horse Embrocation. . . Then if you don't want to take this draft up the line. . . Though I'd advise you to. . . It's merely a Cook's Tour to Hazebrouck. . . No, Bailleul. . . And the sergeant-major will march the men for you. . . And you will have been in the First Army Lines and able to tell all your friends you've been on active service at the real front. . ."

His mind said to himself while his words went on. . .

"Then, good God, if Sylvia is actively paying attention to my career I shall be the laughing-stock of the whole army. I was thinking that ten minutes ago! . . . What's to be done? What in God's name is to be done?" A black crape veil seemed to drop across his vision. . . Liver. . .

Lieutenant Hotchkiss said with dignity:

"I'm going to the front. I'm going to the real front. I was passed A1 this morning. I am going to study the blood reactions of the service horse under fire."

"Well, you're a damn good chap," Tietjens said. There was nothing to be done. The amazing activities of which Sylvia would be capable were just the thing to send laughter raging like fire through a cachinnating army. She could not thank God, get into France: to that place. But she could make scandals in the papers that every Tommie read. There was no game of which she was not capable. That sort of pursuit was called "pulling the strings of shower-baths" in her circle of friends. Nothing. Nothing to be done. . . The beastly hurricane lamp was smoking.

"I'll tell you what to do," he said to Lieutenant Hotchkiss.

Mackenzie had tossed his sheet of rhymes under his nose. Tietjens read: "*Death, moil, coil, breath. . . Saith*—The dirty Cockney!" *Oil, soil, wraith. . .*

"I'd be blowed," Mackenzie said with a vicious grin, "if I was going to give you rhymes you had suggested yourself. . ."

The officer said:

"I don't of course want to be a nuisance if you're busy."

"It's no nuisance," Tietjens said. "It's what we're for. But I'd suggest that now and then you say 'sir' to the officer commanding your unit. It sounds well before the men. . . Now you go to No. XVI I.B.D. Mess ante-room. . . The place where they've got the broken bagatelle-table. . ."

The voice of Sergeant-Major Cowley exclaimed tranquilly from outside:

"Fall in now. Men who've got their ring papers and identity disks— three of them—on the left. Men who haven't, on the right. Any man who has not been able to draw his blankets tell Colour-Sergeant Morgan. Don't forget. You won't get any where you're going. Any man who hasn't made his will in his Soldier's Small Book or elsewhere and wants to, to consult Captain Tietjens. Any man who wants to draw money, ask Captain Mackenzie. Any R.C. who wants to go to confession after he has got his papers signed can find the R.C. padre in the fourth hut from the left in the Main Line from here. . . And damn kind it is of his reverence to put himself out for a set of damn blinking mustard-faced red herrings like you who can't keep from running away to the first baby's bonfire you sees. You'll be running the other way before you're a week older, though what good they as asks for you thinks you'll be out there God knows. You look like a squad of infants' companions from a Wesleyan Sunday school. That's what you look like and, thank God, we've got a Navy."

Under cover of his voice Tietjens had been writing:

"Now we affront the grinning chops of *Death*," and saying to Lieutenant Hotchkiss: "In the I.B.D. ante-room you'll find any number of dirty little squits of Glamorgan-shires drinking themselves blind over *La Vie Parisienne*. . . Ask any one of them you like. . ." He wrote:

"And in between the carcases and the *moil*
Of marts and cities, toil and moil and *coil*. . ."

"You think this difficult!" he said to Mackenzie. "Why, you've written a whole undertaker's mortuary ode in the rhymes alone," and went on to Hotchkiss: "Ask anyone you like as long as he's a P.B. officer. . . Do you know what P.B. means? No, not Poor B——y, Permanent Base. Unfit. . . If he'd like to take a draft to Bailleul."

The hut was filling with devious, slow, ungainly men in yellow-brown. Their feet shuffled desultorily; they lumped dull canvas bags along the floor and held in unliterary hands small open books that they dropped from time to time. From outside came a continuing, swelling and descending chant of voices; at times it would seem to be all one laugh, at times one menace, then the motives mingled fugally, like the sea on a beach of large stones. It seemed to Tietjens suddenly extraordinary how shut in on oneself one was in this life. . . He sat scribbling fast: "Old Spectre blows a cold protecting *breath*. . . Vanity of vanities, the preacher *saith*. . . No more parades, not any more, no *oil*. . ." He was telling Hotchkiss, who was obviously shy of approaching the Glamorganshires in their ante-room. . . "Unambergris'd our limbs in the naked *soil*. . ." that he did not suppose any P.B. officer would object. They would go on a beanfeast up into the giddy line in a first-class carriage and get draft leave and command pay too probably. . . "No funeral struments cast before our wraiths. . ." If any fellow does object, you just send his name to me and I will damn well shove it into extra orders. . .

The advanced wave of the brown tide of men was already at his feet. The extraordinary complications of even the simplest lives. . . A fellow was beside him Private Logan, formerly, of all queer things for a Canadian private, a trooper of the Inniskillings: owner, of all queer things, of a milk-walk or a dairy farm, outside Sydney, which is in Australia. . . A man of sentimental complications, jauntiness as became an Inniskilling, a Cockney accent such as ornaments the inhabitants of Sydney, and a complete distrust of lawyers. On the other hand, with the completest trust in Tietjens. Over his shoulder—he was blond, upright, with his numerals shining like gold, looked a lumpish, *café-au-lait*, eagle-nosed countenance: a half-caste member of one of the Six Nations, who had been a doctor's errand boy in Quebec. . . He had his troubles, but was difficult to understand. Behind him, very black-avised with a high colour, truculent eyes and an Irish accent, was a graduate of McGill University who had been a teacher of languages in Tokyo and had some sort of claim against the Japanese Government. . . And faces, two and two, in a coil round the hut. . . Like dust: like a cloud of dust that would approach and overwhelm a landscape: every one with preposterous troubles and anxieties, even if they did not overwhelm you personally with them. . . Brown dust. . .

He kept the Inniskilling waiting while he scribbled the rapid sestet to his sonnet which ought to make a little plainer what it all meant. Of course the general idea was that, when you got into the line or near it, there was no room for swank: typified by expensive funerals. As you might say: No flowers by compulsion. . . No more parades! . . . He had also to explain, while he did it, to the heroic veterinary sexagenarian that he need not feel shy about going into the Glamorganshire Mess on a man-catching expedition. The Glamorganshires were bound to lend him, Tietjens, P.B. officers if they had not got other jobs. Lieutenant Hotchkiss could speak to Colonel Johnson, whom he would find in the mess and quite good natured over his dinner. A pleasant and sympathetic old gentleman who would appreciate Hotchkiss's desire not to go superfluously into the line. Hotchkiss could offer to take a look at the colonel's charger: a Hun horse, captured on the Marne and called Schomburg, that was off its feed. . . He added: "But don't do anything professional to Schomburg. I ride him myself!"

He threw his sonnet across to Mackenzie, who with a background of huddled khaki limbs and anxious faces was himself anxiously counting out French currency notes and dubious-looking tokens. . . What the deuce did men want to draw money—sometimes quite large sums of money, the Canadians being paid in dollars converted into local coins—when in an hour or so they would be going up? But they always did and their accounts were always in an incredibly entangled state. Mackenzie might well look worried. As like as not he might find himself a fiver or more down at the end of the evening for unauthorized payments. If he had only his pay and an extravagant wife to keep, that might well put the wind up him. But that was his funeral. He told Lieutenant Hotchkiss to come and have a chat with him in his hut, the one next the mess. About horses. He knew a little about horse-illness himself. Only empirically, of course.

Mackenzie was looking at his watch.

"You took two minutes and eleven seconds," he said. "I'll take it for granted it's a sonnet. . . I have not read it because I can't turn it into Latin here. . . I haven't got your knack of doing eleven things at once. . ."

A man with a worried face, encumbered by a bundle and a small book, was studying figures at Mackenzie's elbow. He interrupted Mackenzie in a high American voice to say that he had never drawn fourteen dollars seventy-five cents in Thrasna Barracks, Aldershot.

Mackenzie said to Tietjens:

"You understand. I have not read your sonnet. I shall turn it into Latin in the mess: in the time stipulated. I don't want you to think I've read it and taken time to think about it."

The man besides him said:

"When I went to the Canadian Agent, Strand, London, his office was shut up. . ."

Mackenzie said with white fury:

"How much service have you got? Don't you know better than to interrupt an officer when he is talking? You must settle your own figures with your own confounded Colonial paymaster: I've sixteen dollars thirty cents here for you. Will you take them or leave them?"

Tietjens said:

"I know that man's case. Turn him over to me. It isn't complicated. He's got his paymaster's cheque, but doesn't know how to cash it and of course they won't give him another. . .

The man with slow, broad, brown features looked from one to the other officer's face and back again with a keen black-eyed scrutiny as if he were looking into a wind and dazed by the light. He began a long story of how he owed Fat-Eared Bill fifty dollars lost at House. He was perhaps half Chinese, half Finn. He continued to talk, being in a state of great anxiety about his money. Tietjens addressed himself to the cases of the Sydney Inniskilling ex-trooper and the McGill graduate who had suffered at the hands of the Japanese Educational Ministry. It made altogether a complicated effect. "You would say," Tietjens said to himself, "that, all together, it ought to be enough to take my mind up."

The upright trooper had a very complicated sentimental history. It was difficult to advise him before his fellows. He, however, felt no diffidence. He discussed the points of the girl called Rosie whom he had followed from Sydney to British Columbia, of the girl called Gwen with whom he had taken up in Aberystwyth, of the woman called Mrs. Hosier with whom he had lived maritally, on a sleeping-out pass, at Berwick St. James, near Salisbury Plain. Through the continuing voice of the half-caste Chinaman he discussed them with a large tolerance, ex-p aiming that he wanted them all to have a bit, as a souvenir, if he happened to stop one out there. Tietjens handed him the draft of a will he had written out for him, asked him to read it attentively and copy it with his own hand into his soldier's small book. Then Tietjens would witness it for him. He said:

"Do you think this will make my old woman in Sydney part? I guess it won't. She's a sticker, sir. A regular July bur, God bless her." The McGill graduate was beginning already to introduce a further complication into his story of complications with the Japanese Government. It appeared that in addition to his scholastic performances he had invested a little money in a mineral water spring near Kobe, the water, bottled, being exported to San Francisco. Apparently his company had been indulging in irregularities according to Japanese law, but a pure French Canadian, who had experienced some difficulties in obtaining his baptismal certificate from a mission somewhere in the direction of the Klondike, was allowed by Tietjens to interrupt the story of the graduate; and several men without complications, but anxious to get their papers signed so as to write last letters home before the draft moved, overflowed across Tietjens' table. . .

The tobacco smoke from the pipes of the N.C.O.'s at the other end of the room hung, opalescent, beneath the wire cages of the brilliant hurricane lamps hung over each table; buttons and numerals gleamed in the air that the universal khaki tinge of the limbs seemed to turn brown, as if into a gas of dust. Nasal voices, throat voices, drawling voices, melted into a rustle so that the occasional high, sing-song profanity of a Welsh N.C.O.: Why the *hell* haffn't you got your 124? Why the —— hell haffn't you got your 124? Don't you *know* you haff to haff your bleedin' 124's? seemed to wail tragically through a silence. . . The evening wore on and on. It astounded Tietjens, looking at one time at his watch, to discover that it was only 21 hrs. 19. He seemed to have been thinking drowsily of his own affairs for ten hours. . . For, in the end, these were his own affairs. . . Money, women, testamentary bothers. Each of these complications from over the Atlantic and round the world were his own troubles: a world in labour: an army being moved off in the night. Shoved off. Anyhow. And over the top. A lateral section of the world. . .

He had happened to glance at the medical history of a man beside him and noticed that he had been described as CI. . . It was obviously a slip of the pen on the part of the Medical Board, or one of their orderlies. He had written C instead of A. The man was Pte. 197394 Thomas Johnson, a shining-faced lump of beef, an agricultural odd jobman from British Columbia where he had worked on the immense estates of Sylvia Tietjens' portentous ducal second cousin Rugeley. It was a double annoyance. Tietjens had not wanted to be reminded of his wife's second cousin, because he had not wanted to be reminded of his wife. He had determined to give his thoughts a field day on that subject when he got warm into his flea-bag in his hut that smelt of paraffin whilst the canvas walls crackled with frost and the moon shone. . . He would think of Sylvia beneath the moon. He was determined not to now! But 197394 Pte. Johnson, Thomas, was otherwise a nuisance and Tietjens cursed himself for having glanced at the man's medical history. If this preposterous yokel was C3 he could not go on a draft. . . C1 rather! It was all the same. That would mean finding another man to make up the strength and that would drive Sergeant-Major Cowley out of his mind. He looked up towards the ingenuous, protruding, shining, liquid, bottle-blue eyes of Thomas Johnson. . . The fellow had never had an illness. He could not have had an illness—except from a surfeit of cold, fat, boiled pork—and for that you would give him a horse's blue ball and drench which, ten to one, would not remove the cause of the belly-ache. . .

His eyes met the non-committal glance of a dark, gentlemanly thin fellow with a strikingly scarlet hatband, a lot of gilt about his khaki and little strips of steel chain-armour on his shoulders. . . Levin. . . Colonel Levin, G.S.O. II, or something, attached to General Lord Edward Campion. . . How the hell did fellows get into these intimacies of commanders of units and their men? Swimming in like fishes into the brown air of a tank and there at your elbow. . . —— spies! . . . The men had all been called to attention and stood like gasping codfish. The ever-watchful Sergeant-Major Cowley had drifted to his, Tietjens', elbow. You protect your orfcers from the gawdy Staff as you protect your infant daughters in lambswool from draughts. The dark, bright, cheerful staffwallah said with a slight lisp:

"Busy, I see." He might have been standing there for a century and have a century of the battalion headquarters' time to waste like that. "What draft is this?"

Sergeant-Major Cowley, always ready in case his orfcer should not know the name of his unit or his own name, said:

"No. 16 I.B.D. Canadian First Division Casual Number Four Draft, sir."

Colony Levin let air lispingly out between his teeth.

"No. 16 Draft not off yet. . . Dear, dear! Dear, dear! . . . We shall be strafed to hell by First Army. . ." He used the word hell as if he had first wrapped it in eau-de-cologned cotton-wadding.

Tietjens, on his feet, knew this fellow very well: a fellow who had been a very bad Society water-colour painter of good family on the mother's side: hence the cavalry gadgets on his shoulders. Would it then be good. . . say good taste to explode? He let the sergeant-major do it. Sergeant-Major Cowley was of the type of N.C.O. who carried weight because he knew ten times as much about his job as any Staff officer. The sergeant-major explained that it had been impossible to get off the draft earlier. The colonel said:

"But surely, sergeant-majah. . ."

The sergeant-major, now a deferential shopwalker in a lady's store, pointed out that they had had urgent instructions not to send up the draft without the four hundred Canadian Railway Service men who were to come from Etaples. These men had only arrived that evening at 5.30 . . . at the railway station. Marching them up had taken three-quarters of an hour. The colonel said:

"But surely, sergeant-majah. . ."

Old Cowley might as well have said "madam" as "sir" to the red hat-band. . . The four-hundred had come with only what they stood up in. The unit had had to wangle everything: boots, blankets, tooth-brushes, braces, rifles, iron-rations, identity disks out of the depot store. And it was now only twenty-one twenty. . . Cowley permitted his commanding officer at this point to say:

"You must understand that we work in circumstances of extreme difficulty, sir. . ."

The graceful colonel was lost in an absent contemplation of his perfectly elegant knees.

"I know, of course. . ." he lisped. "Very difficult. . ." He brightened up to add: "But you must admit you're unfortunate. . . You must admit that. . ." The weight settled, however, again on his mind.

Tietjens said:

"Not, I suppose, sir, any more unfortunate than any other unit working under a dual control for supplies. . ."

The colonel said:

"What's that? Dual. . . Ah, I see you're there, Mackenzie. . . Feeling well. . . feeling fit, eh?"

The whole hut stood silent. His anger at the waste of time made Tietjens say:

"If you understand, sir, we are a unit whose principal purpose is drawing things to equip drafts with. . ." This fellow was delaying them atrociously. He was brushing his knees with a handkerchief! "I've had," Tietjens said, "a man killed on my hands this afternoon because we have to draw tin-hats for my orderly room from Dublin on an A.F.B. Canadian from Aldershot. . . Killed here. . . We've only just mopped up the blood from where you're standing. . ."

The cavalry colonel exclaimed:

"Oh, good gracious me! . . ." jumped a little and examined his beautiful shining knee-high aircraft boots. "Killed! . . . Here! . . . But there'll have to be a court of inquiry. . . You certainly are *most* unfortunate, Captain Tietjens. . . Always these mysterious. . . Why wasn't your man in a dug-out? . . . Most unfortunate. . . We cannot have casualties among the Colonial troops. . . Troops from the Dominions, I mean. . ."

Tietjens said grimly:

"The man was from Pontardulias. . . not from any Dominion. . . One of my orderly room. . . We are forbidden on pain of court martial to let any but Dominion Expeditionary Force men go into the dug-outs. . . My Canadians were all there. . . It's an A.C.I. local of the eleventh of November. . ."

The Staff Offcer said:

"It makes of course, a difference! . . . Only a Glamorgan-shire? You say. . . Oh well. . . But these mysterious. . ."

He exclaimed, with the force of an explosion, and the relief:

"Look here. . . can you spare possible ten. . . twenty. . . eh. . . minutes? . . . It's not exactly a service matter. . . so per. . ."

Tietjens exclaimed:

"You see how we're situated, colonel. . ." and like one sowing grass seed on a lawn, extended both hands over his papers and towards his men. . . He was choking with rage. Colonel Levin had, under the chaperonage of an English dowager, who ran a chocolate store down on the quays in Rouen, a little French piece to whom he was quite seriously engaged. In the most naïve manner. And the young woman, fantastically jealous, managed to make endless insults to herself out of her almost too handsome colonel's barbaric French. It was an idyll, but it drove the colonel frantic. At such times Levin would consult Tietjens, who passed for a man of brains and a French scholar as to really nicely turned compliments in a difficult language. . . And as to how you explained that is was necessary for a G.S.O. II, or whatever the colonel was, to be seen quite frequently in the company of very handsome V.A.D.'s and female organizers of all arms. . . It was the sort of silliness as to which no gentleman ought to be consulted. . . And here was Levin with the familiar feminine-agonized wrinkle on his bronzed-alabaster brow. . . Like a beastly soldier-man out of a revue. Why didn't the ass burst into gesture and a throaty tenor. . .

Sergeant-Major Cowley naturally saved the situation. Just as Tietjens was as near saying *Go to hell* as you can be to your remarkably senior officer on parade, the sergeant-major, now a very important solicitor's most confidential clerk, began whispering to the colonel. . .

"The captain might as well take a spell as not. . . We're through with all the men except the Canadian Railway batch, and they can't be issued with blankets not for half an hour. . . not for three-quarters. If then! It depends if our runner can find where Quarter's lance-corporal is having his supper, to issue them. . . ! The sergeant-major had inserted that last speech deftly. The Staff officer, with a vague reminiscence of his regimental days, exclaimed:

"Damn it! . . . I wonder you don't break into the depot blanket store and take what you want. . ."

The sergeant-major, becoming Simon Pure, exclaimed:

"Oh, no, sir, we could never do that, sir. . ."

"But the confounded men are urgently needed in the line," Colonel Levin said. "Damn it, it's touch and go! . . . We're rushing. . ." He appreciated the fact again that he was on the gawdy Staff, and that the sergeant-major and Tietjens, playing like left backs into each other's hands, had trickily let him in.

"We can only pray, sir," the sergeant-major said, "that these 'ere bloomin' 'Uns has got quartermasters and depots and issuing departments, same as ourselves." He lowered his voice into a husky whisper. "Besides, sir, there's a rumour. . . round the telephone in depot orderly room. . . that there's a W.O. order at 'Edquarters. . . countermanding this and other drafts. . ."

Colonel Levin said: "Oh, my God!" and consternation rushed upon both him and Tietjens. The frozen ditches, in the night, out there; the agonized waiting for men; the weight upon the mind like a weight upon the brows; the imminent sense of approaching unthinkableness on the right or the left, according as you looked up or down the trench; the solid protecting earth of the parapet then turns into pierced mist. . . and no reliefs coming from here. . . The men up there thinking naïvely that they were coming, and they not coming. Why not? Good God, why not? Mackenzie said:

"Poor —— old Bird. . . His crowd had been in eleven weeks last Wednesday. . . About all they could stick. . ."

"They'll have to stick a damn lot more," Colonel Levin said. "I'd like to get at some of the brutes. . ." It was at that date the settled conviction of His Majesty's Expeditionary Force that the army in the field was the tool of politicians and civilians. In moments of routine that cloud dissipated itself lightly: when news of ill omen arrived it settled down again heavily like a cloud of black gas. You hung your head impotently. . .

"So that," the sergeant-major said cheerfully, "the captain could very well spare half an hour to get his dinner. Or for anything else. . ." Apart from the domestic desire that Tietjens' digestion should not suffer from irregular meals he had the professional conviction that for his captain to be in intimate private converse with a member of the gawdy Staff was good for the unit. . . "I suppose, sir," he added valedictorily to Tietjens, "I'd better arrange to put this draft, and the nine hundred men that came in this afternoon to replace them, twenty in a tent. . . It's lucky we didn't strike them. . .

Tietjens and the colonel began to push men out of their way, going towards the door. The Inniskilling-Canadian, a small open brown book extended deprecatingly, stood, modestly obtrusive, just beside the door-post. Catching avidly at Tietjens' "Eh?" he said:

"You'd got the names of the girls wrong in your copy, sir. It was Gwen Lewis I had a child by in Aberystwyth that I wanted to have the lease of the cottage and the ten bob a week. Mrs. Hosier that I lived with in Berwick St. James, she was only to have five guineas for a soovneer. . . I've took the liberty of changing the names back again."

Tietjens grabbed the book from him, and bending down at the sergeant-major's table scrawled his signature on the bluish page. He thrust the book back at the man and said:

"There. . . fall out." The man's face shone. He exclaimed:

"Thank you, sir. Thank you kindly, captain. . . I wanted to get off and go to confession. I did bad. . ." The McGill graduate with his arrogant black moustache put himself in the way as Tietjens struggled into his British warm.

"You won't forget, sir, . . ." he began.

Tietjens said:

"Damn you, I've told you I won't forget. I never forget. You instructed the ignorant Jap in Asaki, but the educational authority is in Tokyo. And your flagitious mineral-water company had their headquarters at the Tan Sen spring near Kobe. . . Is that right? Well, I'll do my best for you."

They walked in silence through the groups of men that hung around the orderly room door and gleamed in the moonlight. In the broad country street of the main line of the camp Colonel Levin began to mutter between his teeth:

"You take enough trouble with your beastly crowd. . . a whole lot of trouble. . . Yet. . ."

"Well, what's the matter with us?" Tietjens said. "We get our drafts ready in thirty-six hours less than any other unit in this command."

"I know you do," the other conceded. "It's only all these mysterious rows. Now. . ."

Tietjens said quickly:

"Do you mind my asking: Are we still on parade? Is this a strafe from General Campion as to the way I command my unit?"

The other conceded quite as quickly and much more worriedly:

"God forbid." He added more quickly still: "Old bean!", and prepared to tuck his wrist under Tietjens' elbow. Tietjens, however, continued to face the fellow. He was really in a temper.

"Then tell me," he said, "how the deuce you can manage to do without an overcoat in this weather?" If only he could get the chap off the topics of his mysterious rows they might drift to the matter that had brought him up there on that bitter night when he should be sitting over a good wood fire philandering with Mlle Nanette de Bailly. He sank his neck deeper into the sheepskin collar of his British warm. The other, slim, was with all his badges, ribands and mail, shining darkly in a cold that set all Tietjens' teeth chattering like porcelain. Levin became momentarily animated:

"You should do as I do. . . Regular hours. . . lots of exercise. . . horse exercise. . . I do P.T. every morning at the open window of my room. . . hardening. . ."

"It must be very gratifying for the ladies in the rooms facing yours," Tietjens said grimly. "Is that what's the matter with Mlle Nanette, now? . . . I haven't got time for proper exercise. . .

"Good gracious, no," the colonel, said. He now tucked his hand firmly under Tietjens' arm and began to work him towards the left hand of the road: in the direction leading out of camp. Tietjens worked their steps as firmly towards the right and they leant one against the other. "In fact, old bean," the colonel said, "Campy is working so hard to get the command of a fighting army—though he's indispensable here— that we might pack up bag and baggage any day. . . That is what has made Nanette see reason. . ."

"Then what am I doing in this show?" Tietjens asked. But Colonel Levin continued blissfully:

"In fact I've got her almost practically for certain to promise that next week. . . or the week after next at latest. . . she'll. . . damn it, she'll name the happy day."

Tietjens said:

"Good hunting! . . . How splendidly Victorian!"

"That's, damn it," the colonel exclaimed manfully, "what I say myself. . . Victorian is what it is. . . All these marriage settlements. . . And what is it. . . *Droits du Seigneur*? . . . And notaries. . . And the Count, having his say. . . And the Marchioness. . . And two old grand aunts. . . But. . . Hoopla! . . ." He executed with his gloved right thumb in the moonlight a rapid pirouette. . . "Next week. . . or at least the week after. . ." His voice suddenly dropped.

"At least," he wavered, "that was what it was at lunchtime. . . Since then. . . something happened. . ."

"You've not been caught in bed with a V.A.D.?" Tietjens asked.

The colonel mumbled:

"No. . . not in bed. . . Not with a V.A.D. . . Oh, damn it, at the railway station. . . With. . . The general sent me down to meet her. . . and Nanny of course was seeing off her grandmother, the Duchesse. . . The giddy cut she handed me out. . ."

Tietjens became coldly furious.

"Then it *was* over one of your beastly imbecile rows with Miss de Bailly that you got me out here," he exclaimed. "Do you mind going down with me towards the I.B.D. headquarters? Your final orders may have come in there. The sappers won't let me have a telephone, so I have to look in there the last thing. . ." He felt a yearning towards rooms in huts, warmed by coke-stoves and electrically lit, with acting lance-corporals bending over A.F.B.'s on a background of deal pigeon-holes filled with returns on buff and blue paper. You got quiet and engrossment there. It was a queer thing: the only place where he, Christopher Tietjens of Groby, could be absently satisfied was in some orderly room or other. The only place in the world. . . And why? It was a queer thing. . .

But not queer, really. It was a matter of inevitable selection if you came to think it out. An acting orderly-room lance-corporal was selected for his penmanship, his power of elementary figuring, his trustworthiness amongst innumerable figures and messages, his dependability. For this he differed a hair's breadth in rank from the rank and file. A hairbreadth that was to him the difference between life and death. For, if he proved not to be dependable, back he went—returned to duty! As long as he was dependable he slept under a table in a warm room, his toilette arrangements and washing in a bully-beef case near his head, a billy full of tea always stewing for him on an always burning stove. . . A

paradise! . . . No! Not a paradise: *the* paradise of the Other Ranks! . . .
He might be awakened at one in the morning. Miles away the enemy
might be beginning a strafe. . . He would roll out from among the
blankets under the table amongst the legs of hurrying N.C.O.'s and
officers, the telephone going like hell. . . He would have to manifold
innumerable short orders on buff slips on a typewriter. . . A bore to be
awakened at one in the morning, but not unexciting: the enemy putting
up a tremendous barrage in front of the village of Dranoutre: the whole
nineteenth division to be moved into support along the Bailleul-Nieppe
road. In case. . .

Tietjens considered the sleeping army. . . That country village under
the white moon, all of sackcloth sides, celluloid windows, forty men to a
hut. . . That slumbering Arcadia was one of. . . how many? Thirty-seven
thousand five hundred, say for a million and a half of men. . . But there
were probably more than a million and a half in that base. . . Well, round
the slumbering Arcadias were the fringes of virginly glimmering tents. . .
Fourteen men to a tent. . . For a million. . . Seventy-one thousand four
hundred and twenty-one tents round, say, one hundred and fifty I.B.D.'s,
C.B.D.'s, R.E.B.D.'s. . . Base depots for infantry, cavalry, sappers,
gunners, airmen, anti-airmen, telephone-men, vets, chiropodists, Royal
Army Service Corps men, Pigeon Service men, Sanitary Service men,
Women's Auxiliary Army Corps women, V.A.D. women—what in the
world did V.A.D. stand for?—canteens, rest-tent attendants, barrack
damage superintendents, parsons, priests, rabbis, Mormon bishops,
Brahmins, Lamas, Imams, Fanti men, no doubt, for African troops.
And all ready dependent on the acting orderly-room lance-corporals for
their temporal and spiritual salvation. . . For, if by a slip of the pen a
lance-corporal sent a Papist priest to an Ulster regiment, the Ulster men
would lynch him, and all go to hell. Or, if by a slip of the tongue at the
telephone, or a slip of the typewriter, he sent a division to Westoutre
instead of to Dranoutre at one in the morning, the six or seven thousand
poor devils in front of Dranoutre might all be massacred and nothing
but His Majesty's Navy could save us. . .

Yet, in the end, all this tangle was satisfactorily unravelled; the drafts
moved off, unknotting themselves like snakes, coiling out of inextricable
bunches, sliding vertebrately over the mud to dip into their bowls—the
rabbis found Jews dying to whom to administer; the vets, spavined mules;
the V.A.D.'s, men without jaws and shoulders in C.C.S.'s; the camp-
cookers, frozen beef; the chiropodists, ingrowing toe-nails; the dentists,

decayed molars; the naval howitzers, camouflaged emplacements in picturesquely wooded dingles. . . Somehow they got there—even to the pots of strawberry jam by the ten dozen!

For if the acting lance-corporal, whose life hung by a hair, made a slip of the pen over a dozen pots of jam, back he went, *Returned to duty*. . . back to the frozen rifle, the ground-sheet on the liquid mud, the desperate suction on the ankle as the foot was advanced, the landscapes silhouetted with broken church towers, the continual drone of the planes, the mazes of duckboards in vast plains of slime, the unending Cockney humour, the great shells labelled *Love to Little Willie*. . . Back to the Angel with the Flaming Sword. The wrong side of him! . . . So, on the whole, things moved satisfactorily. . .

He was walking Colonel Levin imperiously between the huts towards the mess quarters, their feet crunching on the freezing gravel, the colonel hanging back a little; but a mere light-weight and without nails in his elegant bootsoles, so he had no grip on the ground. He was remarkably silent. Whatever he wanted to get out he was reluctant to come to. He brought out, however:

"I wonder you don't apply to be returned to duty. . . to your battalion. I jolly well should if I were you. . ."

Tietjens said:

"Why? Because I've had a man killed on me? . . . There must have been a dozen killed tonight."

"Oh, more, very likely," the other answered. "It was one of our own planes that was brought down. . . But it isn't that. . . Oh, damn it! . . . Would you mind walking the other way? . . . I've the greatest respect. . . oh, almost. . . for you personally. . . You're a man of intellect. . ."

Tietjens was reflecting on a nice point of military etiquette.

This lisping, ineffectual fellow—he was a very careful Staff officer or Campion would not have had him about the place!—was given to moulding himself exactly on his general. Physically, in costume as far as possible, in voice—for his lisp was not his own so much as an adaptation of the general's slight stutter—and above all in his uncompleted sentences and point of view. . .

Now, if he said:

"Look here, colonel. . ." or "Look here, Colonel Levin. . ." or "Look here, Stanley, my boy. . ." For the one thing an officer may not say to a superior whatever their intimacy was: "Look here, Levin. . ." If he said then:

"Look here, Stanley, you're a silly ass. It's all very well for Campion to say that I am unsound because I've some brains. He's my godfather and has been saying it to me since I was twelve, and had more brain in my left heel than he had in the whole of his beautifully barbered skull. . . But when you say it you are just a parrot. You did not think that out for yourself. You do not even think it. You know I'm heavy, short in the wind, and self-assertive. . . but you know perfectly well that I'm as good on detail as yourself. And a damned sight more. You've never caught me tripping over a return. Your sergeant in charge of returns may have. But not you. . ."

If Tietjens should say that to this popinjay, would that be going farther than an officer in charge of detachment should go with a member of the Staff set above him, though not on parade and in a conversation of intimacy? Off parade and in intimate conversation all His Majesty's poor —— officers are equals. . . gentlemen having his Majesty's commission: there can be no higher rank and all that Bilge! . . . For how off parade could this descendant of an old-clo' man from Frankfurt be the equal of him, Tietjens of Groby? He wasn't his equal in any way—let alone socially. If Tietjens hit him he would drop dead; if he addressed a little sneering remark to Levin, the fellow would melt so that you would see the old spluttering Jew swimming up through his carefully arranged Gentile features. He couldn't shoot as well as Tietjens, or ride, or play a hand at auction. Why, damn it, he, Tietjens, hadn't the least doubt that he could paint better water-colour-pictures. . . And, as for returns. . . he would undertake to tear the guts out of half a dozen new and contradictory A.C.I.'s—Army Council Instructions—and write twelve correct Command Orders founded on them, before Levin had lisped out the date and serial number of the first one. . . He had done it several times up in the room, arranged like a French blue-stocking's salon, where Levin worked at Garrison headquarters. . . He had written Levin's blessed command order while Levin fussed and fumed about their being delayed for tea with Mlle de Bailly. . . and curled his delicate moustache. . . Mlle de Badly, chaperoned by old Lady Sachse, had tea by a clear wood fire in an eighteenth-century octagonal room, with blue-grey tapestried walls and powdering closets, out of priceless porcelain cups without handles. Pale tea that tasted faintly of cinnamon!

Mlle de Bailly was a long, dark high-coloured Provençale. Not heavy, but precisely long, slow, and cruel; coiled in a deep arm-chair, saying the most wounding, slow things to Levin, she resembled a white Persian cat luxuriating, sticking out a tentative pawful of expanding claws. With eyes slanting pronouncedly upwards and a very thin hooked nose. . . almost Japanese. . . And with a terrific cortege of relatives, swell in a French way. One brother a chauffeur to a Marshal of France. . . An aristocratic way of shirking!

With all that, obviously even off parade, you might well be the social equal of a Staff colonel: but you jolly well had to keep from showing that you were his superior. Especially intellectually. If you let yourself show a Staff officer that he was a silly ass—you could say it as often as you liked as long as you didn't prove it!—you could be certain that you would be for it before long. And quite properly. It was not English to be intellectually adroit. Nay, it was positively un-English. And the duty of field officers is to keep messes as English as possible. . . So a Staff officer would take it out of such a regimental inferior. In a perfectly creditable way. You would never imagine the hash headquarters warrant officers would make of your returns. Until you were worried and badgered and in the end either you were ejected into, or prayed to be transferred to. . . any other command in the whole service. . .

And that was beastly. The process, not the effect. On the whole Tietjens did not care where he was or what he did as long as he kept out of England, the thought of that country, at night, slumbering across the Channel, being sentimentally unbearable to him. . . Still, he was fond of old Campion, and would rather be in his command than any other. He had attached to his staff a very decent set of fellows, as decent as you could be in contact with. . . if you had to be in contact with your kind. . . So he just said:

"Look here, Stanley, you are a silly ass," and left it at that, without demonstrating the truth of the assertion.

The colonel said:

"Why, what have I been doing now? . . . I *wish* you would walk the other way. . .

Tietjens said:

"No, I can't afford to go out of camp. . . I've got to come to witness your fantastic wedding-contract tomorrow afternoon, haven't I? . . . I can't leave camp twice in one week. . .

"You've got to come down to the camp-guard," Levin said. "I hate to keep a woman waiting in the cold. . . though she is in the general's car."

Tietjens exclaimed:

"You've not been. . . oh, extraordinarily enough, to bring Miss de Bailly out here? To talk to me?"

Colonel Levin mumbled, so low Tietjens almost imagined that he was not meant to hear:

"It isn't Miss de Bailly!" Then he exclaimed quite aloud: "Damn it all, Tietjens, haven't you had hints enough?"

For a lunatic moment it went through Tietjens' mind that it must be Miss Wannop in the general's car, at the gate, down the hill beside the camp guard-room. But he knew folly when it presented itself to his mind. He had nevertheless turned and they were going very slowly back along the broad way between the huts. Levin was certainly in no hurry. The broad way would come to an end of the hutments; about two acres of slope would descend blackly before them, white stones to mark a sort of coastguard track glimmering out of sight beneath a moon gone dark with the frost. And, down there in the dark forest, at the end of that track, in a terrific Rolls-Royce, was waiting something of which Levin was certainly deucedly afraid. . .

For a minute Tietjens' backbone stiffened. He didn't intend to interfere between Mlle de Bailly and any married woman Levin had had as a mistress. . . Somehow he was convinced that what was in that car was a married woman. . . He did not dare to think otherwise. If it was not a married woman it might be Miss Wannop. If it was, it couldn't be. . . An immense waft of calm, sentimental happiness had descended upon him. Merely because he had imagined her! He imagined her little, fair, rather pug-nosed face: under a fur cap, he did not know why. Leaning forward she would be, on the seat of the general's illuminated car: glazed in: a regular raree show! Peering out, shortsightedly on account of the reflections on the inside of the glass. . .

He was saying to Levin:

"Look here, Stanley. . . why I said you are a silly ass is because Miss de Bailly has one chief luxury. It's exhibiting jealousy. Not feeling it; exhibiting it."

"*Ought* you," Levin asked ironically, "to discuss my fiancée before me? As an English gentleman. Tietjens of Groby and all."

"Why, of course," Tietjens said. He continued feeling happy. "As a sort of swollen best man, it's my duty to instruct you. Mothers tell their daughters things before marriage. Best men do it for the innocent Benedict. . . woman. . ."

"I'm not doing it now," Levin grumbled direly.

"Then what, in God's name, are you doing? You've got a cast mistress, haven't you, down there in old Campion's car? . . ." They were beside the alley that led down to his orderly room. Knots of men, dim and desultory, still half filled it, a little way down.

"I *haven't*," Levin exclaimed almost tearfully. "I never had a mistress."

"And you're not married?" Tietjens asked. "He used on purpose the schoolboy's exclamation Tummy!" to soften the jibe. "If you'll excuse me," he said, "I must just go and take a look at my crowd. To see if your orders have come down."

He found no orders in a hut as full as ever of the dull mists and odours of khaki, but he found in revenge a fine upstanding, blond, Canadian-born lance-corporal of old Colonial lineage, with a moving story as related by Sergeant-Major Cowley:

"This man, sir, of the Canadian Railway lot, "is mother's just turned up in the town, come on from Eetarpels. Come all the way from Toronto where she was bedridden." Tietjens said:

"Well, what about it? Get a move on."

The man wanted leave to go to his mother who was waiting in a decent estaminet at the end of the tramline just outside the camp where the houses of the town began.

Tietjens said: "It's impossible. It's absolutely impossible. You know that."

The man stood erect and expressionless; his blue eyes looked confoundedly honest to Tietjens who was cursing himself. He said to the man:

"You can see for yourself that it's impossible, can't you?" The man said slowly:

"Not knowing the regulations in these circumstances I can't say, sir. But my mother's is a very special case. . . She's lost two sons already."

Tietjens said:

"A great many people have. . . Do you understand, if you went absent off my pass I might—I quite possibly might—lose my commission? I'm responsible for you fellows getting up the line."

The man looked down at his feet. Tietjens said to himself that it was Valentine Wannop doing this to him. He ought to turn the man down at once. He was pervaded by a sense of her being. It was imbebile. Yet it was so. He said to the man:

"You said good-bye to your mother, didn't you, in Toronto, before you left?"

The man said:

"No, sir." He had not seen his mother in seven years. He had been up in the Chilkoot when war broke out and had not heard of it for ten months. Then he had at once joined up in British Columbia, and had been sent straight through for railway work, on to Aldershot where the Canadians had a camp in building. He had not known that his brothers were killed till he got there and his mother, being bedridden at the news, had not been able to get to Toronto when his batch had passed through. She lived about sixty miles from Toronto. Now she had risen from her bed like a miracle and come all the way. A widow: sixty-two years of age. Very feeble.

It occurred to Tietjens as it occurred to him ten times a day that it was idiotic of him to figure Valentine Wannop to himself. He had not the slightest idea where she was: in what circumstances, or even in what house. He did not suppose she and her mother had stayed on in that dog-kennel of a place in Bedford Park. They would be fairly comfortable. His father had left them money. "It is preposterous," he said to himself, "to persist in figuring a person to yourself when you have no idea of where they are." He said to the man:

"Wouldn't it do if you saw your mother at the camp gate, by the guard-room?"

"Not much of a leave-taking, sir," the man said; "she not allowed in the camp and I not allowed out. Talking under a sentry's nose very likely."

Tietjens said to himself:

"What a monstrous absurdity this is of seeing and talking, for a minute or so! You meet and talk. . ." And next day at the same hour. Nothing. . . As well not to meet or talk. . . Yet the mere fantastic idea of seeing Valentine Wannop for a minute. . . She not allowed in the camp and he not going out. Talking under a sentry's nose, very likely. . . It had made him smell primroses. Primroses, like Miss Wannop. He said to the sergeant-major:

"What sort of a fellow is this?" Cowley, in open-mouthed suspense, gasped like a fish. Tietjens said:

"I suppose your mother is fairly feeble to stand in the cold?"

"A very decent man, sir," the sergeant-major got out, "one of the best. No trouble. A perfectly clean conduct sheet. Very good education. A railway engineer in civil life. . . Volunteered, of course, sir."

"That's the odd thing," Tietjens said to the man, "that the percentages of absentees is as great amongst the volunteers as the Derby men or the compulsorily enlisted. . . Do you understand what will happen to you if you miss the draft?"

The man said soberly:

"Yes, sir. Perfectly well."

"You understand that you will be shot? As certainly as that you stand there. And that you haven't a chance of escape."

He wondered what Valentine Wannop, hot pacifist, would think of him if she heard him. Yet it was his duty to talk like that: his human, not merely his military duty. As much his duty as that of a doctor to warn a man that if he drank of typhoid-contaminated water he would get typhoid. But people are unreasonable. Valentine too was unreasonable. She would consider it brutal to speak to a man of the possibility of his being shot by a firing party. A groan burst from him. At the thought that there was no sense in bothering about what Valentine Wannop would or would not think of him. No sense. No sense. No sense. . .

The man, fortunately, was assuring him that he knew, very soberly, all about the penalty for going absent off a draft. The sergeant-major, catching a sound from Tietjens, said with admirable fussiness to the man:

"There, there! Don't you hear the officer's speaking? Never interrupt an officer."

"You'll be shot," Tietjens said, "at dawn. . . Literally at dawn." Why did they shoot them at dawn? To rub it in that they were never going to see another sunrise. But they drugged the fellows so that they wouldn't know the sun if they saw it: all roped in a chair. . . It was really the worse for the firing party. He added to the man:

"Don't think I'm insulting you. You appear to be a very decent fellow. But very decent fellows have gone absent." He said to the sergeant-major:

"Give this man a two-hours' pass to go to the. . . whatever's the name of the estaminet. . . The draft won't move off for two hours, will it?" He added to the man: "If you see your draft passing the pub you run out and fall in. Like mad, you understand. You'd never get another chance."

There was a mumble like applause and envy of a mate's good luck from a packed audience that had hung on the lips of simple melodrama. . . an audience that seemed to be all enlarged eyes, the khaki was so colourless. . . They came as near applause as they dared, but there was no sense in worrying about whether Valentine Wannop would have applauded or not. . . And there was no knowing whether the fellow would not go absent, either. As likely as not there was no mother. A girl very likely. And very likely the man would desert. . . The man looked you straight in the eyes. But a strong passion, like that for escape—or a girl—will give you control over the muscles of the eyes. A little thing that, before strong passion! One would look God in the face on the day of judgement and lie, in that case.

Because what the devil did he want of Valentine Wannop? Why could he not stall off the thought of her? He could stall off the thought of his wife. . . or his not-wife. But Valentine Wannop came wriggling in. At all hours of the day and night. It was an obsession. A madness. . . What those fools called "a complex"! . . . Due, no doubt, to something your nurse had done, or your parents said to you. At birth. . . A strong passion. . . or no doubt not strong enough. Otherwise he, too, would have gone absent. At any rate, from Sylvia. . . Which he hadn't done. Or hadn't he? There was no saying. . .

It was undoubtedly colder in the alley between the huts. A man was saying: "Hoo. . . Hooo. . . Hoo. . ." A sound like that, and flapping his arms and hopping. . . "Hand and foot, mark time! Somebody ought to fall these poor devils in and give them that to keep their circulations going. But they might not know the command. . . It was a Guards' trick, really. . . What the devil were these fellows kept hanging about here for? he asked.

One or two voices said that they did not know. The majority said gutturally:

"Waiting for our mates, sir. . ."

"I should have thought you could have waited under cover," Tietjens said caustically. "But never mind; it's your funeral, if you like it. . ." This getting together. . . a strong passion. There was a warmed reception-hut for waiting drafts not fifty yards away. . . But they stood, teeth chattering and mumbling "Hoo. . . Hoo. . ." rather than miss thirty seconds of gabble. . . About what the English sergeant-major said and about what the officer said and how many dollars did they give you. . . And of course about what you answered back. . . Or perhaps not that. These Canadian troops were husky, serious fellows, without the swank of the Cockney or the Lincolnshire Moonrakers. They wanted, apparently, to learn the rules of war. They discussed anxiously information that they received in orderly rooms, and looked at you as if you were expounding the gospels. . .

But, damn it, he, he himself, would make a pact with Destiny, at that moment, willingly, to pass thirty months in the frozen circle of hell, for the chance of thirty seconds in which to tell Valentine Wannop what he had answered back. . . to Destiny! . . . What was the fellow in the Inferno who was buried to the neck in ice and begged Dante to clear the icicles out of his eyelids so that he could see out of them? And Dante kicked him in the face because he was a Ghibelline. . . Always a bit of a swine, Dante. . . Rather like. . . like whom? . . . Oh, Sylvia Tietjens. . . A good hater! . . . He imagined hatred coming to him in waves from the convent in which Sylvia had immured herself. . . Gone into retreat. . . He imagined she had gone into retreat. She had said she was going. For the rest of the war. . . For the duration of hostilities or life, whichever were the longer. . . He imagined Sylvia, coiled up on a convent bed. . . Hating. . . Her certainly glorious hair all round her. . . Hating. . . Slowly and coldly. . . Like the head of a snake when you examined it. . . Eyes motionless: mouth closed tight. . . Looking away into the distance and hating. . . She was presumably in Birkenhead. . . A long way to send your hatred. . . Across a country and a sea in an icy night. . . ! Over all that black land and water. . . with the lights out because of air-raids and U-boats. . . Well, he did not have to think of Sylvia at the moment. She was well out of it. . .

It was certainly getting no warmer as the night drew on. . . Even that ass Levin was pacing swiftly up and down in the dusky moon-shadow of the last hutments that looked over the slope and the vanishing trail of white stones. . . In spite of his boasting about not wearing an overcoat; to catch women's eyes with his pretty Staff gadgets he was carrying on like a leopard at feeding time. . .

Tietjens said:

"Sorry to keep you waiting, old man. . . Or rather your lady. . . But there were some men to see to. . . And, you know. . . 'The comfort and—what is it?—of the men comes before every—is it "consideration"?—except the exigencies of actual warfare' . . . My memory's gone phut these days. . . And you want me to slide down this hill and wheeze back again. . . To see a woman!

Levin screeched: "Damn you, you ass! It's your wife who's waiting for you at the bottom there."

III

The one thing that stood out sharply in Tietjens' mind when at last, with a stiff glass of rum punch, his, officer's pocket-book complete with pencil because he had to draft before eleven a report as to the desirability of giving his unit special lectures on the causes of the war, and a cheap French novel on a camp chair beside him, he sat in his fleabag with six army blankets over him—the one thing that stood out as sharply as Staff tabs was that that ass Levin was rather pathetic. His unnailed bootsoles very much cramping his action on the frozen hillside, he had alternately hobbled a step or two, and, reduced to inaction, had grabbed at Tietjens' elbow, while he brought out breathlessly puzzled sentences. . .

There resulted a singular mosaic of extraordinary, bright-coloured and melodramatic statements, for Levin, who first hobbled down the hill with Tietjens and then hobbled back up, clinging to his arm, brought out monstrosities of news about Sylvia's activities, without any sequence, and indeed without any apparent aim except for the great affection he had for Tietjens himself. . . All sorts or singular things seemed to have been going on round him in the vague zone, outside all this engrossed and dust-coloured world—in the vague zone that held. . . Oh, the civilian population, tea-parties short of butter! . . .

And as Tietjens, seated on his hams, his knees up, pulled the soft woolliness of his flea-bag under his chin and damned the paraffin heater for letting out a new and singular stink, it seemed to him that this affair was like coming back after two months and trying to get the hang of battalion orders. . . You come back to the familiar, slightly battered mess ante-room. You tell the mess orderly to bring you the last two months' orders, for it is as much as your life is worth not to know what is or is not in them. . . There might be an A.C.I. ordering you to wear your helmet back to the front, or a battalion order that Mills bombs must always be worn in the left breast pocket. Or there might be the detail for putting on a new gas helmet! . . . The orderly hands you a dishevelled mass of faintly typewritten matter, thumbed out of all chance of legibility, with the orders for November 26 fastened inextricably into the middle of those for the 1st of December, and those for the 10th, 25th and 29th missing altogether. . . And all that you gather is that headquarters has some exceedingly insulting things to say about A Company; that a fellow called Hartopp, whom you don't know, has been deprived of his commission; that at a court of inquiry held to ascertain deficiencies in C Company Captain Wells—poor Wells I—has been assessed at £27 11 4d., which he is requested to pay forthwith to the adjutant. . .

So, on that black hillside, going and returning, what stuck out for Tietjens was that Levin had been taught by the general to consider that he, Tietjens, was an extraordinarily violent chap who would certainly knock Levin down when he told him that his wife was at the camp gates; that Levin considered himself to be the descendant of an ancient Quaker family. . . (Tietjens had said *Good God*! at that); that the mysterious "rows" to which in his fear Levin had been continually referring had been successive letters from Sylvia to the harried general. . . and that Sylvia had accused him, Tietjens, of stealing two pairs of her best sheets. . . There was a great deal more. But having faced what he considered to be the worst of the situation, Tietjens set himself coolly to recapitulate every aspect of his separation from his wife. He had meant to face every aspect, not that merely social one upon which, hitherto, he had automatically imagined their disunion to rest. For, as he saw it, English people of good position consider that the basis of all marital unions or disunions is the maxim: No scenes. Obviously for the sake of the servants—who are the same thing as the public. No scenes, then, for the sake of the public. And indeed, with him, the instinct for privacy—as to his relationships, his passions, or even as to his most unimportant motives—was as strong as the instinct of life itself. He would, literally, rather be dead than an open book.

And, until that afternoon, he had imagined that his wife, too, would rather be dead than have her affairs canvassed by the other ranks. . . But that assumption had to be gone over. Revised. . . Of course he might say she had gone mad. But, if he said she had gone mad he would have to revise a great deal of their relationships, so it would be as broad as it was long. . .

The doctor's batman, from the other end of the hut, said:

"Poor—0 Nine Morgan. . ." in a sing-song, mocking voice. . .

For though, hours before, Tietjens had appointed this moment of physical ease that usually followed on his splurging heavily down on to his creaking camp-bed in the doctor's lent hut, for the cool consideration of his relations with his wife, it was not turning out a very easy matter. The hut was unreasonably warm: he had invited Mackenzie—whose real name turned out to be McKechnie, James Grant McKechnie—to occupy the other end of it. The other end of it was divided from him by a partition of canvas and a striped Indian curtain. And McKechnie, who was unable to sleep, had elected to carry on a long—an interminable—conversation with the doctor's batman.

The doctor's batman also could not sleep and, like McKechnie, was more than a little barmy on the crumpet—an almost non-English-speaking Welshman from God knows what up-country valley. He had shaggy hair like a Caribbean savage and two dark, resentful wall-eyes; being a miner he sat on his heels more comfortably than on a chair and his almost incomprehensible voice went on in a low sort of ululation, with an occasionally and startlingly comprehensible phrase sticking out now and then.

It was troublesome, but orthodox enough. The batman had been blown literally out of most of his senses and the VIth Battalion of the Glamorganshire Regiment by some German high explosive or other, more than a year ago. But before then, it appeared, he had been in McKechnie's own company in that battalion. It was perfectly in order that an officer should gossip with a private formerly of his own platoon or company, especially on first meeting him after long separation caused by a casualty to one or the other. And McKechnie had first re-met this scoundrel Jonce, or Evanns, at eleven that night—two and a half hours before. So there, in the light of a single candle stuck in a stout bottle they were tranquilly at it: the batman sitting on his heels by the officer's head; the officer, in his pyjamas, sprawling half out of bed over his pillows, stretching his arms abroad, occasionally yawning, occasionally asking: "What became of Company-Sergeant-Major Hoyt?" . . . They might talk till half-past three.

But that was troublesome to a gentleman seeking to recapture what exactly were his relations with his wife.

Before the doctor's batman had interrupted him by speaking startlingly of 0 Nine Morgan, Tietjens had got as far as what follows with his recapitulation: The lady, Mrs. Tietjens, was certainly without mitigation a whore; he himself equally certainly and without qualification had been physically faithful to the lady and their marriage tie. In law, then, he was absolutely in the right of it. But that fact had less weight than a cobweb. For after the last of her high-handed divagations from fidelity he had accorded to the lady the shelter of his roof and of his name. She had lived for years beside him, apparently on terms of hatred and miscomprehension. But certainly in conditions of chastity. Then, during the tenuous and lugubrious small hours, before his coming out there again to France, she had given evidence of a madly vindictive passion for his person. A physical passion at any rate.

Well, those were times of mad, fugitive emotions. But even in the calmest times a man could not expect to have a woman live with him as the mistress of his house and mother of his heir without establishing some sort of claim upon him. They hadn't slept together. But was it not possible that a constant measuring together of your minds was as proper to give you a proprietary right as the measuring together of the limb? It was perfectly possible. Well then. . .

What, in the eyes of God, severed a union? . . . Certainly he had imagined—until that very afternoon—that their union had been cut, as the tendon of Achilles is cut in a hamstringing, by Sylvia's clear voice, outside his house, saying in the dawn to a cabman, "Paddington!" . . . He tried to go with extreme care through every detail of their last interview in his still nearly dark drawing-room at the other end of which she had seemed a mere white phosphorescence. . .

They had, then, parted for good on that day. He was going out to France; she into retreat in a convent near Birkenhead—to which place you go from Paddington. Well then, that was one parting. That, surely, set him free for the girl!

He took a sip from the glass of rum and water on the canvas chair beside him. It was tepid and therefore beastly. He had ordered the batman to bring it him hot, strong and sweet, because he had been certain of an incipient cold. He had refrained from drinking it because he had remembered that he was to think cold-bloodedly of Sylvia, and he made a practice of never touching alcohol when about to engage in protracted reflection. That had always been his theory: it had been immensely and empirically strengthened by his warlike experience. On the Somme, in the summer, when stand-to had been at four in the morning, you would come out of your dug-out and survey, with a complete outfit of pessimistic thoughts, a dim, grey, repulsive landscape over a dull and much too thin parapet. There would be repellent posts, altogether too fragile entanglements of barbed wire, broken wheels, detritus, coils of mist over the positions of revolting Germans. Grey stillness; grey horrors, in front, and behind amongst the civilian populations! And clear, hard outlines to every thought. . . Then your batman brought you a cup of tea with a little—quite a little—rum in it. In three of four minutes the whole world changed beneath your eyes. The wire aprons became jolly efficient protections that your skill had devised and for which you might thank God; the broken wheels were convenient landmarks for raiding at night in No Man's Land. You had to confess that, when you had re-erected that parapet, after it had last been jammed in, your company had made a pretty good job of it. And, even as far as the Germans were concerned, you were there to kill the swine; but you didn't feel that the thought of them would make you sick beforehand. . . You were, in fact, a changed man. With a mind of a different specific gravity. You could not even tell that the roseate touches of dawn on the mists were not really the effects of rum. . .

Therefore he had determined not to touch his grog. But his throat had gone completely dry; so, mechanically, he had reached out for something to drink, checking himself when he had realized what he was doing. But why should his throat be dry? He hadn't been on the drink. He had not even had any dinner. And why was he in this extraordinary state? . . . For he was in an extraordinary state. It was because the idea had suddenly occurred to him that his parting from his wife had set him free for his girl. . . The idea had till then never entered his head.

He said to himself: We must go methodically into this! Methodically into the history of his last day on earth. . .

Because he swore that when he had come out to France this time he had imagined that he was cutting loose from this earth. And during the months that he had been there he had seemed to have no connection with any earthly things. He had imagined Sylvia in her convent and done with; Miss Wannop he had not been able to imagine at all. But she had seemed to be done with.

It was difficult to get his mind back to that night. You cannot force your mind to a deliberate, consecutive recollection unless you are in the mood; then it will do whether you want it to or not. . . He had had then, three months or so ago, a very painful morning with his wife, the pain coming from a suddenly growing conviction that his wife was forcing herself into an attitude of caring for him. Only an attitude probably, because, in the end, Sylvia was a lady and would not allow herself really to care for the person in the world for whom it would be least decent of her to care. . . But she would be perfectly capable of forcing herself to take that attitude if she thought that it would enormously inconvenience himself. . .

But that wasn't the way, wasn't the way, wasn't the way, his excited mind said to himself. He was excited because it was possible that Miss Wannop, too, might not have meant their parting to be a permanency. That opened up an immense perspective. Nevertheless, the contemplation of that immense perspective was not the way to set about a calm analysis of his relations with his wife. The facts of the story must be stated before the moral. He said to himself that he must put, in exact language, as if he were making a report for the use of garrison headquarters, the history of himself in his relationship to his wife. . . And to Miss Wannop, of course. "Better put it into writing," he said.

Well then. He clutched at his pocket-book and wrote in large pencilled characters:

"When I married Miss Satterthwaite,"—he was attempting exactly to imitate a report to General Headquarters—"unknown to myself, she imagined herself to be with child by a fellow called Drake. I think she was not. The matter is debatable. I am passionately attached to the child who is my heir and the heir of a family of considerable position. The lady was subsequently, on several occasions, though I do not know how many, unfaithful to me. She left me with a fellow called Perowne, whom she had met constantly at the house of my godfather, General Lord Edward Campion, on whose staff Perowne was. That was long before the war. This intimacy was, of course, certainly unsuspected by the general. Perowne is again on the staff of General Campion, who has the quality of attachment to his old subordinates, but as Perowne is an inefficient officer, he is used only for more decorative jobs. Otherwise, obviously, as he is an old regular, his seniority should make him a general, and he is only a major. I make this diversion about Perowne because his presence in this garrison causes me natural personal annoyance.

"My wife, after an absence of several months with Perowne, wrote and told me that she wished to be taken back into my household. I allowed this. My principles prevent me from divorcing any woman, in particular any woman who is the mother of a child. As I had taken no steps to ensure publicity for the escapade of Mrs. Tietjens, no one, as far as I know, was aware of her absence. Mrs. Tietjens, being a Roman Catholic, is prevented from divorcing me.

"During this absence of Mrs. Tietjens with the man Perowne, I made the acquaintance of a young woman, Miss Wannop, the daughter of my father's oldest friend, who was also an old friend of General Campion's. Our station in Society naturally forms rather a close ring. I was immediately aware that I had formed a sympathetic but not violent attachment for Miss Wannop, and fairly confident that my feeling was returned. Neither Miss Wannop nor myself being persons to talk about the state of our feelings, we exchanged no confidences. . . A disadvantage of being English of a certain station.

"The position continued thus for several years. Six or seven. After her return from her excursion with Perowne, Mrs. Tietjens remained, I believe, perfectly chaste. I saw Miss Wannop sometimes frequently, for a period, in her mother's house or on social occasions, sometimes not for long intervals. No expression of affection on the part of either of us ever passed. Not one. Ever.

"On the day before my second going out to France I had a very painful scene with my wife, during which, for the first time, we went into the question of the parentage of my child and other matters. In the afternoon I met Miss Wannop by appointment outside the War Office. The appointment had been made by my wife, not by me. I knew nothing about it. My wife must have been more aware of my feelings for Miss Wannop than I was myself.

"In St. James's Park I invited Miss Wannop to become my mistress that evening. She consented and made an assignation. It is to be presumed that that was evidence of her affection for me. We have never exchanged words of affection. Presumably a young lady does not consent to go to bed with a married man without feeling affection for him. But I have no proof. It was, of course, only a few hours before my going out to France. Those are emotional sorts of moments for young women. No doubt they consent more easily.

"But we didn't. We were together at one-thirty in the morning, leaning over her suburban garden gate. And nothing happened. We agreed that we were the sort of persons who didn't. I do not know how we agreed. We never finished a sentence. Yet it was a passionate scene. So I touched the brim of my cap and said: *So long*! . . . Or she. . . I don't remember. I remember the thoughts I thought and the thoughts I gave her credit for thinking. But perhaps she did not think them. There is no knowing. It is no good going into them. . . except that I gave her credit for thinking that we were parting for good. Perhaps she did not mean that. Perhaps I could write letters to her. And live. . ."

He exclaimed:

"God, what a sweat I am in! . . ."

The sweat, indeed, was pouring down his temples. He became instinct with a sort of passion to let his thoughts wander into epithets and go about where they would. But he stuck at it. He was determined to get it expressed. He wrote on again:

"I got home towards two in the morning and went into the dining-room in the dark. I did not need a light. I sat thinking for a long time. Then Sylvia spoke from the other end of the room. There was thus an abominable situation. I have never been spoken to with such hatred. She went, perhaps, mad. She had apparently been banking on the idea that if I had physical contact with Miss Wannop I might satisfy my affection for the girl. . . And feel physical desires for *her*. . . But she knew, without my speaking, that I had not had physical contact with the girl. She threatened to ruin me; to ruin me in the Army; to drag my name through the mud. . . I never spoke. I am damn good at not speaking. She struck me in the face. And went away. Afterwards she threw into the room, through the half-open doorway, a gold medallion of St. Michael, the R.C. patron of soldiers in action that she had worn between her breasts. I took it to mean the final act of parting. As if by no longer wearing it she abandoned all prayer for my safety. . . It might just as well mean that she wished me to wear it myself for my personal protection. . . I heard her go down the stairs with her maid. The dawn was just showing through the chimney-pots opposite. I heard her say: *Paddington*. Clear, high syllables! And a motor drove off.

"I got my things together and went to Waterloo. Mrs. Satterthwaite, her mother, was waiting to see me off. She was very distressed that her daughter had not come, too. She was of opinion that it meant we had parted for good. I was astonished to find that Sylvia had told her mother about Miss Wannop because Sylvia had always been extremely reticent, even to her mother. . . Mrs. Satterthwaite, who was *very* distressed—she likes me!—expressed the most gloomy forebodings as to what Sylvia might not be up to. I laughed at her. She began to tell me a long anecdote about what a Father Consett, Sylvia's confessor, had said about Sylvia years before. He had said that if I ever came to care for another woman Sylvia would tear the world to pieces to get at me. . . Meaning, to disturb my equanimity! . . . It was difficult to follow Mrs. Satterthwaite. The side of an officer's train, going off, is not a good place for confidences. So the interview ended rather untidily."

At this point Tietjens groaned so audibly that McKechnie, from the other end of the hut, asked if he had not said anything. Tietjens saved himself with:

"That candle looks from here to be too near the side of the hut. Perhaps it isn't. These buildings are very inflammable."

It was no good going on writing. He was no writer, and this writing gave no sort of psychological pointers. He wasn't himself ever much the man for psychology, but one ought to be as efficient at it as at anything else. . . Well then. . . What was at the bottom of all the madness and cruelty that had distinguished both himself and Sylvia on his last day and night in his native country? . . . For, mark! It was Sylvia who had made, unknown to him, the appointment through which the girl had met him. Sylvia had wanted to force him and Miss Wannop into each other's arms. Quite definitely. She had said as much. But she had only said that afterwards. When the game had not come off. She had had too much knowledge of amatory manoeuvres to show her hand before. . .

Why then had she done it? Partly, undoubtedly, out of pity for him. She had given him a rotten time; she had undoubtedly, at one moment, wanted to give him the consolation of his girl's arms. . . Why, damn it, she, Sylvia, and no one else, had forced out of him the invitation to the girl to become his mistress. Nothing but the infernal cruelty of their interview of the morning could have forced him to the pitch of sexual excitement that would make him make a proposal of illicit intercourse to a young lady to whom hitherto he had spoken not even one word of affection. It was an effect of a Sadic kind. That was the only way to look at it scientifically. And without doubt Sylvia had known what she was doing. The whole morning; at intervals, like a person directing the whiplash to a cruel spot of pain, reiteratedly, she had gone on and on. She had accused him of having Valentine Wannop for his mistress. She had accused him of having Valentine Wannop for his mistress. She had accused him of having Valentine Wannop for his mistress. . . With maddening reiteration, like that. They had disposed of an estate; they had settled up a number of business matters; they had decided that his heir was to be brought up as a Papist—the mother's religion! They had gone, agonizedly enough, into their own relationships and past history. Into the very paternity of his child. . . But always, at moments when his mind was like a blind octopus, squirming in an agony of knife-cuts, she would drop in that accusation. She had accused him of having Valentine Wannop for his mistress. . .

He swore by the living God.. He had never realized that he had a passion for the girl till that morning; that he had a passion deep and boundless like the sea, shaking like a tremor of the whole world, an unquenchable thirst, a thing the thought of which made your bowels turn over. . . But he had not been the sort of fellow who goes into his emotions. . . Why, damn it, even at that moment when he thought of the girl, there, in that beastly camp, in that Rembrandt beshadowed hut, when he thought of the girl he named her to himself Miss Wannop.

It wasn't in that way that a man thought of a young woman whom he was aware of passionately loving. He wasn't aware. He hadn't been aware. Until that morning. . .

Then. . . that let him out. . . Undoubtedly that let him out. . . A woman cannot throw her man, her official husband, into the arms of the first girl that comes along and consider herself as having any further claims upon him. Especially if, on the same day, you part with him, he going out to France! *Did* it let him out? Obviously it did.

He caught with such rapidity at his glass of rum and water that a little of it ran over on to his thumb. He swallowed the lot, being instantly warmed..

What in the world was he doing? Now? With all this introspection? . . . Hang it all, he was not justifying himself. . . He had acted perfectly correctly as far as Sylvia was concerned. Not perhaps to Miss Wannop. . . Why, if he, Christopher Tietjens of Groby, had the need to justify himself, what did it stand for to be Christopher Tietjens of Groby? That was the unthinkable thought.

Obviously he was not immune from the seven deadly sins. In the way of a man. One might lie, yet not bear false witness against a neighbour; one might kill, yet not without fitting provocation or for self-interest; one might conceive of theft as receiving cattle from the false Scots which was the Yorkshireman's duty; one might fornicate, obviously, as long as you did not fuss about it unhealthily. That was the right of the Seigneur in a world of Other Ranks. He hadn't personally committed any of these sins to any great extent. One reserved the right so to do and to take the consequences. . .

But what in the world had gone wrong with Sylvia? She was giving away her own game, and that he had never known her do. But she could not have made more certain, if she had wanted to, of returning him to his allegiance to Miss Wannop than by forcing herself there into his private life, and doing it with such blatant vulgarity. For what she had done had been to make scenes before the servants! All the while he had been in France she had been working up to it. Now she had done it. Before the Tommies of his own unit. But Sylvia did not make mistakes like that. It was a game. What game? He didn't even attempt to conjecture! She could not expect that he would in the future even extend to her the shelter of his roof. . . What then was the game? He could not believe that she could be capable of vulgarity except with a purpose. . .

She was a thoroughbred. He had always credited her with being that. And now she was behaving as if she had every mean vice that a mare could have. Or it looked like it. Was that, then, because she had been in his stable? But how in the world otherwise could he have run their lives? She had been unfaithful to him. She had never been anything but unfaithful to him, before or after marriage. In a high-handed way so that he could not condemn her, though it was disagreeable enough to himself. He took her back into his house after she had been off with the fellow Perowne. What more could she ask? . . . He could find no answer. And it was not his business!

But even if he did not bother about the motives of the poor beast of a woman, she was the mother of his heir. And now she was running about the world declaiming about her wrongs. What sort of a thing was that for a boy to have happen to him? A mother who made scenes before the servants! That was enough to ruin any boy's life. . .

There was no getting away from it that that was what Sylvia had been doing. She had deluged the general with letters for the last two months or so, at first merely contenting herself with asking where he, Tietjens, was and in what state of health, conditions of danger, and the like. Very decently, for some time, the old fellow had said nothing about the matter to him. He had probably taken the letters to be the naturally anxious inquiries of a wife with a husband at the front; he had considered that Tietjens' letters to her must have been insufficiently communicative, or concealed what she imagined to be wounds or a position of desperate danger. That would not have been very pleasant in any case; women should not worry superior officers about the vicissitudes of their menfolk. It was not done. Still, Sylvia was very intimate with Campion and his family—more intimate than he himself was, though Campion was his godfather. But quite obviously her letters had got worse and worse.

It was difficult for Tietjens to make out exactly what she had said. His channel of information had been Levin, who was too gentlemanly ever to say anything direct at all. Too gentlemanly, too implicitly trustful of Tietjens' honour. . . and too bewildered by the charms of Sylvia, who had obviously laid herself out to bewilder the poor Staff-wallah. . . But she had gone pretty far, either in her letters or in her conversation since she had been in that city, to which—it was characteristic—she had come without any sort of passports or papers, just walking past gentlemen in their wooden boxes at pierheads and the like, in conversation with—of all people in the world!—with Perowne, who had been returning from leave with King's dispatches, or something glorified of the Staff sort! In a special train very likely. That was Sylvia all over.

Levin said that Campion had given Perowne the most frightful dressing down he had ever heard mortal man receive. And it really was *damn* hard on the poor general, who, after happenings to one of his predecessors, had been perfectly rabid to keep skirts out of his headquarters. Indeed it was one of the crosses of Levin's worried life that the general had absolutely refused him, Levin, leave to marry Miss de Bailly if he would not undertake that that young woman should leave France by the first boat after the ceremony. Levin, of course, was to go with her, but the young woman was not to return to France for the duration of hostilities. And a fine row all her noble relatives had raised over that. It had cost Levin another hundred and fifty thousand francs in the marriage settlements. The married wives of officers in any case were not allowed in France, though you could not keep out their unmarried ones. . .

Campion, anyhow, had dispatched his furious note to Tietjens after receiving, firstly, in the early morning, a letter from Sylvia in which she said that her ducal second-cousin, the lugubrious Rugeley, highly disapproved of the fact that Tietjens was in France at all, and after later receiving, towards four in the afternoon, a telegram, dispatched by Sylvia herself from Havre, to say that she would be arriving by a noon train. The general had been almost as much upset at the thought that his car would not be there to meet Sylvia as by the thought that she was coming at all. But a strike of French railway civilians had delayed Sylvia's arrival. Campion had dispatched, within five minutes, his snorter to Tietjens, who he was convinced knew all about Sylvia's coming, and his car to Rouen Station with Levin in it.

The general, in fact, was in a fine confusion. He was convinced that Tietjens, as Man of Intellect, had treated Sylvia badly, even to the extent of stealing two pair of her best sheets, and he was also convinced that Tietjens was in close collusion with Sylvia. As Man of Intellect, Campion was convinced, Tietjens was dissatisfied with his lowly job of draft-forwarding officer, and wanted a place of an extravagantly cushy kind in the general's own entourage. . . And Levin had said that it made it all the worse that Campion in his bothered heart thought that Tietjens really ought to have more exalted employment. He had said to Levin:

"Damn it all, the fellow ought to be in command of my Intelligence instead of you. But he's unsound. That's what he is: unsound. He's too brilliant. . . And he'd talk both the hind legs off Sweedlepumpkins." Sweedlepumpkins was the general's favourite charger. The general was afraid of talk. He practically never talked with anyone except about his job—certainly never to Tietjens—without being proved to be in the wrong, and that undermined his belief in himself.

So that altogether he was in a fine fume. And confusion. He was almost ready to believe that Tietjens was at the bottom of every trouble that occurred in his immense command.

But, when all that was gathered, Tietjens was not much farther forward in knowing what his wife's errand in France was.

"She complains," Levin had bleated painfully at some point on the slippery coastguard path, "about your taking her sheets. And about a Miss. . . a Miss Wanostrocht, is it? . . . The general is not inclined to attach much importance to the sheets. . ."

It appeared that a sort of conference on Tietjens' case had taken place in the immense tapestried salon in which Campion lived with the more intimate members of his headquarters, and which was, for the moment, presided over by Sylvia, who had exposed various wrongs to the general and Levin. Major Perowne had excused himself on the ground that he was hardly competent to express an opinion. Really, Levin said, he was sulking, because Campion had accused him of running the risk of getting himself and Mrs. Tietjens "talked about". Levin thought it was a bit thick of the general. Were none of the members of his staff ever to escort a lady anywhere? As if they were sixth-form schoolboys. . .

"But you. . . you. . . you. . ." he stuttered and shivered together, "certainly *do* seem to have been remiss in not writing to Mrs. Tietjens. The poor lady—excuse me!—really appears to have been out of her mind with anxiety. . ." That was why she had been waiting in the general's car at the bottom of the hill. To get a glimpse of Tietjens' living body. For they had been utterly unable, up at H.Q., to convince her that Tietjens was even alive, much less in that town.

She hadn't in fact waited even so long. Having apparently convinced herself by conversation with the sentries outside the guard-room that Tietjens actually still existed, she had told the chauffeur-orderly to drive her back to the Hotel de la Poste, leaving the wretched Levin to make his way back into the town by tram, or as best he might. They had seen the lights of the car below them, turning, with its gaily lit interior, and disappearing among the trees along the road farther down. . . The sentry, rather monosyllabically and gruffly—you can tell all right when a Tommie has something at the back of his mind!—informed them that the sergeant had turned out the guard so that all his men together could assure the lady that the captain was alive and well. The obliging sergeant said that he had adopted that manoeuvre which generally should attend only the visits of general officers and, once a day, for the C.O., because the lady had seemed so distressed at having received no letters from the captain. The guardroom itself, which was unprovided with cells, was decorated by the presence of two drunks who, having taken it into their heads to destroy their clothing, were in a state of complete nudity. The sergeant hoped, therefore, that he had done no wrong. Rightly the Garrison Military Police ought to take drunks picked up outside camp to the A.P.M.'s guard-room, but seeing the state of undress and the violent behaviour of these two, the sergeant had thought right to oblige the Red Caps. The voices of the drunks, singing the martial anthem of the "Men of Harlech", could be heard corroborating the sergeant's opinion as to their states. He added that he would not have turned out the guard if it had not been for its being the captain's lady.

"A damn smart fellow, that sergeant," Colonel Levin had said. "There couldn't have been any better way of convincing Mrs. Tietjens."

Tietjens had said—and even whilst he was saying it he tremendously wished he hadn't:

"Oh, a *damned* smart fellow," for the bitter irony of his tone had given Levin the chance to remonstrate with him as to his attitude towards Sylvia. Not at all as to his actions—for Levin conscientiously stuck to his thesis that Tietjens was the soul of honour—but just as to his tone of voice in talking of the sergeant who had been kind to Sylvia, and, just precisely, because Tietjens' not writing to his wife had given rise to the incident. Tietjens had thought of saying that, considering the terms on which they had parted, he would have considered himself as molesting the lady if he had addressed to her any letter at all. But he said nothing and, for a quarter of an hour, the incident resolved itself into soliloquy on the slippery hillside, delivered by Levin on the subject of matrimony. It was a matter which, naturally, at that moment very much occupied his thoughts. He considered that a man should so live with his wife that she should be able to open all his letters. That was his idea of the idyllic. And when Tietjens remarked with irony that he had never in his life either written or received a letter that his wife might not have read, Levin exclaimed with such enthusiasm as almost to lose his balance in the mist:

"I was sure of it, old fellow. But it enormously cheers me up to hear you say so." He added that he desired as far as possible to model his ideas of life and his behaviour on those of this his friend. For, naturally, about as he was to unite his fortunes with those of Miss de Bailly, that could be considered a turning point of his career.

IV

They had gone back up the hill so that Levin might telephone to headquarters for his own car in case the general's chauffeur should not have the sense to return for him. But that was as far as Tietjens got in uninterrupted reminiscences of that scene. . . He was sitting in his fleabag, digging idly with his pencil into the squared page of his notebook which had remained open on his knees, his eyes going over and over again over the words with which his report on his own case had concluded—the words: *So the interview ended rather untidily.* Over the words went the image of the dark hillside with the lights of the town, now that the air-raid was finished, spreading high up into the sky below them. . .

But at that point the doctor's batman had uttered, as if with a jocular, hoarse irony, the name:

"Poor —— 0 Nine Morgan! . . ." and over the whitish sheet of paper on a level with his nose Tietjens perceived thin films of reddish purple to be wavering, then a glutinous surface of gummy scarlet pigment. Moving! It was once more an effect of fatigue, operating on the retina, that was perfectly familiar to Tietjens. But it filled him with indignation against his own weakness. He said to himself: Wasn't the name of the wretched 0 Nine Morgan to be mentioned in his hearing without his retina presenting him with the glowing image of the fellow's blood? He watched the phenomenon, growing fainter, moving to the right-hand top corner of the paper and turning a faintly luminous green. He watched it with a grim irony.

Was he, he said to himself, to regard himself as responsible for the fellow's death? Was his inner mentality going to present that claim upon him? That would be absurd. The end of the earth! The absurd end of the earth. . . Yet that insignificant ass Levin had that evening asserted the claim to go into his, Tietjens of Groby's, relations with his wife. That was an end of earth as absurd! It was the unthinkable thing, as unthinkable as the theory that the officer can be responsible for the death of the man. . . But the idea had certainly presented itself to him. How could he be responsible for the death? In fact—in literalness—he was. It had depended absolutely upon his discretion whether the man should go home or not. The man's life or death had been in his hands. He had followed the perfectly correct course. He had written to the police of the man's home town, and the police had urged him not to let the man come home. . . Extraordinary morality on the part of a police force! The man, they begged, should not be sent home because a prize-fighter was occupying his bed and laundry. . . Extraordinary common sense, very likely. . . They probably did not want to get drawn into a scrap with Red Evans of the Red Castle. . .

For a moment he seemed to see. . . he actually saw. . . 0 Nine Morgan's eyes, looking at him with a sort of wonder, as they had looked when he had refused the fellow his leave. . . A sort of wonder! Without resentment, but with incredulity. As you might look at God, you being very small and ten feet or so below His throne when He pronounced some inscrutable judgment! . . . The Lord giveth home-leave, and the Lord refuseth. . . Probably not blessed, but queer, be the name of God-Tietjens!

And at the thought of the man as he was alive and of him now, dead, an immense blackness descended all over Tietjens. He said to himself: *I am very tired*. Yet he was not ashamed. . . It was the blackness that descends on you when you think of your dead. . . It comes, at any time, over the brightness of sunlight, in the grey of evening, in the grey of the dawn, at mess, on parade: it comes at the thought of one man or at the thought of half a battalion that you have seen, stretched out, under sheeting, the noses making little pimples: or not stretched out, lying face downwards, half buried. Or at the thought of dead that you have never seen dead at all. . . Suddenly the light goes out. . . In this case it was because of one fellow, a dirty enough man, not even very willing, not in the least endearing, certainly contemplating desertion. . . But your dead. . . *Yours*. . . Your own. As if joined to your own identity by a black cord. . .

In the darkness outside, the brushing, swift, rhythmic pacing of an immense number of men went past, as if they had been phantoms. A great number of men in fours, carried forward, irresistibly, by the overwhelming will of mankind in ruled motion. The sides of the hut were so thin that is was peopled by an innumerable throng. A sodden voice, just at Tietjens' head, chuckled: "For God's sake, sergeant-major, stop these —— I'm too —— drunk to halt them. . ."

It made for the moment no impression on Tietjens' conscious mind. Men were going past. Cries went up in the camp. Not orders, the men were still marching. Cries.

Tietjens' lips—his mind was still with the dead—said:

"That obscene Pitkins! I'll have him cashiered for this. . ." He saw an obscene subaltern, small, with one eyelid that drooped.

He came awake at that. Pitkins was the subaltern he had detailed to march the draft to the station and go on to Bailleul under a boozy field officer of sorts.

McKechnie said from the other bed:

"That's the draft back."

Tietjens said:

"Good God! . . ."

McKechnie said to the batman:

"For God's sake go and see if it is. Come back at once. . ."

The intolerable vision of the line, starving beneath the moon, of grey crowds murderously elbowing back a thin crowd in brown, zigzagged across the bronze light in the hut. The intolerable depression that, in those days, we felt—that all those millions were the play-things of ants busy in the miles of corridors beneath the domes and spires that rise up over the central heart of our comity, that intolerable weight upon the brain and the limbs, descended once more on those two men lying upon their elbows. As they listened their jaws fell open. The long, polyphonic babble, rushing in from an extended line of men stood easy, alone rewarded their ears.

Tietjens said:

"That fellow won't come back. . . He can never do an errand and come back. . ." He thrust one of his legs cumbrously out of the top of his flea-bag. He said:

"By God, the Germans will be all over here in a week's time!"

He said to himself:

"If they so betray us from Whitehall that fellow Levin has no right to pry into my matrimonial affairs. It is proper that one's individual feelings should be sacrificed to the necessities of a collective entity. But not if that entity is to be betrayed from above. Not if it hasn't the ten-millionth of a chance. . ." He regarded Levin's late incursion on his privacy as inquiries set afoot by the general. . . Incredibly painful to him. . . like a medical examination into nudities, but perfectly proper. Old Campion had to assure himself that the other ranks were not demoralized by the spectacle of officers' matrimonial infidelities. . . But such inquiries were not to be submitted to if the whole show were one gigantic demoralization!

McKechnie said, in reference to Tietjens' protruded foot:

"There's no good your going out. . . . Cowley will get the men into their lines. He was prepared." He added: "If the fellows in Whitehall are determined to do old Puffles in, why don't they recall him?"

The legend was that an eminent personage in the Government had a great personal dislike for the general in command of one army—the general being nicknamed Puffles. The Government, therefore, were said to be starving his command of men so that disaster should fall upon his command.

"They can recall generals easy enough," McKechnie went on, "or anyone else!"

A heavy dislike that this member of the lower middle classes should have opinions on public affairs overcame Tietjens. He exclaimed: "Oh, that's all tripe!"

He was himself outside all contact with affairs by now. But the other rumour in that troubled host had it that, as a political manoeuvre, the heads round Whitehall—the civilian heads—were starving the army of troops in order to hold over the allies of Great Britain the threat of abandoning altogether the Western Front. They were credited with threatening a strategic manoeuvre on an immense scale in the Near East, perhaps really intending it, or perhaps to force the hands of their allies over some political intrigue. These atrocious rumours reverberated backwards and forwards in the ears of all those millions under the black vault of heaven. All their comrades in the line were to be sacrificed as a rearguard to their departing host. That whole land was to be annihilated as a sacrifice to one vanity. Now the draft had been called back. That seemed proof that the Government meant to starve the line! McKechnie groaned:

"Poor —— old Bird! . . . He's booked. Eleven months in the front line, he's been. . . Eleven *months!*. . . I was nine, this stretch. With him."

He added:

"Get back into bed, old bean. . . I'll go and look after the men if it's necessary. . ."

Tietjens said:

"You don't so much as know where their lines are. . ." And sat listening. Nothing but the long roll of tongues came to him. He said:

"Damn it 1 The men ought not to be kept standing in the cold like that. . ." Fury filled him beneath despair. His eyes filled with tears. "God," he said to himself, "the fellow Levin presumes to interfere in my private affair. . . Damn it," he said again, "it's like doing a little impertinence in a world that's foundering. . ."

"I'd go out," he said, "but I don't want to have to put that filthy little Pitkins under arrest. He only drinks because he's shellshocked. He's not man enough else, the unclean little Nonconformist. . ."

McKechnie said:

"Hold on! . . . I'm a Presbyterian myself. . ."

Tietjens answered:

"You would be! . . ." He said: "I beg your pardon. . . There will be no more parades. . . The British Army is dishonoured for ever. . ."

McKechnie said:

"That's all right, old bean. . ."

Tietjens exclaimed with sudden violence:

"What the hell are you doing in the officers' lines? . . . Don't you know it's a court-martial offence?"

He was confronted with the broad, mealy face of his regimental quartermaster-sergeant, the sort of fellow who wore an officer's cap against the regulations, with a Tommie's silver-plated badge. A man determined to get Sergeant-Major Cowley's job. The man had come in unheard under the roll of voices outside. He said:

"Excuse me, sir, I took the liberty of knocking. . . The sergeant-major is in an epileptic fit. . . I wanted your directions before putting the draft into the tents with the other men. . ." Having said that tentatively he hazarded cautiously: "The sergeant-major throws these fits, sir, if he is suddenly woke up. . . And Second-Lieutenant Pitkins woke him very suddenly. . ."

Tietjens said:

"So you took on you the job of a beastly informer against both of them. . . I shan't forget it." He said to himself:

"I'll get this fellow one day. . ." and he seemed to hear with pleasure the clicking and tearing of the scissors as, inside three parts of a hollow square, they cut off his stripes and badges.

McKechnie exclaimed:

"Good God, man, you aren't going out in nothing but your pyjamas. Put your slacks on under your British warm. . ."

Tietjens said:

"Send the Canadian sergeant-major to me at the double. . ." to the quarter. "My slacks are at the tailor's, being pressed." His slacks were being pressed for the ceremony of the signing of the marriage contract of

Levin, the fellow who had interfered in his private affairs. He continued into the mealy broad face and vague eyes of the quartermaster: "You know as well as I do that it was the Canadian sergeant-major's job to report to me. . . I'll let you off this time, but, by God, if I catch you spying round the officers' lines again you are for a D.C.M. . ."

He wrapped a coarse, Red Cross, grey-wool muffler under the turned-up collar of his British warm.

"That swine," he said to McKechnie, "spies on the officers' lines in the hope of getting a commission by catching out —— little squits like Pitkins, when they're drunk. . . I'm seven hundred braces down. Morgan does not know that I know that I'm that much down. But you can bet he knows where they have gone. . ."

McKechnie said:

"I wish you would not go out like that. . . I'll make you some cocoa. . ."

Tietjens said:

"I can't keep the men waiting while I dress. . . I'm as strong as a horse. . ."

He was out amongst the bitterness, the mist, and the moongleams on three thousand rifle barrels, and the voices. . . He was seeing the Germans pour through a thin line, and his heart was leaden. . . A tall, graceful man swam up against him and said, through his nose, like an American: "There has been a railway accident, due to the French strikers. The draft is put back till three pip emma the day after tomorrow, sir."

Tietjens exclaimed:

"It isn't countermanded?" breathlessly.

The Canadian sergeant-major said:

"No, sir. . . A railway accident. . . Sabotage by the French, they say. . . Four Glamorganshire sergeants, all nineteen-fourteen men, killed, sir, going home on leave. But the draft is not cancelled. . ." Tietjens said:

"Thank God!"

The slim Canadian with his educated voice said:

"You're thanking God, sir, for what's very much to our detriment. Our draft was ordered for Salonika till this morning. The sergeant in charge of draft returns showed me the name *Salonika* scored off in his draft roster. Sergeant-Major Cowley had got hold of the wrong story. Now it's going up the line. The other would have been a full two months' more life for us."

The man's rather slow voice seemed to continue for a long time. As it went on Tietjens felt the sunlight dwelling on his nearly coverless limbs, and the tide of youth returning to his veins. It was like champagne. He said:

"You sergeants get a great deal too much information. The sergeant in charge of returns had no business to show you his roster. It's not your fault, of course. But you are an intelligent man. You can see how useful that news might be to certain people: people that it's not to your own interest should know these things. . ." He said to himself: "A landmark in history. . ." And then: "Where the devil did my mind get hold of that expression at this moment?"

They were walking in mist, down an immense lane, one hedge of which was topped by the serrated heads and irregularly held rifles that showed here and there. He said to the sergeant-major: "Call 'em to attention. Never mind their dressing, we've got to get 'em into bed. Roll-call will be at nine tomorrow."

His mind said:

"If this means the single command. . . And it's bound to mean the single command, it's the turning point. . . Why the hell am I so extraordinarily glad? What's it to me?"

He was shouting in a round voice:

"Now then, men, you've got to go six extra in a tent. See if you can fall out six at a time at each tent. It's not in the drill book, but see if you can do it for yourselves. You're smart men: use your intelligences. The sooner you get to bed the sooner you will be warm. I wish I was. Don't disturb the men who're already in the tents. They've got to be up for fatigues tomorrow at five, poor devils. You can lie soft till three hours after that. . . The draft will move to the left in fours. . . Form fours. . . Left. . ." Whilst the voices of the sergeants in charge of companies yelped varyingly to a distance in the quick march order he said to himself:

"Extraordinarily glad. . . A strong passion. . . How damn well these fellows move! . . . Cannon fodder. . . Cannon fodder. . . That's what their steps say. . ." His whole body shook in the grip of the cold that beneath his loose overcoat gnawed his pyjamaed limbs. He could not leave the men, but cantered beside them with the sergeant-major till he came to the head of the column in the open in time to wheel the first double company into a line of ghosts that were tents, silent and austere in the moon's very shadowy light. . . It appeared to him a magic spectacle. He said to the sergeant-major: "Move the second company to B line, and so on," and stood at the side of the men as they wheeled, stamping, like a wall in motion. He thrust his stick half-way down between the second and third files. "Now then, a four and half a four to the right; remaining half-four and next four to the left. Fall out into first tents to right and left. . ." He continued saying "First four and half, this four to the right Damn you, by the left! How can you tell which beastly four you belong to if you don't march by the left. . . Remember you're soldiers, not new-chum lumbermen. . .

It was sheer exhilaration to freeze there on the downside of the extraordinary pure air with the extraordinarily fine men. They came round, marking time with the stamp of guardsmen. He said, with tears in his voice:

"Damn it all, I gave them that extra bit of smartness. . . Damn it all, there's something I've done. . ." Getting cattle into condition for the slaughter-house. . . They were as eager as bullocks running down by Camden Town to Smithfield Market. . . Seventy per cent. of them would never come back. . . But it's better to go to heaven with your skin shining and master of your limbs than as a hulking lout. . . The Almighty's orderly room will welcome you better in all probability. . . He continued exclaiming monotonously. . . "Remaining half-four and next four to the left. . . Hold your beastly tongues when you fall out. I can't hear myself give orders. . ." It lasted a long time. Then they were all swallowed up.

He staggered, his knees wooden-stiff with the cold, and the cold more intense now the wall of men no longer sheltered him from the wind, out along the brink of the plateau to the other lines. It gave him satisfaction to observe that he had got his men into their lines seventy-five per cent. quicker than the best of the N.C.O.'s who had had charge of the other lines. Nevertheless, he swore bitingly at the sergeants: their men were in knots round the entrance to the alleys of ghost-pyramids. . . Then there were no more, and he drifted with regret across the plain towards his country street of huts. One of them had a coarse evergreen rose growing over it. He picked a leaf, pressed it to his lips and threw it up into the wind. . . "That's for Valentine," he said meditatively. "Why did I do that? . . . Or perhaps it's for England. . ." He said: "Damn it all, this is patriotism? . . . *This* is patriotism. . ." It wasn't what you took patriotism as a rule to be. There were supposed to be more parades, about that job! . . . But this was just a broke to the wide, wheezy, half-frozen Yorkshireman, who despised every one in England not a Yorkshireman, or from more to the North, at two in the morning picking a leaf from a rose-tree and slobbering over it, without knowing what he was doing. And then discovering that it was half for a pug-nosed girl whom he presumed, but didn't know, to smell like a primrose; and half for. . . England! . . . At two in the morning with the thermometer ten degrees below zero. . . Damn, it was cold! . . .

And why these emotions? . . . Because England, not before it was time, had been allowed to decide not to do the dirty on her associates! . . . He said to himself: "It is probably because a hundred thousand sentimentalists like myself commit similar excesses of the subconscious that we persevere in this glorious but atrocious undertaking. All the same, I didn't know I had it in me!" A strong passion! . . . For his girl and his country! . . . Nevertheless, his girl was a pro-German. . . It was a queer mix-up. . . Not of course a pro-German, but disapproving of the preparation of men, like bullocks, with sleek healthy skins for the abattoirs in Smithfield. . . Agreeing presumably with the squits who had been hitherto starving the B.E.F. of men. . . A queer mix-up. . .

At half-past one the next day, in chastened winter sunlight, he mounted Schomburg, a coffin-headed, bright chestnut, captured from the Germans on the Marne by the second battalion of the Glamorganshires. He had not been on the back of the animal two minutes before he remembered that he had forgotten to look it over. It was the first time in his life that he had ever forgotten to look at an animal's hoofs, fetlocks, knees, nostrils and eyes, and to take a pull at the girth before climbing into the saddle. But he had ordered the horse for a quarter to one and, even though he had bolted his cold lunch like a cannibal in haste, there he was three-quarters of an hour late, and with his head still full of teasing problems. He had meant to clear his head by a long canter over the be-hutted downs, dropping down into the city by a bypath.

But the ride did not clear his head—rather, the sleeplessness of the night began for the first time then to tell on him after a morning of fatigues, during which he had managed to keep the thought of Sylvia at arm's length. He had to wait to see Sylvia before he could see what Sylvia wanted. And morning had brought the common-sense idea that probably she wanted to do nothing more than pull the string of the showerbath—which meant committing herself to the first extravagant action that came into her head—and exulting in the consequences.

He had not managed to get to bed at all the night before. Captain McKechnie, who had had some cocoa—a beverage Tietjens had never before tasted—hot and ready for him on his return from the lines, had kept him till past half-past four, relating with a male fury his really very painful story. It appeared that he had obtained leave to go home and divorce his wife, who, during his absence in France, had been living with an Egyptologist in Government service. Then, acting under conscientious scruples of the younger school of the day, he had refrained from divorcing her. Campion had in consequence threatened to deprive him of his commission. . . The poor devil—who had actually consented to contribute to the costs of the household of his wife and the Egyptologist—had gone raving mad and had showered an extraordinary torrent of abuse at the decent old fellow that Campion was. . . A decent old fellow, really. For the interview, being delicate, had taken place in the general's bedroom and the general had not felt it necessary, there being no orderlies or junior officers present, to take any official notice of McKechnie's outburst. McKechnie was a fellow with an excellent military record; you could in fact hardly have found a regimental officer with a better record. So Campion had decided to deal with the man as suffering from a temporary brain-storm and had sent him to Tietjens' unit for rest and recuperation. It was an irregularity, but the general was of a rank to risk what irregularities he considered to be of use to the service.

It had turned out that McKechnie was actually the nephew of Tietjens' very old intimate, Sir Vincent Mac-master, of the Department of Statistics, being the son of his sister who had married the assistant to the elder Macmaster, a small grocer in the Port of Leith in Scotland. . . That indeed had been why Campion had been interested in him. Determined as he was to show his godson no unreasonable military favours, the general was perfectly ready, to do a kindness that he thought would please Tietjens. All these pieces of information Tietjens had packed away in his mind for future consideration and, it being after four-thirty before McKechnie had calmed himself down, Tietjens had taken the opportunity to inspect the breakfasts of the various fatigues ordered for duty in the town, these being detailed for various hours from a quarter to five to seven. It was a matter of satisfaction to Tietjens to have seen to the breakfasts, and inspected his cook-houses, since he did not often manage to make the opportunity and he could by no means trust his orderly officers.

At breakfast in the depot mess-hut he was detained by the colonel in command of the depot, the Anglican padre and McKechnie; the colonel, very old, so frail that you would have thought that a shudder or a cough would have shaken his bones one from another, had yet a passionate belief that the Greek Church should exchange communicants with the Anglican: the padre, a stout, militant Churchman, had a gloomy contempt for Orthodox theology. McKechnie from time to time essayed to define the communion according to the Presbyterian rite. They all listened to Tietjens whilst he dilated on the historic aspects of the various schisms of Christianity and accepted his rough definition to the effect that, in transubstantiation, the host actually became the divine presence, whereas in consubstantiation the substance of the host, as if miraculously become porous, was suffused with the presence as a sponge is with water. . . They all agreed that the breakfast bacon supplied from store was uneatable and agreed to put up half a crown a week apiece to get better for their table.

Tietjens had walked in the sunlight down the lines, past the hut with the evergreen climbing rose, in the sunlight, thinking in an interval good humouredly about his official religion: about the Almighty as, on a colossal scale, a great English Landowner, benevolently awful, a colossal duke who never left his study and was thus invisible, but knowing all about the estate down to the last hind at the home farm and the last oak: Christ, an almost too benevolent Land-Steward, son of the Owner, knowing all about the estate down to the last child at the porter's lodge, apt to be got round by the more detrimental tenants: the Third Person of the Trinity, the spirit of the estate, the Game as it were, as distinct from the players of the game: the atmosphere of the estate, that of the interior of Winchester Cathedral just after a Handel anthem has been finished, a perpetual Sunday, with, probably, a little cricket for the young men. Like Yorkshire of a Saturday afternoon; if you looked down on the whole broad county you would not see a single village green without its white flannels. That was why Yorkshire always leads the averages. . . Probably by the time you got to heaven you would be so worn out by work on this planet that you would accept the English Sunday, for ever, with extreme relief!

With his belief that all that was good in English literature ended with the seventeenth century, his imaginations of heaven must be materialist—like Bunyan's. He laughed good-humouredly at his projection of a hereafter. It was probably done with. Along with cricket. There would be no more parades of that sort. Probably they would play some beastly yelping game. . . Like baseball or Association football. . .

And heaven? . . . Oh, it would be a revival meeting on a Welsh hillside. Or Chautauqua, wherever that was. . . And God? A Real Estate Agent, with Marxist views. . . He hoped to be out of it before the cessation of hostilities, in which case he might be just in time for the last train to the old heaven. . .

In his orderly hut he found an immense number of papers. On the top an envelope marked *Urgent. Private* with a huge rubber stamp. From Levin. Levin, too, must have been up pretty late. It was not about Mrs. Tietjens, or even Miss de Bailly. It was a private warning that Tietjens would probably have his draft on his hands another week or ten days, and very likely another couple of thousand men extra as well. He warned Tietjens to draw all the tents he could get hold of as soon as possible. . . Tietjens called to a subaltern with pimples who was picking his teeth with a pen-nib at the other end of the hut: "Here, you! . . . Take two companies of the Canadians to the depot store and draw all the tents you can get up to two hundred and fifty. . . Have 'em put alongside my D lines. . . Do you know how to look after putting up tents? . . . Well then, get Thompson. . . no, Pitkins, to help you. . ." The subaltern drifted out sulkily. Levin said that the French railway strikers, for some political reason, had sabotaged a mile of railway, the accident of the night before had completely blocked up all the lines, and the French civilians would not let their own breakdown gangs make any repairs. German prisoners had been detailed for that fatigue, but probably Tietjens' Canadian railway corps would be wanted. He had better hold them in readiness. The strike was said to be a manoeuvre for forcing our hands—to get us to take over more of the line. In that case they had jolly well dished themselves, for how could we take over more of the line without more men, and how could we send up more men without the railway to send them by? We had half a dozen army corps all ready to go. Now they were all jammed. Fortunately the weather at the front was so beastly that the Germans could not move. He finished up "Four in the morning, old bean, à tantot!" the last phrase having been learned from Mlle de Bailly. Tietjens grumbled that if they went on piling up the work on him like this he would never get down to the signing of that marriage contract.

He called the Canadian sergeant-major to him.

"See," he said, "that you keep the Railway Service Corps in camp with their arms ready, whatever their arms are. Tools, I suppose. Are their tools all complete? And their muster roll?"

"Girtin has gone absent, sir," the slim dark fellow said, with an air of destiny. Girtin was the respectable man with the mother to whom Tietjens had given the two hours' leave the night before.

Tietjens answered:

"He would have!" with a sour grin. It enhanced his views of strictly respectable humanity. They blackmailed you with lamentable and pathetic tales and then did the dirty on you. He said to the sergeant-major:

"You will be here for another week or ten days. See that you get your tents up all right and the men comfortable. I will inspect them as soon as I have taken my orderly room. Full marching order. Captain McKechnie will inspect their kits at two."

The sergeant-major, stiff but graceful, had something at the back of his mind. It came out:

"I have my marching orders for two-thirty this afternoon. The notice for inserting my commission in depot orders is on your table. I leave for the O.T.C. by the three train. . ."

Tietjens said:

"Your commission! . . ." It was a confounded nuisance.

The sergeant-major said:

"Sergeant-Major Cowley and I applied for our commissions three months ago. The communications granting them are both on your table together. . ."

Tietjens said:

"Sergeant-Major Cowley. . . Good God! Who recommended you?"

The whole organization of his confounded battalion fell to pieces. It appeared that a circular had come round three months before—before Tietjens had been given command of that unit—asking for experienced first-class warrant officers capable of serving as instructors in Officers' Training Corps, with commissions. Sergeant-Major Cowley had been recommended by the colonel of the depot, Sergeant-Major Ledoux by his own colonel. Tietjens felt as if he had been let down—but of course he had not been. It was just the way of the army, all the time. You got a platoon, or a battalion, or, for the matter of that, a dug-out or a tent, by herculean labours into good fettle. It ran all right for a day or two, then it all fell to pieces, the personnel scattered to the four winds by what appeared merely wanton orders, coming from the most unexpected headquarters, or the premises were smashed up by a chance shell that might just as well have fallen somewhere else. . . The finger of Fate! . . .

But it put a confounded lot more work on him. . . He said to Sergeant-Major Cowley, whom he found in the next hut where all the paper work of the unit was done:

"I should have thought you would have been enormously better off as regimental sergeant-major than with a commission. I know I would rather have the job." Cowley answered—he was very pallid and shaken—that with his unfortunate infirmity, coming on at any moment of shock, he would be better in a job where he could slack off, like an O.T.C. He had always been subject to small fits, over in a minute, or couple of seconds even. . . But getting too near a H.E. shell—after Noircourt, which had knocked out Tietjens himself—had brought them on, violent. There was also, he finished, the gentility to be considered. Tietjens said:

"Oh, the gentility! . . . That's not worth a flea's jump. . . There won't be any more parades after this war. There aren't any now. Look at who your companions will be in an officer's quarters; you'd be in a great deal better society in any self-respecting sergeants' mess." Cowley answered that he knew the service had gone to the dogs. All the same his missis liked it. And there was his daughter Winnie to be considered. She had always been a bit wild, and his missis wrote that she had gone wilder than ever, all due to the war. Cowley thought that the bad boys would be a little more careful how they monkeyed with her if she was an officer's daughter. . . There was probably something in that!

Coming out into the open, confidentially with Tietjens, Cowley dropped his voice huskily to say:

"Take Quartermaster-Sergeant Morgan for R.S.M., sir." Tietjens said explosively:

"I'm damned if I will." Then he asked: "Why?" The wisdom of an old N.C.O.'s is a thing no prudent officer neglects.

"He can do the work, sir," Cowley said. "He's out for a commission, and he'll do his best. . . He dropped his husky voice to a still greater depth of mystery:

"You're over two hundred—I should say nearer three hundred—pounds down in your battalion stores. I don't suppose you want to lose a sum of money like that?"

Tietjens said:

"I'm damned if I do. . . But I don't see. . . Oh, yes, I do. . . If I make him sergeant-major he has to hand over the stores all complete. . . Today. . . Can he do it?"

Cowley said that Morgan could have till the day after tomorrow. He would look after things till then.

"But you'll want to have a flutter before you go," Tietjens said. "Don't stop for me."

Cowley said that he would stop and see the job through. He had thought of going down into the town and having a flutter. But the girls down there were a common sort, and it was bad for his complaint. . . He would stop and see what could be done with Morgan. Of course it was possible that Morgan might decide to face things out. He might prefer to stick to the money he'd got by disposing of Tietjens' stores to other battalions that were down, or to civilian contractors. And stand a court martial! But it wasn't likely. He was a Nonconformist deacon, or pew-opener, or even a minister possibly, at home in Wales. . . From near Denbigh! And Cowley had got a very good man, a first-class man, an Oxford professor, now a lance-corporal at the depot, for Morgan's place. The colonel would lend him to Tietjens and would get him rated acting quartermaster-sergeant unpaid. . . Cowley had it all arranged. . . Lance-Corporal Caldicott was a first-class man, only he could not tell his right hand from his left on parade. Literally could not tell them. . .

So the battalion settled itself down. . . Whilst Cowley and he were at the colonel's orderly room arranging for the transfer of the professor—he was really only a fellow of his college—who did not know his right hand from his left, Tietjens was engaged in the remains of the colonel's furious argument as to the union of the Anglican and Eastern rites. The colonel—he was a full colonel—sat in his lovely private office, a light, gay compartment of a tin-hutment, the walls being papered in scarlet, with, on the purplish, thick, soft baize of his table-cover, a tall glass vase from which sprayed out pale Riviera roses, the gift of young lady admirers amongst the V.A.D.'s in the town because he was a darling, and an open, very gilt and leather-bound volume of a biblical encyclopaedia beneath his delicate septuagenarian features. He was confirming his opinion that a union between the Church of England and the Greek Orthodox Church was the only thing that could save civilization. The whole war turned on that. The Central Empires represented Roman Catholicism, the Allies Protestantism and Orthodoxy. Let them unite. The papacy was a traitor to the cause of civilization. Why had the Vatican not protested with no uncertain voice about the abominations practised on the Belgian Catholics? . . .

Tietjens pointed out languidly objections to this theory. The first thing our ambassador to the Vatican had found out on arriving in Rome and protesting about massacres of Catholic laymen in Belgium was that the Russians before they had been a day in Austrian Poland had hanged twelve Roman Catholic bishops in front of their palaces.

Cowley was engaged with the adjutant at another table. The colonel ended his theologico-political tirade by saying:

"I shall be very sorry to lose you, Tietjens. I don't know what we shall do without you. I never had a moment's peace with your unit until you came."

Tietjens said:

"Well, you aren't losing me, sir, as far as I know." The colonel said:

"Oh, yes, we are. You are going up the line next week. . ." He added: "Now, don't get angry with me. . . I've protested very strongly to old Campion—General Campion—that I cannot do without you." And he made, with his delicate, thin, hairy-backed, white hands a motion as of washing.

The ground moved under Tietjens' feet. He felt himself clambering over slopes of mud with his heavy legs and labouring chest. He said:

"Damn it all! . . . I'm not fit. . . I'm C3 . . . I was ordered to live in an hotel in the town. . . I only mess here to be near the battalion."

The colonel said with some eagerness:

"Then you can protest to Garrison. . . I hope you will. . . But I suppose you are the sort of fellow that won't." Tietjens said:

"No, sir. . . Of course I cannot protest. . . Though it's probably a mistake of some clerk. . . I could not stand a week in the line. . ." The profound misery of brooding apprehension in the line was less on his mind than, precisely, the appalling labour of the lower limbs when you live in mud to the neck. . . Besides, whilst he had been in hospital, practically the whole of his equipment had disappeared from his kitbag—including Sylvia's two pairs of sheets!—and he had no money with which to get more. He had not even any trench-boots. Fantastic financial troubles settled on his mind.

The colonel said to the adjutant at the other purple baize-covered table:

"Show Captain Tietjens those marching orders of his. . . They're from Whitehall, aren't they? . . . You never know where these things come from nowadays. I call them the arrow that flieth by night!"

The adjutant, a diminutive, a positively miniature gentleman with Coldstream badges up and a dreadfully worried brow, drifted a quarto sheet of paper out of a pile, across his tablecloth towards Tietjens. His tiny hands seemed about to fall off at the wrists; his temples shuddered with neuralgia. He said:

"For God's sake do protest to Garrison if you feel you can. . . We *can't* have more work shoved on us. . . Major Lawrence and Major Halkett left the whole of the work of your unit to us. . .

The sumptuous paper, with the royal arms embossed at the top, informed Tietjens that he would report to his VIth battalion on the Wednesday of next week in preparation for taking up the duties of divisional transport officer to the XIX division. The order came from Room G 14 R, at the War Office. He asked what the deuce G 14 R was, of the adjutant, who in an access of neuralgic agony, shook his head miserably, between his two hands, his elbows on the tablecloth.

Sergeant-Major Cowley, with his air of a solicitor's clerk, said the room G 14 R was the department that dealt with civilian requests for the services of officers. To the adjutant who asked what the devil a civilian request for the employment of officers could have to do with sending Captain Tietjens to the XIX division, Sergeant-Major Cowley presumed that it was because of the activities of the Earl of Beichan. The Earl of Beichan, a Levantine financier and race-horse owner, was interesting himself in army horses, after a short visit to the lines of communication. He also owned several newspapers. So they had been waking up the army transport-animals' department to please him. The adjutant would no doubt have observed a Veterinary-Lieutenant Hotchkiss or Hitchcock. He had come to them through G 14 R. At the request of Lord Beichan, who was personally interested in Lieutenant Hotchkiss's theories, he was to make experiments on the horses of the Fourth Army—in which the XIXth division was then to be found. . . "So," Cowley said, "you'll be under him as far as your horse lines go. If you go up." Perhaps Lord Beichan was a friend of Captain Tietjens and had asked for him, too: Captain Tietjens was known to be wonderful with horses.

Tietjens, his breath rushing through his nostrils, swore he would not go up the line at the bidding of a hog like Beichan, whose real name was Stavropolides, formerly Nathan.

He said the army was reeling to its base because of the continual interference of civilians. He said it was absolutely impossible to get through his programme of parades because of the perpetual extra drills that were forced on them at the biddings of civilians. Any fool who owned a newspaper, nay, any fool who could write to a newspaper, or any beastly little squit of a novelist could frighten the Government and the War Office into taking up one more hour of the men's parade time for patent manoeuvres with jampots or fancy underclothing. Now he was asked if his men wanted lecturing on the causes of the war and whether he—he, good God!—would not like to give the men cosy chats on the nature of the Enemy nations. . .

The colonel said:

"There, there, Tietjens! . . . There, there! . . . We all suffer alike. *We've* got to lecture our men on the uses of a new patent sawdust stove. If you don't want that job, you can easily get the general to take you off it. They say you can turn him round your little finger. . .

"He's my godfather," Tietjens thought it wise to say. "I never asked him for a job, but I'm damned if it isn't his duty as a Christian to keep me out of the clutches of this Greek-'Ebrew pagan peer. . . He's not even Orthodox, colonel."

The adjutant here said that Colour-Sergeant Morgan of their orderly room wanted a word with Tietjens. Tietjens said he hoped to goodness that Morgan had some money for him! The adjutant said he understood that Morgan had unearthed quite a little money that ought to have been paid to Tietjens by his agents and hadn't.

Colour-Sergeant Morgan was the regimental magician with figures. Inordinately tall and thin, his body, whilst his eyes peered into distant columns of cyphers, appeared to be always parallel with the surface of his table and, as he always answered the several officers whom he benefited without raising his head, his face was very little known to his superiors. He was, however, in appearance a very ordinary, thin N.C.O. whose spidery legs, when very rarely he appeared on parade, had the air of running away with him as a race-horse might do. He told Tietjens that, pursuant to his instructions and the A.C.P. i 96 b that Tietjens had signed, he had ascertained that command pay at the rate of two guineas a day and supplementary fuel and light allowance at the rate of 6s. 8*d*. was being paid weekly by the Paymaster-General's Department to his, Tietjens', account at his agents'. He suggested that Tietjens should write to his agents that if they did not immediately pay to his account the sum of £194 13s. 4d., by them received from the Paymaster's Department, he would proceed against the Crown by Petition of Right. And he strongly recommended Tietjens to draw a cheque on his own bank for the whole of the money because, if by any chance the agents had not paid the money in, he could sue them for damages and get them cast in several thousand pounds. And serve the devils right. They must have a million or so in hand in unpaid command and detention allowances due to officers. He only wished he could advertise in the papers offering to recover unpaid sums due by agents. He added that he had a nice little computation as to variations in the course of Gunter's Second Comet that he would like to ask Tietjens' advice about one of these days. The colour-sergeant was an impassioned amateur astronomer.

So Tietjens' morning went up and down. . . The money at the moment, Sylvia being in that town, was of tremendous importance to him and came like an answer to prayer. It was not so agreeable, however, even in a world in which, never, never, never for ten minutes did you know whether you stood on your head or your heels, for Tietjens, on going back to the colonel's private office, to find Sergeant-Major Cowley coming out of the next room in which, on account of the adjutant's neuralgia, the telephone was kept. Cowley announced to the three of them that the general had the day before ordered his correspondence-corporal to send a very emphatic note to Colonel Gillum to the effect that he was informing the competent authority that he had no intention whatever of parting with Captain Tietjens, who was invaluable in his command. The correspondence-corporal had informed Cowley that neither he nor the general knew who was the competent authority for telling Room G 14 R at the War Office to go to hell, but the matter would be looked up and put all right before the chit was sent off. . .

That was good as far as it went. Tietjens was really interested in his present job, and although he would have liked well enough to have the job of looking after the horses of a division, or even an army, he felt he would rather it was put off till the spring, given the weather they were having and the state of his chest. And the complication of possible troubles with Lieutenant Hotchkiss who, being a professor, had never really seen a horse—or not for ten years!—was something to be thought about very seriously. But all this appeared quite another matter when Cowley announced that the civilian authority who had asked for Tietjens' transfer was the permanent secretary to the Ministry of Transport. . .

Colonel Gillum said:

"That's your brother, Mark. . ." And indeed the permanent secretary to the Ministry of Transport was Tietjens' brother Mark, known as the indispensable Official. Tietjens felt a real instant of dismay. He considered that his violent protest against the job would appear rather a smack in the face for poor old wooden-featured Mark who had probably taken a good deal of trouble to get him the job. Even if Mark should never hear of it, a man should not slap his brother in the face! Moreover, when he came to think of his last day in London, he remembered that Valentine Wannop, who had exaggerated ideas as to the safety of First Line Transport, had begged Mark to get him a job as divisional officer. . . And he imagined Valentine's despair if she heard that he—Tietjens—had moved heaven and earth to get out of it. He saw her lower lip quivering and the tears in her eyes. . . But he probably had got that from some novel, because he had never seen her lower lip quiver. He had seen tears in her eyes!

He hurried back to his lines to take his orderly room. In the long hut McKechnie was taking that miniature court of drunks and defaulters for him and, just as Tietjens reached it, he was taking the case of Girtin and two other Canadian privates. . . The case of Girtin interested him, and when McKechnie slid out of his seat Tietjens occupied it. The prisoners were only just being marched in by a Sergeant Davis, an admirable N.C.O. whose rifle appeared to be part of his rigid body and who executed an amazing number of stamps in seriously turning in front of the C.O.'s table. It gave the impression of an Indian war dance. . .

Tietjens glanced at the charge sheet, which was marked as coming from the Provost-Marshal's Office. Instead of the charge of absence from draft he read that of conduct prejudicial to good order and military discipline in that. . . The charge was written in a very illiterate hand; an immense beery lance-corporal of Garrison Military Police, with a red hat-band, attended to give evidence. . . It was a tenuous and disagreeable affair. Girtin had not gone absent, so Tietjens had to revise his views of the respectable. At any rate of the respectable Colonial private soldier with mother complete. For there really had been a mother, and Girtin had been seeing her into the last tram down into the town. A frail old lady. Apparently, trying to annoy the Canadian, the beery lance-corporal of the Garrison Military Police had hustled the mother. Girtin had remonstrated; very moderately, he said. The lance-corporal had shouted at him. Two other Canadians returning to camp had intervened and two more police. The police had called the Canadians —— conscripts, which was almost more than the Canadians could stand, they being voluntarily enlisted 1914 or 1915 men. The police—it was an old trick—had kept the men talking until two minutes after the last post had sounded and then had run them in for being absent off pass—and for disrespect to their red hat-bands.

Tietjens, with a carefully measured fury, first cross-examined and then damned the police witness to hell. Then he marked the charge sheets with the words, "Case explained", and told the Canadians to go and get ready for his parade. It meant he was in for a frightful row with the provost-marshal, who was a port-winey old general called O'Hara and loved his police as if they had been ewe-lambs.

He took his parade, the Canadian troops looking like real soldiers in the sunlight, went round his lines with the new Canadian sergeant-major, who had his appointment, thank goodness, from his own authorities; wrote a report on the extreme undesirability of lecturing his men on the causes of the war, since his men were either graduates of one or other Canadian university and thus knew twice as much about the causes of the war as any lecturer the civilian authorities could provide, or else they were half-breed Micamuc Indians, Esquimaux, Japanese, or Alaskan Russians, none of whom could understand any English lecturer. . . He was aware that he would have to re-write his report so as to make it more respectful to the newspaper proprietor peer who, at that time, was urging on the home Government the necessity of lecturing all the subjects of His Majesty on the causes of the war. But he wanted to get that grouse off his chest and its disrespect would pain Levin, who would have to deal with these reports if he did not get married first. Then he lunched off army sausage-meat and potatoes, mashed with their skins complete, watered with an admirable 1906 brut champagne which they bought themselves, and an appalling Canadian cheese—at the headquarters table to which the colonel had invited all the subalterns who that day were going up the line for the first time. They had some h's in their compositions, but in revenge they must have boasted of a pint of adenoid growths between them. There was, however, a charming young half-caste Goa second-lieutenant, who afterwards proved of an heroic bravery. He gave Tietjens a lot of amusing information as to the working of the purdah in Portuguese India.

So, at half-past one Tietjens sat on Schomburg, the coffin-headed, bright chestnut from the Prussian horse-raising establishment near Celle. Almost a pure thoroughbred, this animal had usually the paces of a dining-room table, its legs being fully as stiff. But today its legs might have been made of cotton-wool, it lumbered over frosty ground breathing stertorously and, at the jumping ground of the Deccan Horse, a mile above and behind Rouen, it did not so much refuse a very moderate jump as come together in a lugubrious crumple. It was, in the light of a red, jocular sun, like being mounted on a broken-hearted camel. In addition, the fatigues of the morning beginning to tell, Tietjens was troubled by an obsession of 0 Nine Morgan which he found tiresome to have to stall off.

"What the hell," he asked of the orderly, a very silent private on a roan beside him, "what the hell is the matter with this horse? . . . Have you been keeping him warm?" He imagined that the clumsy paces of the animal beneath him added to his gloomy obsessions.

The orderly looked straight in front of him over a valley full of hutments. He said:

"No, sir." The 'oss 'ad been put in the 'oss-standings of G depot. By the orders of Lieutenant 'Itchcock. 'Osses, Lieutenant 'Itchcock said, 'ad to be 'ardened.

Tietjens said:

"Did you tell him that it was my orders that Schomburg was to be kept warm? In the stables of the farm behind No. XVI I.B.D."

"The lieutenant," the orderly explained woodenly, "said as 'ow henny departure f'm 'is orders would be visited by the extreme displeasure of Lord Breech'em, K.C.V.O., K.C.B., etcetera.'" The orderly was quivering with rage.

"You," Tietjens said very carefully, "when you fall out with the horses at the Hotel de la Poste, take Schomburg and the roan to the stables of La Volonté Farm, behind No. XVI I.B.D." The orderly was to close all the windows of the stable, stopping up any chinks with wadding. He would procure, if possible, a sawdust stove, new pattern, from Colonel Gillum's store and light it in the stables. He was also to give Schomburg and the roan oatmeal and water warmed as hot as the horses would take it. . . And Tietjens finished sharply, "If Lieutenant Hotchkiss makes any comments, you will refer him to me. As his CO."

The orderly seeking information as to horse-ailments, Tietjens said:

"The school of horse-copers, to which Lord Beichan belongs, believes in the hardening of all horse-flesh other than racing cattle." They bred racing-cattle. Under six blankets apiece! Personally Tietjens did not believe in the hardening process and would not permit any animal over which he had control to be submitted to it.—It had been observed that if any animal was kept at a lower temperature than that of its normal climatic condition it would contract diseases to which ordinarily it was not susceptible. . . If you keep a chicken for two days in a pail of water it will contract human scarlet-fever or mumps if injected with either bacillus. If you remove the chicken from the water, dry it, and restore it to its normal conditions, the scarlet-fever or the mumps will die out of the animal. . . He said to the orderly: "You arc an intelligent man. What deduction do you draw?"

The orderly looked away over the valley of the Seine.

"I suppose, sir," he said, "that our 'osses, being kept alwise cold in their standings, as hillnesses they wouldn't otherwise 'ave."

"Well, then," Tietjens said, "keep the poor animals warm."

He considered that here was the makings of a very nasty row for himself if, by any means, his sayings came round to the ears of Lord Beichan. But that he had to chance. He coud not let a horse for which he was responsible be martyred. . . There was too much to think about. . . so that nothing at all stood out to be thought of. The sun was glowing. The valley of the Seine was blue-grey, like a Gobelin tapestry. Over it all hung the shadow of a deceased Welsh soldier. An odd skylark was declaiming over an empty field behind the incinerators' headquarters. . . An odd lark. For as a rule larks do not sing in December. Larks sing only when courting, or over the nest. . . The bird must be oversexed. 0 Nine Morgan was the other thing, that accounting for the prize-fighter!

They dropped down a mud lane between brick walls into the town. . .

PART II

I

In the admirably appointed, white-enamelled, wicker-worked, bemirrored lounge of the best hotel of that town Sylvia Tietjens sat in a wickerwork chair, not listening rather abstractedly to a staff-major who was lachrymosely and continuously begging her to leave her bedroom door unlocked that night. She said:

"I don't know. . . Yes, perhaps. . . I don't know. . . And looked distantly into a bluish wall-mirror that, like all the rest, was framed with white-painted cork bark. She stiffened a little and said:

"There's Christopher!"

The staff-major dropped his hat, his stick and his gloves. His black hair, which was without parting and heavy with some preparation of a glutinous kind, moved agitatedly on his scalp. He had been saying that Sylvia had ruined his life. Didn't Sylvia know that she had ruined his life? But for her he might have married some pure young thing. Now he exclaimed:

"But what does he want? . . . Good God! . . . what does he want?"

"He wants," Sylvia said, "to play the part of Jesus Christ."

Major Perowne exclaimed:

"Jesus Christ! . . . But he's the most foul-mouthed officer in the general's command. . .

"Well," Sylvia said, "if you had married your pure young thing she'd have. . . What is it? . . . cuckolded you within nine months. . .

Perowne shuddered a little at the word. He mumbled:

"I don't see. . . It seems to be the other way. . ."

"Oh, no, it isn't," Sylvia said. "Think it over. . . Morally, *you're* the husband. . . *Immorally*, I should say. . . Because he's the man I want. . . He looks ill. . . Do hospital authorities always tell wives what is the matter with their husbands?"

From his angle in the chair from which he had half-emerged Sylvia seemed to him to be looking at a blank wall. "I don't see him," Perowne said.

"I can see him in the glass," Sylvia said. "Look! From here you can see him."

Perowne shuddered a little more.

"I don't want to see him. . . I have to see him sometimes in the course of duty. . . I don't like to. . .

Sylvia said:

"*You*," in a tone of very deep contempt. "You only carry chocolate boxes to flappers. . . How can he come across you in the course of duty? . . . You're not a *soldier*!"

Perowne said:

"But what are we going to do? What will *he* do?"

"I," Sylvia answered, "shall tell the page-boy when he comes with his card to say that I'm engaged. . . I don't know what *he'll* do. Hit you, very likely. . . He's looking at your back now. . .

Perowne became rigid, sunk into his deep chair.

"But he *couldn't*!" he exclaimed agitatedly. "You said that he was playing the part of Jesus Christ. Our Lord wouldn't hit people in an hotel lounge. . .

"Our Lord!" Sylvia said contemptuously. "What do you know about our Lord? . . . Our Lord was a gentleman. . . Christopher is playing at being our Lord calling on the woman taken in adultery. . . He's giving me the social backing that his being my husband seems to him to call for."

A one-armed, bearded *maitre d'hôtel* approached them through groups of arm-chairs arranged for *tête-à-tête*. He said:

"Pardon.. I did not see madame at first. . ." And displayed a card on a salver. Without looking at it, Sylvia said:

"*Dites à ce monsieur*. . . that I am occupied." The *maitre d'hôtel* moved austerely away.

"But he'll smash me to pieces. . ." Perowne exclaimed. "What am I to do? . . . What the deuce am I to do?" There would have been no way of exit for him except across Tietjens' face.

With her spine very rigid and the expression of a snake that fixes a bird, Sylvia gazed straight in front of her and said nothing until she exclaimed:

"For God's sake leave off trembling. . . He would not do anything to a girl like you. . . He's a man. . ." The wickerwork of Perowne's chair had been crepitating as if it had been in a railway car. The sound ceased with a jerk. . . Suddenly she clenched both her hands and let out a hateful little breath of air between her teeth.

"By the immortal saints," she exclaimed, "I swear I'll make his wooden face wince yet."

In the bluish looking-glass, a few minutes before, she had seen the agate-blue eyes of her husband, thirty feet away, over arm-chairs and between the fans of palms. He was standing, holding a riding-whip, looking rather clumsy in the uniform that did not suit him. Rather clumsy and worn out, but completely expressionless! He had looked straight into the reflection of her eyes and then looked away. He moved so that his profile was towards her, and continued gazing motionless at an elk's head that decorated the space of wall above glazed doors giving into the interior of the hotel. The hotel servant approaching him, he had produced a card and had given it to the servant, uttering three words. She saw his lips move in the three words: Mrs. Christopher Tietjens. She said, beneath her breath:

"Damn his chivalry! . . . Oh, God damn his chivalry She knew what was going on in his mind. He had seen her, with Perowne, so he had neither come towards her nor directed the servant to where she sat. For fear of embarrassing her! He would leave it to her to come to him if she wished.

The servant, visible in the mirror, had come and gone deviously back, Tietjens still gazing at the elk's head. He had taken the card and restored it to his pocket-book and then had spoken to the servant. The servant had shrugged his shoulders with the formal hospitality of his class and, with his shoulders still shrugged and his one hand pointing towards the inner door, had preceded Tietjens into the hotel. Not one line of Tietjens' face had moved when he had received back his card. It had been then that Sylvia had sworn that she would yet make his wooden face wince. . .

His face was intolerable. Heavy; fixed. Not insolent, but simply gazing over the heads of all things and created beings, into a world too distant for them to enter. . . And yet it seemed to her, since he was so clumsy and worn out, almost not sporting to persecute him. It was like whipping a dying bulldog. . .

She sank back into her chair with a movement almost of discouragement. She said:

"He's gone into the hotel. . ."

Perowne lurched agitatedly forward in his chair. He exclaimed that he was going. Then he sank discouragedly back again:

"No, I'm not," he said, "I'm probably much safer here. I might run against him going out."

"You've realized that my petticoats protect you," Sylvia said contemptuously. "Of course, Christopher would never hit anyone in my presence."

Major Perowne was interrupting her by asking:

"What's he going to do? What's he doing in the hotel?" Mrs. Tietjens said:

"Guess!" She added: "What would you do in similar circumstances?"

"Go and wreck your bedroom," Perowne answered with promptitude. "It's what I did when I found you had left Yssingueux."

Sylvia said:

"Ah, that was what the place was called."

Perowne groaned:

"You're callous," he said. "There's no other word for it. Callous. That's what you are."

Sylvia asked absently why he called her callous at just that juncture. She was imagining Christopher stumping clumsily along the hotel corridor looking at bedrooms, and then giving the hotel servant a handsome tip to ensure that he should be put on the same floor as herself. She could almost hear his not disagreeable male voice that vibrated a little from the chest and made her vibrate.

Perowne was grumbling on. Sylvia was callous because she had forgotten the name of the Brittany hamlet in which they had spent three blissful weeks together, though she had left it so suddenly that all her outfit remained in the hotel.

"Well, it wasn't any kind of a beanfeast for me." Sylvia went on, when she again gave him her attention. "Good heavens! . . . Do you think it would be any kind of a beanfeast with you, *pour tout potage*? Why should I remember the name of the hateful place?"

Perowne said:

"Yssingueux-les-Pervenches, such a pretty name," reproachfully.

"It's no good," Sylvia answered, "your trying to awaken sentimental memories in me. You will have to make me forget what you were like if you want to carry on with me. . . I'm stopping here and listening to your corncrake of a voice because I want to wait until Christopher goes out of the hotel. . . Then I am going to my room to tidy up for Lady Sachse's party and you will sit here and wait for me."

"I'm *not*," Perowne said, "going to Lady Sachse's. Why, *he* is going to be one of the principal witnesses to sign the marriage contract. And Old Campion and all the rest of the staff are going to be there. . . You don't catch *me*. . . An unexpected prior engagement is my line. No fear."

"You'll come with me, my little man," Sylvia said, "if you ever want to bask in my smile again. . . I'm not going to Lady Sachse's alone, looking as if I couldn't catch a man to escort me, under the eyes of half the French house of peers. . . If they've got a house of peers! . . . You don't catch *me*. . . No fear!" she mimicked his creaky voice. "You can go away as soon as you've shown yourself as my escort. . .

"But, good God!" Perowne cried out, "that's just what I mustn't do. Campion said that if he heard any more of my being seen about with you he would have me sent back to my beastly regiment. And my beastly regiment is in the trenches. . . You don't see me in the trenches, do you?"

"I'd rather see you there than in my own room," Sylvia said. "Any day!"

"Ah, there you are!" Perowne exclaimed with animation. "What guarantee have I that if I do what you want I shall bask in your smile as you call it? I've got myself into a most awful hole, bringing you here without papers. You never told me you hadn't any papers. General O'Hara, the P.M., has raised a most awful strafe about it. . . And what have I got for it? . . . Not the ghost of a smile. . . And you should see old O'Hara's purple face! . . . Someone woke him from his afternoon nap to report to him about your heinous case and he hasn't recovered from the indigestion yet. . . Besides, he hates Tietjens Tietjens is always chipping away at his military police. . . O'Hara's lambs. . ."

Sylvia was not listening, but she was smiling a slow smile at an inward thought. It maddened him.

"What's your game?" he exclaimed. "Hell and hounds, what's your game? . . . You can't have come here to see. . . *him*. You don't come here to see me, as far as I can see. Well then. . ."

Sylvia looked round at him with all her eyes, wide open as if she had just awakened from a deep sleep.

"I didn't know I was coming," she said. "It came into my head to come suddenly. Ten minutes before I started. And I came. I didn't know papers were wanted. I suppose I could have got them if I had wanted them. . . You never asked me if I had any papers. You just froze on to me and had me into your special carriage. . . I didn't know you were coming."

That seemed to Perowne the last insult. He exclaimed:

"Oh, damn it, Sylvia! you *must* have known. . . You were at the Quirks' squash on Wednesday evening. And *they* knew. My best friends."

"Since you ask for it," she said, "I didn't know. . . And I would not have come by that train if I had known you would be going by it. You force me to say rude things to you." She added: "Why can't you be more conciliatory?" to keep him quiet for a little. His jaw dropped down.

She was wondering where Christopher had got the money to pay for a bed at the hotel. Only a very short time before she had drawn all the balance of his banking account, except for a shilling. It was the middle of the month and he could not have drawn any more pay. . . That, of course, was a try on her part. He might be forced into remonstrating. In the same way she had tried on the accusation that he had carried off her sheets. It was sheer wilfulness, and when she looked again at his motionless features she knew that she had been rather stupid. . . But she was at the end of her tether: she had before now tried making accusations against her husband, but she had never tried inconveniencing him. . . Now she suddenly realized the full stupidity of which she had been guilty. He would know perfectly well that those petty frightfulnesses of hers were not in the least her note; so he would know, too, that each of them was just a try on. He would say: "She is trying to make me squeal. I'm damned if I will!"

She would have to adopt much more formidable methods. She said: "He shall. . . he shall. . . he *shall* come to heel."

Major Perowne had now closed his jaw. He was reflecting. Once he mumbled: "More conciliatory! Holy smoke!"

She was feeling suddenly in spirits: it was the sight of Christopher had done it: the perfect assurance that they were going to live under the same roof again. She would have betted all she possessed and her immortal soul on the chance that he would not take up with the Wannop girl. And it would have been betting on a certainty! . . . But she had had no idea what their relations were to be, after the war. At first she had thought that they had parted for good when she had gone off from their flat at four o'clock in the morning. It had seemed logical. But, gradually, in retreat at Birkenhead, in the still, white, nun's room, doubt had come upon her. It was one of the disadvantages of living as they did that they seldom spoke their thoughts. But that was also at times an advantage. She had certainly meant their parting to be for good. She had certainly raised her voice in giving the name of her station to the taxi-man with the pretty firm conviction that he would hear her; and she had been pretty well certain that he would take it as a sign that the breath had gone out of their union. . . Pretty certain. But not quite! . . .

She would have died rather than write to him; she would die, now, rather than give any inkling that she wanted them to live under the same roof again. . . She said to herself:

"Is he writing to that girl?" And then: "No! . . . I'm certain that he isn't." . . . She had had all his letters stopped at the flat, except for a few circulars that she let dribble through to him, so that he might imagine that all his correspondence was coming through. From the letters to him that she did read she was pretty sure that he had given no other address than the flat in Gray's Inn. . . But there had been no letters from Valentine Wannop. . . Two from Mrs. Wannop, two from his brother Mark, one from Port Scatho, one or two from brother officers and some official chits. . . She said to herself that, if there *had* been any letters from that girl, she would have let all his letters go through, including the girl's. . . Now she was not so certain that she would have.

In the glass she saw Christopher marching woodenly out of the hotel, along the path that led from door to door behind her. . . It came to her with extraordinary gladness—the absolute conviction that he was not corresponding with Miss Wannop. The absolute conviction. . . If he had come alive enough to do that he would have looked different. She did not know how he would have looked. But different. . . Alive! Perhaps self-conscious: perhaps. . . satisfied. . .

For some time the major had been grumbling about his wrongs. He said that he followed her about all day, like a lap-dog, and got nothing for it. Now she wanted him to be conciliatory. She said she wanted to have a man on show as escort. Well then, an escort got something. . . At just this moment he was beginning again with:

"Look here. . . will you let me come to your room tonight or will you not?"

She burst into high, loud laughter. He said:

"Damn it all, it isn't any laughing matter! . . . Look here! You don't know what I risk. . . There are A.P.M.'s and P.M.'s and deputy sub-acting A.P.M.'s walking about the corridors of all the hotels in this town, all night long. . . It's as much as my job is worth. . ."

She put her handkerchief to her lips to hide a smile that she knew would be too cruel for him not to notice. And even when she took it away, he said:

"Hang it all, what a cruel-looking fiend you are! . . . Why the devil do I hang around you? . . . There's a picture that my mother's got, by

Burne-Jones. . . A cruel-looking woman with a distant smile. . . Some vampire. . . La Belle Dame sans Merci. . . That's what you're like."

She looked at him suddenly with considerable seriousness. . .

"See here, Potty. . ." she began. He groaned:

"I believe you'd like me to be sent to the beastly trenches. . . Yet a big, distinguished-looking chap like me wouldn't have a chance. . . At the first volley the Germans fired, they'd pick me off. . .

"Oh, Potty," she exclaimed, "try to be serious for a minute. . . I tell you I'm a woman who's trying. . . who's desperately wanting. . . to be reconciled to her husband! . . . I would not tell that to another soul. . . I would not tell it to myself. . . But one owes something. . . a parting scene, if nothing else. . . Well, something. . . to a man one's been in bed with. . . I didn't give you a parting scene at. . . ah, Yssingueux-les-Pervenches. . . so I give you this tip instead. . ."

He said:

"Will you leave your bedroom door unlocked, or won't you?"

She said:

"If that man would throw his handkerchief to me, I would follow him round the world in my shift! . . . Look here. . . see me shake when I think of it. . ." She held out her hand at the end of her long arm: hand and arm trembled together, minutely, then very much. . . "Well," she finished, "if you see that and still want to come to my room. . . your blood be on your own head. . ." She paused for a breath or two and then said:

"You can come. . . I won't lock my door. . . But I don't say that you'll get anything. . . or that you'll like what you get. . . That's a fair tip. . ." She added suddenly: "You *sale fat*. . . take what you get and be damned to you!"

Major Perowne had suddenly taken to twirling his moustaches; he said:

"Oh, I'll chance the A.P.M.'s. . ."

She suddenly coiled her legs into her chair.

"I know now what I came here for," she said.

Major Wilfrid Fosbrooke Eddicker Perowne of Perowne, the son of his mother, was one of those individuals who have no history, no strong proclivities, nothing. His knowledge seemed to be bounded by the contents of his newspaper for the immediate day; at any rate, his conversation never went any farther. He was not bold, he was not shy; he was neither markedly courageous nor markedly cowardly. His mother was immoderately wealthy, owned an immense castle that hung over crags, above a western sea, much as a bird-cage hangs from a window of a high tenement building, but she received few or no visitors, her cuisine being indifferent and her wine atrocious. She had strong temperance opinions and, immediately after the death of her husband, she had emptied the contents of his cellar, which were almost as historic as his castle, into the sea, a shudder going through county-family England. But even this was not enough to make Perowne himself notorious.

His mother allowed him—after an eyeopener in early youth—the income of a junior royalty, but he did nothing with it. He lived in a great house in Palace Gardens, Kensington, and he lived all alone with rather a large staff of servants who had been selected by his mother, but they did nothing at all, for he ate all his meals, and even took his bath and dressed for dinner at the Bath Club. He was otherwise parsimonious.

He had, after the fashion of his day, passed a year or two in the army when young. He had been first gazetted to His Majesty's Forty-second Regiment, but on the Black Watch proceeding to India he had exchanged into the Glamorgan-shires, at that time commanded by General Campion and recruiting in and around Lincolnshire. The general had been an old friend of Perowne's mother, and, on being promoted to brigadier, had taken Perowne on to his staff as his galloper, for, although Perowne rode rather indifferently, he had a certain social knowledge and could be counted on to know how correctly to address a regimental invitation to a dowager countess who had married a viscount's third son. . . As a military figure otherwise he had a very indifferent word of command, a very poor drill and next to no control of his men, but he was popular with his batmen, and in a rather stiff way was presentable in the old scarlet uniform or the blue mess jacket. He was exactly six-foot, to a hairbreadth, in his stockings, had very dark eyes, and a rather grating voice; the fact that his limbs were a shade too bulky for his trunk, which was not at all corpulent, made him appear a little clumsy. If in a club you asked what sort of a fellow he was your interlocutor would tell you, most probably, that he had or was supposed to have warts on his head, this to account for his hair which all his life he had combed back, unparted from his forehead. But as a matter of fact he had no warts on his head.

He had once started out on an expedition to shoot big game in Portuguese East Africa. But on its arrival his expedition was met with the news that the natives of the interior were in revolt, so Perowne had returned to Kensington Palace Gardens. He had had several mild successes with women, but, owing to his habits of economy and fear of imbroglios, until the age of thirty-four, he had limited the field of his amours to young women of the lower social orders. . .

His affair with Sylvia Tietjens might have been something to boast about, but he was not boastful, and indeed he had been too hard hit when she had left him even to bear to account lyingly for the employment of the time he had spent with her in Brittany. Fortunately no one took sufficient interest in his movements to wait for his answer to their indifferent questions as to where he had spent the summer. When his mind reverted to her desertion of him moisture would come out of his eyes, undemonstratively, as water leaves the surface of a sponge. . .

Sylvia had left him by the simple expedient of stepping without so much as a reticule on to the little French tramway that took you to the main railway line. From there she had written to him in pencil on a closed correspondence card that she had left him because she simply could not bear either his dullness or his craking voice. She said they would probably run up against each other in the course of the autumn season in town and, after purchase of some night things, had made straight for the German spa to which her mother had retreated.

At the later date Sylvia had no difficulty in accounting to herself for her having gone off with such an oaf: she had simply reacted in a violent fit of sexual hatred, from her husband's mind. And she could not have found a mind more utterly dissimilar than Perowne's in any decently groomed man to be found in London. She could recall, even in the French hotel lounge, years after, the almost painful emotion of joyful hatred that had visited her when she had first thought of going off with him. It was the self-applause of one who has just hit upon an excruciatingly inspiring intellectual discovery. In her previous transitory infidelities to Christopher she had discovered that, however presentable the man with whom she might have been having an affair, and however short the affair, even if it were only a matter of a week-end. . . Christopher had spoilt her for the other man. It was the most damnable of his qualities that to hear any other man talk of any subject—any, any subject—from stable form to the balance of power, or from the voice of a given opera singer to the recurrence of a comet—to have to pass a week-end with any other man and hear his talk after having spent the inside of the week with Christopher, hate his ideas how you might, was the difference between listening to a grown man and, with an intense boredom, trying to entertain an inarticulate schoolboy. As beside him, other men simply did not seem ever to have grown up. . .

Just before, with an extreme suddenness, consenting to go away with Perowne, the illuminating idea had struck her: If I did go away with him it would be the most humiliating thing I could do to Christopher. . . And just when the idea *had* struck her, beside her chair in the conservatory at a dance given by the general's sister, Lady Claudine Sandbach, Perowne, his voice rendered more throaty and less disagreeable than usual by emotion, had been going on and on begging her to elope with him. . . She had suddenly said:

"Very well. . . let's. . ."

His emotion had been so unbridled in its astonishment that she had, even at that, almost been inclined to treat her own speech as a joke and to give up the revenge. . . But the idea of the humiliation that Christopher must feel proved too much for her. For, for your wife to throw you over for an attractive man is naturally humiliating, but that she should leave you publicly for a man of hardly any intelligence at all, you priding yourself on your brains, must be nearly as mortifying a thing as can happen to you.

But she had hardly set out upon her escapade before two very serious defects in her plan occurred to her with extreme force: the one that, however humiliated Christopher might feel, she would not be with him to witness his humiliation; the other that, oaf as she had taken Perowne to be in casual society, in close daily relationship he was such an oaf as to be almost insufferable. She had imagined that he would prove a person out of whom it might be possible to make *something* by a judicious course of alternated mothering and scorn: she discovered that his mother had already done for him almost all that woman could do. For, when he had been an already rather backward boy at a private school, his mother had kept him so extremely short of pocket-money that he had robbed other boys' desks of a few shillings here and there— in order to subscribe towards a birthday present for the headmaster's wife. His mother, to give him a salutary lesson, had given so much publicity to the affair that he had become afflicted with a permanent bent towards shyness that rendered him by turns very mistrustful of himself or very boastful and, although he repressed manifestations of either tendency towards the outside world, the continual repression rendered him almost incapable of any vigorous thought or action. . .

That discovery did not soften Sylvia towards him: it was, as she expressed it, *his* funeral and, although she would have been ready for any normal job of smartening up a roughish man, she was by no means prepared to readjust other women's hopeless maternal misfits.

So she had got no farther than Ostend, where they had proposed to spend a week or so at the tables, before she found herself explaining to some acquaintances whom she met that she was in that gay city merely for an hour or two, between trains, on the way to join her mother in a German health resort. The impulse to say that had come upon her by surprise, for, until that moment, being completely indifferent to criticism, she had intended to cast no veil at all over her proceedings. But, quite suddenly, on seeing some well-known English faces in the casino it had come over her to think that, however much she imagined Christopher to be humiliated by her going off with an oaf like Perowne, that humiliation must be as nothing compared with that which she might be expected to feel at having found no one better than an oaf like Perowne to go off with. Moreover. . . she began to miss Christopher.

These feelings did not grow any less intense in the rather stuffy but inconspicuous hotel in the Rue St. Roque in Paris to which she immediately transported the bewildered but uncomplaining Perowne, who had imagined that he was to be taken to Wiesbaden for a course of light gaieties. And Paris, when you avoid the more conspicuous resorts, and when you are unprovided with congenial companionship, can prove nearly as overwhelming as is, say, Birmingham on a Sunday.

So that Sylvia waited for only just long enough to convince herself that her husband had no apparent intention of applying for an immediate divorce and had, indeed, no apparent intention of doing anything at all. She sent him, that is to say, a postcard saying that all letters and other communications would reach her at her inconspicuous hotel—and it mortified her not a little to have to reveal the fact that her hotel was so inconspicuous. But, except that her own correspondence was forwarded to her with regularity, no communications at all came from Tietjens.

In an air-resort in the centre of France to which she next removed Perowne, she found herself considering rather seriously what it might be expected that Tietjens would do. Through indirect and unsuspecting allusions in letters from her personal friends she found that if Tietjens did not put up, he certainly did not deny, the story that she had gone to nurse or be with her mother, who was supposed to be seriously ill. . . That is to say, her friends said how rotten it was that her mother, Mrs. Satterthwaite, should be so seriously ill; how rotten it must be for her to be shut up in a potty little German kur-ort when the world could be so otherwise amusing; and how well Christopher whom they saw from time to time seemed to be getting on considering how rotten it must be for him to be left all alone. . .

At about this time Perowne began to become, if possible, more irritating than ever. In their air-resort, although the guests were almost entirely French, there was a newly opened golf-course, and at the game of golf Perowne displayed an inefficiency and at the same time a morbid conceit that were surprising in one naturally lymphatic. He would sulk for a whole evening if either Sylvia or any Frenchman beat him in a round, and, though Sylvia was by then completely indifferent to his sulking, what was very much worse was that he became gloomily and loudvoicedly quarrelsome over his games with foreign opponents.

Three events, falling within ten minutes of each other, made her determined to get as far away from that air-resort as was feasible. In the first place she observed at the end of the street some English people called Thurston, whose faces she faintly knew, and the emotion she suddenly felt let her know how extremely anxious she was that she should let it remain feasible for Tietjens to take her back. Then, in the golf club-house, to which she found herself fiercely hurrying in order to pay her bill and get her clubs, she overheard the conversation of two players that left no doubt in her mind that Perowne had been detected in little meannesses of moving his ball at golf or juggling with his score. . . This was almost more than she could stand. And, at the same moment, her mind, as it were, condescended to let her remember Christopher's voice as it had once uttered the haughty opinion that no man one could speak to would ever think of divorcing any woman. If he could not defend the sanctity of his hearth he must lump it unless the woman wanted to divorce him. . .

At the time when he had said it her mind—she had been just then hating him a good deal—had seemed to take no notice of the utterance. But now that it presented itself forcibly to her again it brought with it the thought: Supposing he wasn't really only talking through his hat! . . . She dragged the wretched Perowne off his bed where he had been lost in an after-lunch slumber and told him that they must both leave that place at once, and, that as soon as they reached Paris or some larger town where he could find waiters and people to understand his French, she herself was going to leave him for good. They did not, in consequence, get away from the air-resort until the six o'clock train next morning. Perowne's passion of rage and despair at the news that she wished to leave him took an inconvenient form, for instead of announcing any intention of committing suicide, as might have been expected, he became gloomily and fantastically murderous. He said that unless Sylvia swore on a little relic of St. Anthony she carried that she had no intention of leaving him he would incontinently kill her. He said, as he said for the rest of his days, that she had ruined his life and caused great moral deterioration in himself. But for her he might have married some pure young thing. Moreover, influencing him against his mother's doctrines, she had forced him to drink wine, by an effect of pure scorn. Thus he had done harm, he was convinced, both to his health and to his manly proportions. . . It was indeed for Sylvia one of the most unbearable things about this man—the way he took wine. With every glass he put to his lips he would exclaim with an unbearable titter some such imbecility as: Here is another nail in my coffin. And he had taken to wine, and even to stronger liquor, very well.

Sylvia had refused to swear by St. Anthony. She definitely was not going to introduce the saint into her amorous affairs, and she definitely was not going to take on any relic an oath that she meant to break at an early opportunity. There was such a thing as playing it too low down: there are dishonours to which death is preferable. So, getting hold of his revolver at a time when he was wringing his hands, she dropped it into the water-jug and then felt reasonably safe.

Perowne knew no French and next to nothing about France, but he had discovered that the French did nothing to you for killing a woman who intended to leave you. Sylvia, on the other hand, was pretty certain that, without a weapon, he could not do much to her. If she had had no other training at her very expensive school she had had so much drilling in calisthenics as to be singularly mistress of her limbs, and, in the interests of her beauty she had always kept herself very fit. . .

She said at last:

"Very well. We will go to Yssingueux-les-Pervenches. . ."

A rather pleasant French couple in the hotel had spoken of this little place in the extreme west of France as a lonely paradise, they having spent their honeymoon there. . . And Sylvia wanted a lonely paradise if there was going to be any scrapping before she got away from Perowne. . .

She had no hesitation as to what she was going to do: the long journey across half France by miserable trains had caused her an agony of home-sickness! Nothing less! . . . It was a humiliating disease from which to suffer. But it was unavoidable, like mumps. You had to put up with it. Besides, she even found herself wanting to see her child, whom she imagined herself to hate, as having been the cause of all her misfortunes. . .

She therefore prepared, after great thought, a letter telling Tietjens that she intended to return to him. She made the letter as nearly as possible like one she would write announcing her return from a country house to which she should have been invited for an indefinite period, and she added some rather hard instructions about her maid, these being intended to remove from the letter any possible trace of emotion. She was certain that, if she showed any emotion at all, Christopher would never take her under his roof again. . . She was pretty certain that no gossip had been caused by her escapade. Major Thurston had been at the railway station when they had left, but they had not spoken—and Thurston was a very decentish, brown-moustached fellow, of the sort that does not gossip.

It had proved a little difficult to get away, for Perowne during several weeks watched her like an attendant in a lunatic asylum. But at last the idea presented itself to him that she would never go without her frocks, and, one day, in a fit of intense somnolence after a lunch, washed down with rather a large quantity of the local and fiery cordial, he let her take a walk alone. . .

She was by that time tired of men. . . or she imagined that she was; for she was not prepared to be certain, considering the muckers she saw women coming all round her over the most unpresentable individuals. Men, at any rate never fulfilled expectations. They might, upon acquaintance, turn out more entertaining than they appeared; but almost always taking up with a man was like reading a book you had read when you had forgotten that you had read it. You had not been for ten minutes in any sort of intimacy with any man before you said: "But I've read all this before. . ." You knew the opening, you were already bored by the middle, and, especially, you knew the end. . .

She remembered, years ago, trying to shock her mother's spiritual adviser, Father Consett, whom they had lately murdered in Ireland, along with Casement. . . The poor saint had not in the least been shocked. He had gone her one better. For when she had said something like that her idea of a divvy life—they used in those days to say divvy—would be to go off with a different man every week-end, he had told her that after a short time she would be bored already by the time the poor dear fellow was buying the railway ticket. . .

And, by heavens, he had been right. . . For when she came to think of it, from the day that poor saint had said that thing in her mother's sitting-room in the little German spa—Lobscheid, it must have been called—in the candlelight, his shadow denouncing her from all over the walls, to now when she sat in the palmish brickwork of that hotel that had been new-whitely decorated to celebrate hostilities, never once had she sat in a train with a man who had any right to look upon himself as justified in mauling her about. . . She wondered if, from where he sat in heaven, Father Consett would be satisfied with her as he looked down into that lounge. . . Perhaps it was really he that had pulled off that change in her. . .

Never once till yesterday. . . For perhaps the unfortunate Perowne might just faintly have had the right yesterday to make himself for about two minutes—before she froze him into a choking, pallid snowman with goggle eyes—the perfectly loathsome thing that a man in a railway train becomes. . . Much too bold and yet stupidly awkward with the fear of the guard looking in at the window, the train doing over sixty, without corridors. . . No, never again for *me*, father, she addressed her voice towards the ceiling. . .

Why in the world couldn't you get a man to go away with you and be just—oh, light comedy—for a whole, a whole blessed week-end. For a whole blessed life. . . Why not? . . . Think of it. . . A whole blessed life with a good sort and yet didn't go all gurgly in the voice, and cod-fish-eyed and all-overish—to the extent of not being able to find the tickets when asked for them. . . Father, dear, she said again upwards, if I could find men like that, that would be just heaven. . . where there is no marrying. . . But, of course, she went on almost resignedly, he would not be faithful to you. . . And then: one would have to stand it. . .

She sat up so suddenly in her chair that beside her, too, Major Perowne nearly jumped out of his wicker-work, and asked if *he* had come back. . . She exclaimed:

"No, I'd be damned if I would. . . I'd be damned, I'd be damned, I'd be damned if I would. . . Never. Never. By the living God!"

She asked fiercely of the agitated major:

"Has Christopher got a girl in this town? . . . You'd better tell me the truth!"

The major mumbled:

"He. . . No. . . He's too much of a stick. . . He never even goes to Suzette's. . . Except once to fetch out some miserable little squit of a subaltern who was smashing up Mother Hardelot's furniture. . ."

He grumbled:

"But you shouldn't give a man the jumps like that! . . . Be conciliatory, you said. . . He went on to grumble that her manners had not improved since she had been at Yssingueux-les-Pervenches, . . . and then went on to tell her that in French the words *yeux des pervenches* meant eyes of periwinkle blue. And that was the only French he knew, because a Frenchman he had met in the train had told him so and he had always thought that if *her* eyes had been periwinkle blue. . . "But you're not listening. . . Hardly polite, I call it," he had mumbled to a conclusion. . .

She was sitting forward in her chair still clenching her hand under her chin at the thought that perhaps Christopher had Valentine Wannop in that town. That was perhaps why he elected to remain there. She asked:

"Why does Christopher stay on in this God-forsaken hole? . . . The inglorious base, they call it. . ."

"Because he's jolly well got to. . ." Major Perowne said. "He's got to do what he's told. . ."

She said: "Christopher! . . . You mean to say they'd keep a man like Christopher anywhere he didn't want to be. . ."

"They'd jolly well knock spots off him if he went away," Major Perowne exclaimed. . . "What the deuce do you think your blessed fellow is? . . . The King of England?" He added with a sudden sombre ferocity: "They'd shoot him like anybody else if he bolted. . . What do *you* think?"

She said: "But all that wouldn't prevent his having a girl in this town?"

"Well, he hasn't got one," Perowne said. "He sticks up in that blessed old camp of his like a blessed she-chicken sitting on addled eggs. . . That's what they say of him. . . I don't know anything about the fellow. . ."

Listening vindictively and indolently, she thought she caught in his droning tones a touch of the homicidal lunacy that had used to underlie his voice in the bedroom at Yssingueux. The fellow had undoubtedly about him a touch of the dull, mad murderer of the police-courts. With a sudden animation she thought:

"Suppose he tried to murder Christopher. . ." And she imagined her husband breaking the fellow's back across his knee, the idea going across her mind as fire traverses the opal. Then, with a dry throat, she said to herself:

"I've got to find out whether he has that girl in Rouen. . ." Men stuck together. The fellow Perowne might well be protecting Tietjens. It would be unthinkable that any rules of the service could keep Christopher in that place. They could not shut up the upper classes. If Perowne had any sense he would know that to shield Tietjens was the way not to get her. . . But he had no sense. . . Besides, sexual solidarity was a terribly strong thing. . . She knew that she herself would not give a woman's secrets away in order to get her man. Then. . . how was she to ascertain whether the girl was not in that town? How? . . . She imagined Tietjens going home every night to her. . . But he was going to spend that night with herself. . . She knew that. . . Under that roof. . . Fresh from the other. . .

She imagined him there, now. . . In the parlour of one of the little villas you see from the tram on the top of the town. . . They were undoubtedly, now, discussing her. . . Her whole body writhed, muscle on muscle, in her chair. . . She must discover. . . But how do you discover? Against a universal conspiracy. . . This whole war was an agapemone. . . You went to war when you desired to rape innumerable women. . . It was what war was for. . . All these men, crowded in this narrow space. . . She stood up:

"I'm going," she said, "to put on a little powder for Lady Sachse's feast. . . You needn't stay if you don't want to. . ." She was going to watch every face she saw until it gave up the secret of where in that town Christopher had the Wannop girl hidden. . . She imagined her freckled, snubnosed faced pressed—squashed was the word—against his cheek. . . She was going to investigate. . .

II

S he found an early opportunity to carry on her investigations. For, at dinner that night, she found herself, Tietjens having gone to the telephone with a lance-corporal, opposite what she took to be a small tradesman, with fresh-coloured cheeks, and a great, grey, forward-sprouting moustache, in a uniform so creased that the creases resembled the veins of a leaf. . . A very trustworthy small tradesman: the grocer from round the corner whom, sometimes, you allow to supply you with paraffin. . . He was saying to her:

"If, ma'am, you multiply two-thousand nine hundred and something by ten you arrive at twenty-nine thousand odd. . .

And she had exclaimed:

"You really mean that my husband, Captain Tietjens, spent yesterday afternoon in examining twenty-nine thousand toe-nails. . . And two thousand nine hundred toothbrushes. . .

"I told him," her interlocutor answered with deep seriousness, "that these being Colonial troops it was not so necessary to examine their toothbrushes. . . Imperial troops *will* use the brush they clean their buttons with for their teeth so as to have a clean toothbrush to show the medical officer. . .

"It sounds," she said with a little shudder, "as if you were all schoolboys playing a game. . . And you say my husband really occupies his mind with such things. . ."

Second-Lieutenant Cowley, dreadfully conscious that the shoulder-strap of his Sam Browne belt, purchased that afternoon at the Ordnance, and therefore brand-new, did not match the abdominal part of the belt that he had had for nearly ten years—a splendid bit of leather, that!—answered nevertheless stoutly:

"Madam! If the brains of an army aren't, the life of an army is. . . in its feet. . . And nowadays, the medical officers say, in its teeth. . . Your husband, ma'am, is an admirable officer. . . He says that no draft he turns out shall. . .

She said:

"He spent three hours in. . . You say, foot and kit inspection. . ."

Second-Lieutenant Cowley said:

"Of course he had other officers to help him with the kit. . . but he looked at every foot himself. . ."

She said:

"That took him from two till five. . . Then he had tea, I suppose. . . And went to. . . What is it? . . . The papers of the draft. . ."

Second-Lieutenant Cowley said, muffled through his moustache:

"If the captain is a little remiss in writing letters. . . I *have* heard. . . You might, madam. . . I'm a married man myself. . . with a daughter. . . And the army is not very good at writing letters. . . You might say, in that respect, that thank God we have got a navy, ma'am. . ."

She let him stagger on for a sentence or two, imagining that, in his confusion, she might come upon traces of Miss Wannop in Rouen. Then she said handsomely:

"Of course you have explained everything, Mr. Cowley, and I am very much obliged. . . Of course my husband would not have time to write very full letters. . . He is not like the giddy young subalterns who run after. . ."

He exclaimed in a great roar of laughter:

"The captain run after skirts. . . Why, I can number on my hands the times he's been out of my sight since he's had the battalion!"

A deep wave of depression went over Sylvia.

"Why," Lieutenant Cowley laughed on, "if we *had* a laugh against him it was that he mothered the lot of us as if he was a hen sitting on addled eggs. . . For it's only a ragtime army, as the saying is, when you've said the best for it that you can. . . And look at the other commanding officers we've had before we had him. . . There was Major Brooks. . . Never up before noon, if then, and out of camp by two-thirty. Get your returns ready for signing before then or never get 'em signed. . . And Colonel Potter. . . Bless my soul. . . 'e wouldn't sign any blessed papers at all. . . He lived down here in this hotel, and we never saw him up at the camp at all. . . But the captain. . . We always say that. . . if 'e was a Chelsea adjutant getting off a draft of the Second Coldstreams. . ."

With her indolent and gracious beauty—Sylvia knew that she was displaying indolent and gracious beauty—Sylvia leaned over the tablecloth listening for items in the terrible indictment that, presently, she was going to bring against Tietjens. . . For the morality of these matters is this: . . . If you have an incomparably beautiful woman on your hands you must occupy yourself solely with her. . . Nature exacts that of you. . . until you are unfaithful to her with a snubnosed girl with freckles: that, of course, being a reaction, is still in a way occupying yourself with your woman! . . . But to betray her with a battalion. . .

That is against decency, against Nature. . . And for him, Christopher Tietjens, to come down to the level of the men you met here! . . .

Tietjens, mooning down the room between tables, had more than his usually aloof air since he had just come out of a telephone box. He slipped, a weary mass, into the polished chair between her and the lieutenant. He said:

"I've got the washing arranged for. . ." and Sylvia gave to herself a little hiss between the teeth, of vindictive pleasure! This was indeed betrayal to a battalion. He added: "I shall have to be up in camp before four-thirty tomorrow morning. . .

Sylvia could not resist saying:

"Isn't there a poem. . . *Ah me, the dawn, the dawn, it comes too soon*! . . . said of course by lovers in bed? . . . Who was the poet?"

Cowley went visibly red to the roots of his hair and evidently beyond. Tietjens finished his speech to Cowley, who had remonstrated against his going up to the camp so early by saying that he had not been able to get hold of an officer to march the draft. He then said in his leisurely way:

"There were a great many poems with that refrain in the Middle Ages. . . You are probably thinking of an albade by Arnaut Daniel, which someone translated lately. . . An albade was a song to be sung at dawn when, presumably, no one but lovers would be likely to sing. . ."

"Will there," Sylvia asked, "be anyone but you singing up in your camp tomorrow at four?"

She could not help it. . . She knew that Tietjens had adopted his slow pomposity in order to give the grotesque object at the table with them time to recover from his confusion. She hated him for it. What right had he to make himself appear a pompous ass in order to shield the confusion of anybody?

The second-lieutenant came out of his confusion to exclaim, actually slapping his thigh:

"There you are, madam. . . Trust the captain to know everything! . . . I don't believe there's a question under the sun you could ask him that he couldn't answer. . . They say up at the camp. . ." He went on with long stories of all the questions Tietjens *had* answered up at the camp. . .

Emotion was going all over Sylvia. . . at the proximity of Tietjens. She said to herself: "Is this to go on for ever?" Her hands were ice-cold. She touched the back of her left hand with the fingers of her right. It *was* ice-cold. She looked at her hands. They were bloodless. . . She said to herself:

"It's pure sexual passion. . . it's pure sexual passion. . . God! Can't I get over this?" She said: "Father! . . . You used to be fond of Christopher. . . *Get* our Lady to get me over this. . . It's the ruin of him and the ruin of me. But, oh *damn*, don't! . . . For it's all I have to live for. . ." She said: "When he came mooning back from the telephone I thought it was all right. . . I thought what a heavy wooden-horse he looked. . . For two minutes. . . Then it's all over me again. . . I want to swallow my saliva and I can't. My throat won't work. . .

She leaned one of her white bare arms on the tablecloth towards the walrus-moustache that was still snuffling gloriously:

"They used to call him Old Sol at school." she said. "But there's one question of Solomon's he could not answer. . . The one about the way of a man with. . . Oh, a maid! . . . Ask him what happened before the dawn ninety-six—no, ninety-eight days ago. . ."

She said to herself: "I can't help it. . . Oh, I *can't* help it. . ."

The ex-sergeant-major was exclaiming happily:

"Oh, no one ever said the captain was one of these thought-readers. . . It's real solid knowledge of men and things he has. . . Wonderful how he knows the men considering he was not born in the service. . . But there, your born gentleman mixes with men all his days and knows them. Down to the ground and inside their puttees. . ."

Tietjens was looking straight in front of him, his face perfectly expressionless.

"But I bet I got him. . ." she said to herself and then to the sergeant-major:

"I suppose now an army officer—one of your born gentlemen—when a back-from-leave train goes out from any of the great stations—Paddington, say—to the front. . . He knows how all the men are feeling. . . But not what the married women think. . . or the. . . the girl. . ."

She said to herself: "Damn it, how clumsy I am getting! . . . I used to be able to take his hide off with a word. Now I take sentences at a time. . ."

She went on with her uninterrupted sentence to Cowley: "Of course he may never be going to see his only son again, so it makes him sensitive. . . The officer at Paddington, I mean. . ."

She said to herself: "By God, if that beast does not give in to me tonight he never *shall* see Michael again. . . Ah, but I got him. . . Tietjens had his eyes closed, round each of his high-coloured nostrils a crescent of whiteness was beginning. And increasing. . . She felt a sudden alarm and held the edge of the table with her extended arm to steady herself. . . Men went white at the nose like that when they were going to faint. . . She did not want him to faint. . . But he *had* noticed the word Paddington. . . Ninety-eight days before. . . She had counted every day since. . . She had got that much information. . . She had said *Paddington* outside the house at dawn and he had taken it as a farewell. He *had*. . . He had imagined himself free to do what he liked with the girl. . . Well, he wasn't. . . That was why he was white about the gills. . .

Cowley exclaimed loudly:

"Paddington! . . . It isn't from there that back-from-leave trains go. Not for the front: the B.E.F. . . Not from Paddington. . . The Glamorganshires go from there to the depot. . . And the Liverpools. . . They've got a depot at Birkenhead. . . Or is that the Cheshires? . . ." He asked of Tietjens: "Is it the Liverpools or the Cheshires that have a depot at Birkenhead, sir? . . . You remember we recruited a draft from there when we were at Penhally. . . At any rate, you go to Birkenhead from Paddington. . . I was never there myself. . . They say it's a nice place. . ."

Sylvia said—she did not want to say it:

"It's quite a nice place. . . but I should not think of staying there for ever. . ."

Tietjens said:

"The Cheshires have a training camp—not a depot—near Birkenhead. And of course there are R.G.A.'s there. . ." She had been looking away from him. . . Cowley exclaimed:

"You were nearly off, sir," hilariously. "You had your peepers shut. . ." Lifting a champagne glass, he inclined himself towards her. "You must excuse the captain, ma'am," he said. "He had no sleep last night. . . Largely owing to my fault. . . Which is what makes it so kind of him. . . I tell you, ma'am, there are few things I would not do for the captain. . ." He drank his champagne and began an explanation: "You may not know, ma'am, this is a great day for me. . . And you and the captain are making it the greatest day of my life. . ." Why, at four this morning there hadn't been a wretcheder man in Ruin town. . . And now. . . He must tell her that he suffered from an unfortunate—a miserable—complaint. . . One that makes one have to be careful of celebrations. . . And today was a day that he had to celebrate. . . But he dare not have done it where Sergeant-Major Ledoux is along with a lot of their old mates. . . "I dare not. . . I dussn't!" he finished. . . "So I might have been sitting, now, at this very moment, up in the cold camp. . . But for you and the captain. . . Up in the cold camp. . . You'll excuse me, ma'am. . ."

Sylvia felt that her lids were suddenly wavering:

"I might have been myself," she said, "in a cold camp, too. . . if I hadn't thrown myself on the captain's mercy! . . . At Birkenhead, you know. . . I happened to be there till three weeks ago. . . It's strange that you mentioned it. . . There are things like signs. . . but you're not a Catholic! They could hardly be coincidences. . ."

She was trembling. . . She looked, fumblingly opening it, into the little mirror of her powder-box—of chased, very thin gold with a small blue stone, like a forget-me-not in the centre of the concentric engravings. . . Drake—the possible father of Michael—had given it to her. . . The first thing he had ever given her. She had brought it down tonight out of defiance. She imagined that Tietjens disliked it. . . She said breathlessly to herself: perhaps the damn thing is an ill omen. . . Drake had been the first man who had ever. . . A hot-breathed brute! . . . In the little glass her features were chalk-white. . . She looked like. . . she looked like. . . She had a dress of golden tissue. . . The breath was short between her white set teeth. . . Her face was as white as her teeth. . . And. . . Yes! Nearly! Her lips. . . What was her face like? . . . In the chapel of the convent of Birkenhead there was a tomb all of alabaster. . . She said to herself:

"He was near fainting. . . I'm near fainting. . . What's this beastly thing that's between us? . . . If I let myself faint. . . But it would not make that beast's face any less wooden! . . ."

She leaned across the table and patted the ex-sergeant major's black-haired hand:

"I'm sure," she said, "you're a very good man. . ." She did not try to keep the tears out of her eyes, remembering his words: "Up in the cold camp." . . . "I'm glad the captain, as you call him, did not leave you in the cold camp. . . You're devoted to him, aren't you? . . . There are others he does leave. . . up in. . . the cold camp. . . For punishment, you know. . ."

The ex-sergeant-major, the tears in his eyes too, said: "Well, there *is* men you 'as to give the C.B. to' . . . C.B. means confined to barracks."

"Oh, there are!" she exclaimed. "There are! . . . And women, too. . . Surely there are women, too? . . ."

The sergeant-major said:

"Wacks, per'aps. . . I don't know. . . They say women's discipline is like ours. . . Founded on hours!"

She said:

"Do you know what they used to say of the captain? . . ." She said to herself: "I pray to God the stiff, fatuous beast likes sitting here listening to this stuff. . . Blessed Virgin, mother of God, make him take me. . . Before midnight. Before eleven. . . As soon as we get rid of this. . . No, he's a decent little man. . . Blessed Virgin!" . . . "Do you know what they used to say of the captain? . . . I heard the warmest banker in England say it of him. . ."

The sergeant-major, his eyes enormously opened, said: "Did you know the warmest banker in England? But there, we always knew the captain was well connected. . ." She went on:

"They said of him. . . He was always helping people." . . . "Holy Mary, mother of God! . . . He's my *husband*. . . It's not a sin. . . Before midnight. . . Oh, give me a sign. . . Or before. . . the termination of hostilities. . . If you give me a sign I could wait." . . . "He helped virtuous Scotch students, and broken-down gentry. . . And women taken in adultery. . . All of them. . . Like. . . You know Who. . . That is his model. . ." She said to herself: "Curse him! . . . I hope he likes it. . . You'd think the only thing he thinks about is the beastly duck he's wolfing down." . . . And then aloud: "They used to say: 'He saved others; himself he could not save. . .'"

The ex-sergeant-major looked at her gravely:

"Ma'am," he said, we couldn't say exactly that of the captain. . . For I fancy it was said of our Redeemer. . . But we 'ave said that if ever there was a poor bloke the captain could 'elp, 'elp 'im 'e would. . . Yet the unit was always getting "ellish strafe from headquarters. . ."

Suddenly Sylvia began to laugh. . . As she began to laugh she had remembered. . . The alabaster image in the nun's chapel at Birkenhead the vision of which had just presented itself to her, had been the recumbent tomb of an honourable Mrs. Tremayne-Warlock. . . She was said to have sinned in her youth. . . And her husband had never forgiven her. . . That was what the nuns said. . . She said aloud:

"A sign. . ." Then to herself: "Blessed Mary! . . . You've given it me in the neck. . . Yet you could not name a father for your child, and I can name two. . . I'm going mad. . . Both I and he are going to go mad. . ."

She thought of dashing an enormous patch of red upon either cheek. Then she thought it would be rather melodramatic. . .

She made in the smoking-room, whilst she was waiting for both Tietjens and Cowley to come back from the telephone, another pact. . . This time with Father Consett in heaven! She was fairly sure that Father Consett—and quite possibly other of the heavenly powers—wanted Christopher not to be worried, so that he could get on with the war— or because he was a good sort of dullish man such as the heavenly authorities are apt to like. . . Something like that. . .

She was by that time fairly calm again. You cannot keep up fits of emotion by the hour: at any rate, with her, the fits of emotion were periodical and unexpected, though her colder passion remained always the same. . . Thus, when Christopher had come into Lady Sachse's that afternoon, she had been perfectly calm. He had mooned through a number of officers, both French and English, in a great octagonal, bluish salon where Lady Sachse gave her teas, and had come to her side with just a nod—the merest inflexion of the head! . . . Perowne had melted away somewhere behind the disagreeable duchess. The general, very splendid and white-headed and scarlet-tipped and gilt, had also borne down upon her at that. . . At the sight of Perowne with her he had been sniffing and snorting whilst he talked to the young nobleman—a dark fellow in blue with a new belt who seemed just a shade too theatrical, he being chauffeur to a marshal of France and first cousin and nearest relative, except for parents and grandparents, of the prospective bride. . .

The general had told her that he was running the show pretty strong on purpose because he thought it might do something to cement the Entente Cordiale. But it did not seem to be doing it. The French—officers, soldiers and women—kept pretty well all on the one side of the room—the English on the other. The French were as a rule more gloomy than men and women are expected to be. A marquis of sorts—she understood that these were all Bonapartist nobility—having been introduced to her had distinguished himself no more than by saying that, for his part, he thought the duchess was right, and by saying that to Perowne who, knowing no French, had choked exactly as if his tongue had suddenly got too big for his mouth. . .

She had not heard what the duchess—a very disagreeable duchess who sat on a sofa and appeared savagely careworn—had been saying, so that she had inclined herself, in the courtly manner that at school she had been taught to reserve for the French legitimist nobility, but that she thought she might expend upon a rather state function even for the Bonapartists, and had replied that without the least doubt the duchess had the right of the matter. . . The marquis had given her from dark eyes one long glance, and she had returned it with a long cold glance that certainly told him she was meat for his masters. It extinguished him. . .

Tietjens had staged his meeting with herself remarkably well. It was the sort of lymphatic thing he *could* do, so that, for the fifth of a minute, she wondered if he had any feelings or emotions at all. But she knew that he had. . . The general, at any rate, bearing down upon them with satisfaction, had remarked:

"Ah, I see you've seen each other before today. . . I thought perhaps you wouldn't have found time before, Tietjens. . . Your draft must be a great nuisance. . ."

Tietjens said without expression:

"Yes, we have seen each other before. . . I made time to call at Sylvia's hotel, sir."

It was at Tietjens' terrifying expressionlessness, at that completely being up to a situation, that the first wave of emotion had come over her. . . For, till that very moment, she had been merely sardonically making the constatation that there was not a single presentable man in the room. . . There was not even one that you could call a gentleman. . . for you cannot size up the French. . . ever! . . . But, suddenly, she was despairing! . . . How, she said to herself, could she ever move, put emotion into, this lump! It was like trying to move an immense mattress filled with feathers. You pulled at one end, but the whole mass sagged down and remained immobile until you seemed to have no strength at all. . . Until virtue went out from you. . .

It was as if he had the evil eye; or some special protector. He was so appallingly competent, so appallingly always in the centre of his own picture.

The general said, rather joyfully:

"Then you can spare a minute, Tietjens, to talk to the duchess! About coal! . . . For goodness' sake, man, save the situation! I'm worn out. . ."

Sylvia bit the inside of her lower lip—she never bit her lip itself!—to keep herself from exclaiming aloud. It was just exactly what should not happen to Tietjens at that juncture. . . She heard the general explaining to her, in his courtly manner, that the duchess was holding up the whole ceremony because of the price of coal. The general loved her desperately. Her, Sylvia! In quite a proper manner for an elderly general. . . But he would go to no small extremes in her interests! So would his sister!

She looked hard at the room to get her senses into order again. She said:

"It's like a Hogarth picture. . ."

The undissolvable air of the eighteenth century that the French contrive to retain in all their effects kept the scene singularly together. On a sofa sat the duchess, relatives leaning over her. She was a duchess with one of those impossible names: Beauchain-Radigutz or something like it. The bluish room was octagonal and vaulted, up to a rosette in the centre of the ceiling. English officers and V.A.D.'s of some evident presence opened out to the left, French military and very black-clothed women of all ages, but all apparently widows, opened out to the right, as if the duchess shone down a sea at sunset. Beside her on the sofa you did not see Lady Sachse: leaning over her you did not see the prospective bride. This stoutish, unpresentable, coldly venomous woman, in black clothes so shabby that they might have been grey tweed, extinguished other personalities as the sun conceals planets. A fattish, brilliantined personality, in mufti, with a scarlet rosette, stood sideways to the duchess's right, his hands extended forward as if in an invitation to a dance; an extremely squat lady, also apparently a widow, extended, on the left of the duchess, both her black-gloved hands, as if she too were giving an invitation to the dance. . .

The general, with Sylvia beside him, stood glorious in the centre of the clearing that led to the open doorway of a much smaller room. Through the doorway you could see a table with a white damask cloth; a silver-gilt inkpot, fretted, like a porcupine with pens, a fat, flat leather case for the transportation of documents and two notaries: one in black, fat, and bald-headed; one in blue uniform, with a shining monocle, and a brown moustache that he continued to twirl. . .

Looking round that scene Sylvia's humour calmed her and she heard the general say:

"She's supposed to walk on my arm to that table and sign the settlement. . . We're supposed to be the first to sign it together. . . But she won't. Because of the price of coal. It appears that she has hothouses in miles. And she thinks the English have put up the price of coal as if. . . damn it you'd think we did it just to keep her hothouse stoves out."

The duchess had delivered, apparently, a vindictive, cold, calm, and uninterruptible oration on the wickedness of her country's allies as people who should have allowed France to be devastated and the flower of her youth slain in order that they might put up the price of a comestible that was absolutely needed in her life. There was no arguing with her. There was no British soul there who both knew anything about economics and spoke French. And there she sat, apparently immovable. She did not refuse to sign the marriage contract. She just made no motion to go to it and, apparently, the resulting marriage would be illegal if that document were brought to her!

The general said:

"Now, what the deuce will Christopher find to say to her? He'll find something because he could talk the hind legs off anything. But what the deuce will it be?"

It almost broke Sylvia's heart to see how exactly Christopher did the right thing. He walked up that path to the sun and made in front of the duchess a little awkward nick with his head and shoulders that was rather more like a curtsy than a bow. It appeared that he knew the duchess quite well. . . as he knew everybody in the world quite well. He smiled at her and then became just suitably grave. Then he began to speak an admirable, very old-fashioned French with an atrocious English accent. Sylvia had no idea that he knew a word of the language—that she herself knew very well indeed. She said to herself that upon her word it was like hearing Chateaubriand talk—if Chateaubriand had been brought up in an English hunting country. . . Of course Christopher *would* cultivate an English accent: to show that he was an English country gentleman. And he would speak correctly— to show that an English Tory can do anything in the world if he wants to. . .

The British faces in the room looked blank: the French faces turned electrically upon him. Sylvia said:

"Who would have thought. . . ?" The duchess jumped to her feet and took Christopher's arm. She sailed with him imperiously past the general and past Sylvia. She was saying that that was just what she would have expected of *a milor Anglais. . . Avec un spleen tel que vous l'avez*!

Christopher, in short, had told the duchess that as his family owned almost the largest stretch of hot-house coal-burning land in England and her family the largest stretch of hothouses in the sister-country of France, what could they do better than make an alliance? He would instruct his brother's manager to see that the duchess was supplied for the duration of hostilities and as long after as she pleased with all the coal needed for her glass at the pithead prices of the Middlesbrough-Cleveland district as the prices were on the 3rd of August, nineteen fourteen. . . He repeated: "The pit-head price. . . *livrable au prix de l'houillemaigre dans l'enceinte des puits de ma campagne*." . . . Much to the satisfaction of the duchess, who knew all about prices. . . A triumph for Christopher was at that moment so exactly what Sylvia thought she did not want that she decided to tell the general that Christopher was a Socialist. That might well take him down a peg or two in the general's esteem. . . for the general's arm-patting admiration for Tietjens, the man who did not argue but acted over the price of coal, was as much as she could bear. . . But, thinking it over in the smoking-room after dinner, by which time she was a good deal more aware of what she did want, she was not so certain that she had done what she wanted. . . Indeed, even in the octagonal room during the economical festivities that followed the signatures, she had been far from certain that she had not done almost exactly what she did not want. . .

It had begun with the general's exclaiming to her:

"You know your man's the most unaccountable fellow. . . He wears the damn-shabbiest uniform of any officer I ever have to talk to. He's said to be unholily hard up. . . I even heard he had a cheque sent back to the club. . . Then he goes and makes a princely gift like that—just to get Levin out of ten minutes' awkwardness. . . I wish to goodness I could understand the fellow. . . He's got a positive genius for getting all sorts of things out of the most beastly muddles. . . Why, he's even been useful to me. . . And then he's got a positive genius for getting into the most disgusting messes. . . You're too young to have heard of Dreyfus. . . But I always say that Christopher is a regular Dreyfus. . . I shouldn't be astonished if he didn't end by being drummed out of the army. . . which heaven forfend!"

It had been then that Sylvia had said:

"Hasn't it ever occurred to you that Christopher was a Socialist?"

For the first time in her life Sylvia saw her husband's godfather look grotesque. . . His jaw dropped down, his white hair became disarrayed, and he dropped his pretty cap with all the gold oakleaves and the scarlet. When he rose from picking it up his thin old face was purple and distorted. She wished she hadn't said it: she wished she hadn't said it. He exclaimed:

"Christopher! . . . A So. . ." He gasped as if he could not pronounce the word. He said: "Damn it all! . . . I've loved that boy. . . He's my only godson. . . His father was my best friend. . . I've watched over him. . . I'd have married his mother if she would have had me. . . Damn it all, he's down in my will as residuary legatee after a few small things left to my sister and my collection of horns to the regiment I commanded. . ."

Sylvia—they were sitting on the sofa the duchess had left—patted him on the forearm and said:

"But general. . . godfather. . ."

"It explains everything," he said with a mortification that was painful. His white moustache drooped and trembled. "And what makes it all the worse—he's never had the courage to tell me his opinions." He stopped, snorted and exclaimed: "By God, I *will* have him drummed out of the service. . . By God, I will. I can do that much. . ."

His grief so shut him in on himself that she could say nothing to him. . .

"You tell me he seduced the little Wannop girl. . . The last person in the world he should have seduced. . . Ain't there millions of other women? . . . He got you sold up, didn't he? . . . Along with keeping a girl in a tobacco-shop. . . By jove, I almost lent him. . . offered to lend him money on that occasion. . . You can forgive a young man for going wrong with women. . . We all do. . . We've all set up girls in tobacco-shops in our time. . . But, damn it all, if the fellow's a Socialist it puts a different complexion. . . I could forgive him even for the little Wannop girl, if he wasn't. . . But. . . Good God, isn't it just the thing that a dirty-minded Socialist would do? . . . To seduce the daughter of his father's oldest friend, next to me. . . Or perhaps Wannop was an older friend than me. . ."

He had calmed himself a little—and he was not such a fool. He looked at her now with a certain keenness in his blue eyes that showed no sign of age. He said:

"See here, Sylvia. . . You aren't on terms with Christopher for all the good game you put up here this afternoon. . . I shall have to go into this. It's a serious charge to bring against one of His Majesty's officers. . . Women do say things against their husbands when they are not on good terms with them. . ." He went on to say that he did not say she wasn't justified. If Christopher had seduced the little

Wannop girl it was enough to make her wish to harm him. Had always found her the soul of honour, straight as a die, straight as she rode to hounds. And if she wished to nag against her husband, even if in little things it wasn't quite the truth, she was perhaps within her rights as a woman. She had said, for instance, that Tietjens had taken two pairs of her best sheets. Well, his own sister, her friend, raised Cain if he took anything out of the house they lived in. She had made an atrocious row because he had taken his own shaving-glass out of his own bedroom at Mounts-by. Women liked to have sets of things. Perhaps she, Sylvia, had sets of pairs of sheets. His sister had linen sheets with the date of the battle of Waterloo on them. . . Naturally you would not want a set spoiled. . . But this was another matter. He ended up very seriously:

"I have not got time to go into this now. . . I ought not to be another minute away from my office. These are very serious days. . ." He broke off to utter against the Prime Minister and the Cabinet at home a series of violent imprecations. He went on:

"But this will have to be gone into. . . It's heart-breaking that my time should be taken up by matters like this in my own family. . . But these fellows aim at sapping the heart of the army. . . They say they distribute thousands of pamphlets recommending the rank and file to shoot their officers and go over to the Germans. . . Do you seriously mean that Christopher belongs to an organization? What is it you are going on? What evidence have you? . . ."

She said:

"Only that he is heir to one of the biggest fortunes in England, for a commoner, and he refuses to touch a penny. . . His brother Mark tells me Christopher could have. . . Oh, a fabulous sum a year. . . But he has made over Groby to me. . ."

The general nodded his head as if he were ticking off ideas.

"Of course, refusing property is a sign of being one of these fellows. By jove, I must go. . . But as for his not going to live at Groby: if he is setting up house with Miss Wannop. . . Well, he could not flaunt her in the face of the country. . . And, of course, those sheets! . . . As you put it it looked as if he'd beggared himself with his dissipations. . . But of course, if he is refusing money from Mark, it's another matter. . . Mark would make up a couple of hundred dozen pairs of sheets without turning a hair. . . Of course there are the extraordinary things Christopher says. . . I've often heard you complain of the immoral way he looks at the serious affairs of life. . . You said he once talked of lethal-chambering unfit children."

He exclaimed:

"I must go. There's Thurston looking at me. . . But what then is it that Christopher has said? . . . Hang it all: what is at the bottom of that fellow's mind? . . ."

"He desires," Sylvia said, and she had no idea when she said it, "to model himself upon our Lord. . ."

The general leant back in the sofa. He said almost indulgently:

"Who's that. . . our *Lord?*"

Sylvia said:

"Upon our Lord Jesus Christ. . ."

He sprang to his feet as if she had stabbed him with a hatpin.

"Our. . ." he exclaimed. "Good God! . . . I always knew he had a screw loose. . . But. . ." He said briskly: "Give all his goods to the poor! . . . But He wasn't a. . . Not a Socialist! What was it He said: Render unto Caesar. . . It wouldn't be necessary to drum Him out of the Army. . ." He said: "Good Lord! . . . Good Lord! . . . Of course his poor dear mother was a little. . . But, hang it! . . . The Wannop girl! . . ." Extreme discomfort overcame him. . . Tietjens was half-way across from the inner room, coming towards them.

He said:

"Major Thurston is looking for you, sir. Very urgently. . ." The general regarded him as if he had been the unicorn of the royal arms, come alive. He exclaimed:

"Major Thurston! . . . Yes! Yes! . . ." and, Tietjens saying to him:

"I wanted to ask you, sir. . ." he pushed Tietjens away as if he dreaded an assault and went off with short, agitated steps.

So sitting there, in the smoking-lounge of the hotel which was cram-jam full of officers, and no doubt perfectly respectable, but over-giggling women—the sort of place and environment which she had certainly never expected to be called upon to sit in; and waiting for the return of Tietjens and the ex-sergeant-major—who again was certainly not the sort of person that she had ever expected to be asked to wait for, though for long years she had put up with Tietjens' protégé, the odious Sir Vincent Macmaster, at all sorts of meals and all sorts of places. . . but of course that was only Christopher's rights. . . to have in his own house, which, in the circumstances, wasn't morally hers, any snuffling, nervous, walrus-moustached or orientally obsequious protégé that he chose to patronize. . . And she quite believed that Tietjens, when he had invited the sergeant-major to celebrate his commission with himself at dinner, hadn't expected to dine with her. . . It was the sort of obtuseness of which he was disconcertingly capable, though at other times he was much more disconcertingly capable of reading your thoughts to the last hairsbreadth. . . And, as a matter of fact, she objected much less to dining with the absolute lower classes than with merely snuffly little official critics like Macmaster, and the sergeant-major had served her turn very well when it had come to flaying the hide off Christopher. . . So, sitting there, she made a new pact, this time with Father Consett in heaven. . .

Father Consett was very much in her mind, for she was very much in the midst of the British military authorities who had hanged him. . . She had never seemed before to be so in the midst of these negligible, odious, unpresentable, horse-laughing schoolboys. It antagonized her, and it was a weight upon her, for hitherto she had completely ignored them: in this place they seemed to have a coherence, a mass. . . almost a life. . . They rushed in and out of rooms occupied, as incomprehensibly, as unpresentably, with things like boots, washing, vaccination certificates. . . Even with old tins! . . . A man with prematurely white hair and a pasty face, with a tunic that bulged both above and below his belt, would walk into the drawing-room of a lady who superintended all the acid-drop and cigarette stalls of that city and remark to a thin-haired, deaf man with an amazingly red nose—a nose that had a perfectly definite purple and scarlet diagonal demarcation running from the bridge to the upper side of the nostrils—that he had got his old tins off his hands at last. He would have to repeat it in a shout because the red-nosed man, his head hanging down, would have heard nothing at all. The deaf man would say Humph! Humph! Snuffle. The woman giving the tea—a Mrs. Hemmerdine, of Tarbolton, whom you might have met at home, would be saying that at last she had got twelve reams of notepaper with forget-me-nots in the top corners when the deaf-faced man would begin, gruffly and uninterruptedly, a monologue on his urgent need for twenty thousand tons of sawdust for the new slow-burning stoves in the men's huts. . .

It was undeniably like something moving. . . All these things going in one direction. . . A disagreeable force set in motion by gawky schoolboys—but schoolboys of the Sixth Form, sinister, hobbledehoy, waiting in the corners of playgrounds to torture someone, weak and unfortunate. . . In one or other corner of their world-wide playground they had come upon Father Consett and hanged him. No doubt they tortured him first. And, if he made an offering of his sufferings, then and there to Heaven, no doubt he was already in paradise. . . Or, if he was not yet in heaven, certain of these souls in purgatory were yet listened to in the midst of their torments. . .

So she said:

"Blessed and martyred father, I know that you loved Christopher and wish to save him from trouble. I will make this pact with you. Since I have been in this room I have kept my eyes in the boat—almost in my lap. I will agree to leave off torturing Christopher and I will go into retreat in a convent of Ursuline Dames Nobles—for I can't stand the nuns of that other convent—for the rest of my life. . . And I know that will please you, too, for you were always anxious for the good of my soul. . ." She was going to do that if when she raised her eyes and really looked round the room she saw in it one man that looked presentable. She did not ask that he should more than look presentable, for she wanted nothing to do with the creature. He was to be a sign: not a prey!

She explained to the dead priest that she could not go all the world over to see if it contained a presentable man, but she could not bear to be in a convent for ever, and have the thought that there wasn't, for other women, one presentable man in the world. . . For Christopher would be no good to them. He would be mooning for ever over the Wannop girl. Or her memory. That was all one. . . He was content with LOVE. . . If he knew that the Wannop girl was loving him in Bedford Park, and he in the Khyber States with the Himalayas between them, he would be quite content. . . That would be correct in its way, but not very helpful for other women. . . Besides, if he were the only presentable man in the world, half the women would be in love with him. . . And that would be disastrous, because he was no more responsive than a bullock in a fatting pen.

"So, father," she said, "work a miracle. . . It's not very much of a little miracle. . . Even if a presentable man doesn't exist you could put him there. . . I'll give you ten minutes before I look. . ."

She thought it was pretty sporting of her, for, she said to herself, she was perfectly in earnest. If in that long, dim, green-lamp-shaded, and of course be-palm-leaved, badly-proportioned, glazed, ignoble public room, there appeared one decentish man, as decentish men went before this beanfeast began, she would go into retreat for the rest of her life. . .

She fell into a sort of dim trance after she had looked at her watch. Often she went into these dim trances. . . ever since she had been a girl at school with Father Consett for her spiritual adviser! . . . She seemed to be aware of the father moving about the room, lifting up a book and putting it down. . . Her ghostly friend! . . . Goodness, he was unpresentable enough, with his broad, open face that always looked dirtyish, his great dark eyes, and his great mouth. . . But a saint and a martyr. . . She felt him there. . . What had they murdered him for? Hanged at the word of a half-mad, half-drunk subaltern, because he had heard the confession of some of the rebels the night before they were taken. . . He was over in the far corner of the room. . . She heard him say: they had not understood, the men that had hanged him. That is what you would say, father. . . Have mercy on them, for they know not what they do. . .

Then have mercy on me, for half the time I don't know what I'm doing! . . . It was like a spell you put on me. At Lobscheid. Where my mother was, when I came back from that place without my clothes. . . You said, didn't you, to mother, but she told me afterwards: The real hell for that poor boy, meaning Christopher, will come when he falls in love with some young girl—as, mark me, he will. . . For she, meaning me, will tear the world down to get at him. . . And when mother said she was certain I would never do anything vulgar you obstinately did not agree. . . You knew me. . .

She tried to rouse herself and said: He *knew* me. . . Damn it he knew me! . . . What's vulgarity to me, Sylvia Tietjens, born Satterthwaite? I do what I want and that's good enough for anyone. Except a priest. Vulgarity! I wonder mother could be so obtuse. If I am vulgar I'm vulgar with a purpose. Then it's not vulgarity. It may be vice. Or viciousness. . . But if you commit a mortal sin with your eyes open it's not vulgarity. . . You chance hell fire for ever. . . Good enough!

The weariness sank over her again and the sense of the father's presence. . . She was back again in Lobscheid, thirty-six hours free of Perowne with the father and her mother in the dim sitting-room, all antlers, candle-lit, with the father's shadow waving over the pitchpine walls and ceilings. . . It was a bewitched place, in the deep forest of Germany. The father himself said it was the last place in Europe to be Christianized. Or perhaps it was never Christianized. . . That was perhaps why those people, the Germans, coming from those deep, devil-infested woods, did all these wickednesses. Or maybe they were not wicked. . . One would never know properly. . . But maybe the father had put a spell on her. . . His words had never been out of her mind, much. . . At the back of her brain, as the saying was. . .

Some man drifted near her and said:

"How do you do, Mrs. Tietjens? Who would have thought of seeing you here?"

She answered:

"I have to look after Christopher now and then." He remained hanging over her with a schoolboy grin for a minute, then he drifted away as an object sinks into deep water. . . Father Consett again hovered near her. She exclaimed:

"But the real point is, father. . . Is it sporting? . . . Sporting or whatever it is?" And Father Consett breathed: "Ah! . . ." with his terrible power of arousing doubts. . . She said:

"When I saw Christopher. . . Last night? . . . Yes, it *was* last night. . . Turning back to go up that hill. . . And I had been talking about him to a lot of grinning private soldiers. . . To *madden* him. . . You *mustn't* make scenes before the servants. . . A heavy man, tired. . . come down the hill and lumbering up again. . . There was a searchlight turned on him just as he turned. . . I remembered the white bulldog I thrashed on the night before it died. . . A tired, silent beast. . . with a fat white behind. . . Tired out. . . You couldn't see its tail because it was turned down, the stump. . . A great, silent beast. . . The vet said it had been poisoned with red lead by burglars. . . It's beastly to die of red lead. . . It eats up the liver. . . And you think you're getting better for a fortnight. And you're always cold. . . freezing in the blood-vessels. . . And the poor beast had left its kennel to try and be let in to the fire. . . And I found it at the door when I came in from a dance without Christopher. . . And got the rhinoceros whip and lashed into it. . . There's a pleasure in lashing into a naked white beast. . . Obese and silent. . . Like Christopher. . . I thought Christopher might. . . That night. . . It went through my head. . . It hung down its head. . . A great head, room for a whole British encyclopaedia of mis-information, as Christopher used to put it. . . It said: 'What a hope!' . . . As I hope to be saved, though I never shall be, the dog said: 'What a hope!' . . . Snow-white in quite black bushes. . . And it went under a bush. . . They found it dead there in the morning. . . You can't imagine what it looked like, with its head over its shoulder, as it looked back and said: What a hope to me. . . Under a dark bush. An eu. . . eu. . . euonymus, isn't it? . . . In thirty degrees of frost with all the blood-vessels exposed on the naked surface of the skin. . . It's the seventh circle of hell, isn't it? the frozen one. . . The last stud-white bulldog of that breed. . . As Christopher is the last stud-white hope of the Groby Tory breed. . . Modelling himself on our Lord. . . But our Lord was never married. He never touched on topics of sex. Good for Him. . .

She said: "The ten minutes is up, father. . ." and looked at the round, starred surface between the diamonds of her wrist watch. She said: "Good God! . . . Only one minute. . . I've thought all that in only one minute. . . I understand how hell can be an eternity. . ."

Christopher, very weary, and ex-Sergeant-Major Cowley, very talkative by now, loomed down between palms. Cowley was saying: "It's infamous! . . . It's past bearing. . . To re-order the draft at eleven. . ." They sank into chairs. . . Sylvia extended towards Tietjens a small packet of letters. She said: "You had better look at these. . . I had your letters sent to me from the flat as there was so much uncertainty about your movements. . ." She found that she did not dare, under Father Consett's eyes, to look at Tietjens as she said that. She said to Cowley: "We might be quiet for a minute or two while the captain reads his letters. . . Have another liqueur? . . ."

She then observed that Tietjens just bent open the top of the letters from Mrs. Wannop and then opened that from his brother Mark.

"Curse it," she said, "I've given him what he wants! . . . He knows. . . He's seen the address. . . that they're still in Bedford Park. . . He can think of the Wannop girl as there. . . He has not been able to know, till now, where she is. . . He'll be imagining himself in bed with her there. . ."

Father Consett, his broad, unmodelled dark face full of intelligence and with the blissful unction of the saint and martyr, was leaning over Tietjens' shoulder. . . He must be breathing down Christopher's back as, her mother said, he always did when she held a hand at auction and he could not play because it was between midnight and his celebrating the holy mass. . .

She said:

"No, I am not going mad. . . This is an effect of fatigue on the optic nerves. . . Christopher has explained that to me. . . He says that when his eyes have been very tired with making one of his senior wrangler's calculations he has often seen a woman in an eighteenth-century dress looking into a drawer in his bureau. . . Thank God, I've had Christopher to explain things to me. . . I'll never let him go. . . Never, never, let him go. . ."

It was not, however, until several hours later that the significance of the father's apparition came to her and those intervening hours were extraordinarily occupied—with emotions, and even with action. To begin with, before he had read the fewest possible words of his brother's letter, Tietjens looked up over it and said:

"Of course you will occupy Groby. . . With Michael. . . Naturally the proper business arrangements will be made. . ." He went on reading the letter, sunk in his chair under the green shade of a lamp. . .

The letter, Sylvia knew, began with the words: "Your —— of a wife has been to see me with the idea of getting any allowance I might be minded to make you transferred to herself. Of course she can have Groby, for I shan't let it, and could not be bothered with it myself. On the other hand, you may want to live at Groby with that girl and chance the racket. I should if I were you. You would probably find the place worth the. . . what is it? ostracism, if there was any. . . But I'm forgetting that the girl is not your mistress unless anything has happened since I saw you. . . And you probably would want Michael to be brought up at Groby, in which case you couldn't keep the girl there, even if you camouflaged her as governess. At least I think that kind of arrangement always turns out badly: there's bound to be a stink, though Crosby of Ulick did it and nobody much minded. . . But it was mucky for the Crosby children. Of course if you want your wife to have Groby she must have enough to run it with credit, and expenses are rising damnably. Still, our incomings rise not a little, too, which is not the case with some. The only thing I insist on is that you make plain to that baggage that whatever I allow her, even if it's no end of a hot income, not one penny of it comes out of what I wish you would allow me to allow you. I mean I want you to make plain to that rouged piece—or perhaps it's really natural, my eyes are not what they were—that what you have is absolutely independent of what she sucks up as the mother of our father's heir and to keep our father's heir in the state of life that is his due. . . I hope you feel satisfied that the boy is your son, for it's more than I should be, looking at the party. . . But even if he is not he is our father's heir all right and must be so treated."

"But be plain about that, for the trollop came to me, if you please, with the proposal that I should dock you of any income I might propose to allow you—and to which of course you are absolutely entitled under our father's will, though it is no good reminding you of that!—as a token from me that I disapproved of your behaviour when, damn it, there is not an action of yours that I would not be proud to have to my credit. At any rate in this affair, for I cannot help thinking that you could be of more service to the country if you were anywhere else but where you are. But you know what your conscience demands of you better than I, and I dare say these hell-cats have so mauled you that you are glad to be able to get away into any hole. But don't let yourself die in your hole. Groby will have to be looked after, and even if you do not live there you can keep a strong hand on Sanders, or whoever you elect to have as manager. That monstrosity you honour with your name— which is also mine, thank you!—suggested that if I consented to let her live at Groby she would have her mother to live with her, in which case her mother would be good to look after the estate. I dare say she would, though she has had to let her own place. But then almost everyone else has. She seems anyhow a notable woman, with her head screwed on the right way. I did not tell the discreditable daughter that she—her mother—had come to see me at breakfast immediately after seeing you off, she was so upset. And she *keawert ho down i' th' ingle and had a gradely pow*. You remember how Gobbles the gardener used to say that. A good chap, though he came from Lancasheere! . . . The mother has no illusions about the daughter and is heart and soul for you. She was dreadfully upset at your going, the more so as she believes that it's her offspring has driven you out of the country and that you purpose. . . isn't stopping one the phrase? Don't do that.

"I saw your girl yesterday. . . She looked peaky. But of course I have seen her several times, and she always looks peaky. I do not understand why you do not write to them. The mother is clamorous because you have not answered several letters and have not sent her military information she wants for some article she is writing for a Swiss magazine. . ."

Sylvia knew the letter almost by heart as far as that because in the unbearable white room of the convent near Birkenhead she had twice begun to copy it out, with the idea of keeping the copies for use in some sort of publicity. But, at that point, she had twice been overcome by the idea that it was not a very sporting thing to do, if you really think about it. Besides, the letter after that—she had glanced through it—occupied itself almost entirely with the affairs of Mrs. Wannop. Mark, in his nave way, was concerned that the old lady, although now enjoying the income from the legacy left her by their father, had not immediately settled down to write a deathless novel; although, as he added, he knew nothing about novels. . .

Christopher was reading away at his letters beneath the green-shaded lamp; the ex-quartermaster had begun several sentences and dropped into demonstrative silence at the reminder that Tietjens was reading. Christopher's face was completely without expression; he might have been reading a return from the office of statistics in the old days at breakfast. She wondered, vaguely, if he would see fit to apologize for the epithets that his brother had applied to her. Probably he would not. He would consider that she having opened the letter must take the responsibility of the contents. Something like that. Thumps and rumbles began to exist in the relative silence. Cowley said: "They're coming again then!" Several couples passed them on the way out of the room. Amongst them there was certainly no presentable man; they were all either too old or too hobbledehoy, with disproportionate noses and vacant, half-opened mouths.

Accompanying Christopher's mind, as it were, whilst he read his letter had induced in her a rather different mood. The pictures in her own mind were rather of Mark's dingy breakfast-room in which she had had her interview with him—and of the outside of the dingy house in which the Wannops lived, at Bedford Park. . . But she was still conscious of her pact with the father and, looking at her wrist watch, saw that by now six minutes had passed. . . It was astonishing that Mark, who was a millionaire at least, and probably a good deal more, should live in such a dingy apartment—it had for its chief decoration the hoofs of several deceased race-winners, mounted as ink-stands, as pen-racks, as paper-weights—and afford himself only such a lugubrious breakfast of fat slabs of ham over which bled pallid eggs. . . For she too, like her mother, had looked in on Mark at breakfast-time—her mother because she had just seen Christopher off to France, and she because, after a sleepless night—the third of a series—she had been walking about St. James's Park and, passing under Mark's windows, it had occurred to her that she might do Christopher some damage by putting his brother wise about the entanglement with Miss Wannop. So, on the spur of the moment, she had invented a desire to live at Groby with the accompanying necessity for additional means. For, although she was a pretty wealthy woman, she was not wealthy enough to live at Groby and keep it up. The immense old place was not so immense because of its room-space, though, as far as she could remember, there must be anything between forty and sixty rooms, but because of the vast old grounds, the warren of stabling, wells, rose-walks and fencing. . . A man's place, really, the furniture very grim and the corridors on the ground floor all slabbed with great stones. So she had looked in on Mark, reading his correspondence with his copy of *The Times* airing on a chair-back before the fire—for he was just the man to retain the eighteen-forty idea that you catch cold by reading a damp newspaper. His grim, tight, brown-wooden features that might have been carved out of an old chair, had expressed no emotion at all during the interview. He had offered to have up some more ham and eggs for her and had asked one or two questions as to how she meant to live at Groby if she went there. Otherwise he had said nothing about the information she had given him as to the Wannop girl having had a baby by Christopher—for purposes of conversation she had adhered to that old story, at any rate till that interview. He had said nothing at all. Not one word. . . At the end of the interview, when he had risen and produced from an adjoining room a bowler hat and an umbrella, saying that he must now go to his office, he had put to her without any expression pretty well what stood in the letter, as far as business was concerned. He said that she could have Groby, but she must understand that, his father being now dead and he a public official, without children and occupied in London with work that suited him, Groby was practically Christopher's property to do what he liked with as long as—which he certainly would—he kept it in proper style. So that, if she wished to live there, she must produce Christopher's authorization to that effect. And he added, with an equableness so masking the proposition that it was not until she was well out of the house and down the street that its true amazingness took her breath away:

"Of course, Christopher, if what you say is true, might want to live at Groby with Miss Wannop. In that case he would have to." And he had offered her an expressionless hand and shepherded her, rather fussily, through his dingy and awkward front passages that were lit only from ground-glass windows giving apparently on to his bathroom. . .

It wasn't until that moment, really, that, at once with exhilaration and also with a sinking at the heart, she realized what she was up against in the way of a combination. For, when she had gone to Mark's, she had been more than half-maddened by the news that Christopher at Rouen was in hospital and, although the hospital authorities had assured her, at first by telegram and then by letter, that it was nothing more than his chest, she had not had any knowledge of to what extent Red Cross authorities did or did not mislead the relatives of casualties.

So it had seemed natural that she should want to inflict on him all the injuries that she could at the moment, the thought that he was probably in pain making her wish to add all she could to that pain. . . Otherwise, of course, she would not have gone to Mark's. . . For it was a mistake in strategy. But then she said to herself: "Confound it! . . . What strategy was it a mistake in? What do I care about strategy? What am I out for? . . ." She did what she wanted to, on the spur of the moment! . . .

Now she certainly realized. How Christopher had got round Mark she did not know or much care, but there Christopher certainly was, although his father had certainly died of a broken heart at the rumours that were going round about his son—rumours she, almost as efficiently as the man called Ruggles and more irresponsible gossips, had set going about Christopher. They had been meant to smash Christopher: they had smashed his father instead. . .

But Christopher had got round Mark, whom he had not seen for ten years. . . Well, he probably would. Christopher was perfectly immaculate, that was a fact, and Mark, though he appeared half-witted in a North Country way, was no fool. He could not be a fool. He was a really august public official. And, although as a rule Sylvia gave nothing at all for any public official, if a man like Mark had the position by birth amongst presentable men that he certainly ought to have and was also the head of a department and reputed absolutely indispensable—you could not ignore him. . . He said, indeed, in the later, more gossipy parts of his letter that he had been offered a baronetcy, but he wanted Christopher to agree with his refusing it. Christopher would not want the beastly title after his death, and for himself he would be rather struck with the pip than let that harlot—meaning herself—become Lady T. by any means of his. He had added, with his queer solicitude, "Of course if you thought of divorcing—which I wish to God you would, though I agree that you are right not to—and the title would go to the girl after my decease I'd take it gladly, for a title is a bit of a help after a divorce. But as it is I propose to refuse it and ask for a knighthood, if it won't too sicken you to have me a Sir. . . For I hold no man ought to refuse an honour in times like these, as has been done by certain sickening intellectuals, because it is like slapping the sovereign in the face and bound to hearten the other side, which no doubt was what was meant by those fellows."

There was no doubt that Mark—with the possible addition of the Wannops—made a very strong backing for Christopher if she decided to make a public scandal about him. . . As for the Wannops. . . the girl was negligible. Or possibly not, if she turned nasty and twisted Christopher round her fingers. But the old mother was a formidable figure—with a bad tongue, and viewed with a certain respect in places where people talked. . . both on account of her late husband's position and of the solid sort of articles she wrote. . . She, Sylvia, had gone to take a look at the place where these people lived. . . a dreary street in an outer suburb, the houses—she knew enough about estates to know—what is called tile-healed, the upper parts of tile, the lower flimsy brick and the tiles in bad condition. Oldish houses really, in spite of their sham artistic aspect, and very much shadowed by old trees that must have been left to add to the picturesqueness. . . The rooms poky, and they must be very dark. . . The residence of extreme indigence, or of absolute poverty. . . She understood that the old lady's income had so fallen off during the war that they had nothing to live on but what the girl made as a schoolteacher, or a teacher of athletics in a girls' school. . . She had walked two or three times up and down the street with the idea that the girl might come out: then it had struck her that that was rather an ignoble proceeding, really. . . It was, for the matter of that, ignoble that she should have a rival who starved in an ashbin. . . But that was what men were like: she might think herself lucky that the girl did not inhabit a sweetshop. . . And the man, Mac-master, said that the girl had a good head and talked well, though the woman Macmaster said that she was a shallow ignoramus. . . That last was probably not true; at any rate the girl had been the Macmaster woman's most intimate friend for many years—as long as they were sponging on Christopher and until, lower middle-class snobs as they were, they began to think that they could get into Society by carneying to herself. . . Still, the girl probably was a good talker and, if little, yet physically uncommonly fit. . . A good homespun article. . . She wished her no ill!

What was incredible was that Christopher should let her go on starving in such a poverty-stricken place when he had something like the wealth of the Indies at his disposal. . . But the Tietjens were hard people! You could see that in Mark's rooms. . . and Christopher would lie on the floor as lief as in a goose-feather bed. And probably the girl would not take his money. She was quite right. That was the way to keep him. . . She herself had no want of comprehension of the stimulation to be got out of parsimonious living. . . In retreat at her convent she lay as hard and as cold as any anchorite, and rose to the nuns' matins at four.

It was not, in fact, their fittings or food that she objected to—it was that the lay-sisters, and some of the nuns, were altogether too much of the lower classes for her to like to have always about her. . . That was why it was to the Dames Nobles that she would go, if she had to go into retreat for the rest of her life, according to contract. . .

A gun manned by exhilarated anti-aircraft fellows, and so close that it must have been in the hotel garden, shook her physically at almost the same moment as an immense maroon popped off on the quay at the bottom of the street in which the hotel was. She was filled with annoyance at these schoolboy exercises. A tall, purple-faced, white-moustached general of the more odious type, appeared in the doorway and said that all the lights but two must be extinguished and, if they took his advice, they would go somewhere else. There were good cellars in the hotel. He loafed about the room extinguishing the lights, couples and groups passing him on the way to the door. . . Tietjens looked up from his letter—he was now reading one of Mrs. Wannop's—but seeing that Sylvia made no motion he remained sunk in his chair. . .

The old general said:

"Don't get up, Tietjens. . . Sit down, lieutenant. . . Mrs. Tietjens, I presume. . . But of course I know you are Mrs. Tietjens. . . There's a portrait of you in this week's. . . I forget the name. . ." He sat down on the arm of a great leather chair and told her of all the trouble her escapade to that city had caused him. . . He had been awakened immediately after a good lunch by some young officer on his staff who was scared to death by her having arrived without papers. His digestion had been deranged ever since. . . Sylvia said she was very sorry. He should drink hot water and no alcohol with lunch. She had had very important business to discuss with Tietjens, and she had really not understood that they wanted papers of grown-up people. The general began to expatiate on the importance of his office and the number of enemy agents his perspicacity caused to be arrested every day in that city and the lines of communication. . .

Sylvia was overwhelmed at the ingenuity of Father Consett. She looked at her watch. The ten minutes were up, but there did not appear to be a soul in the dim place. . . The father had—and no doubt as a Sign that there could be no mistaking!—completely emptied that room. It was like his humour!

To make certain, she stood up. At the far end of the room, in the dimness of the one other reading lamp that the general had not extinguished, two figures were rather indistinguishable. She walked towards them, the general at her side extending civilities all over her. He said that she need not be under any apprehension there. He adopted that device of clearing the room in order to get rid of the beastly young subalterns who would use the place to spoon in when the lights were turned down. She said she was only going to get a timetable from the far end of the room. . .

The stab of hope that she had that one of the two figures would turn out to be the presentable man died. . . They were a young mournful subaltern, with an incipient moustache and practically tears in his eyes, and an elderly, violently indignant baldheaded man in evening civilian clothes that must have been made by a country tailor. He was smacking his hands together to emphasize what, with great agitation, he was saying.

The general said that it was one of the young cubs on his own staff getting a dressing down from his dad for spending too much money. The young devils would get amongst the girls—and the old ones too. There was no stopping it. The place was a hotbed of. . . He left the sentence unfinished. She would not believe the trouble it gave him. . . That hotel itself. . . The scandals. . .

He said she would excuse him if he took a little nap in one of the arm-chairs too far away to interfere with their business talk. He would have to be up half the night. He seemed to Sylvia a blazingly contemptible personage—too contemptible really for Father Consett to employ as an agent, in clearing the room. . . But the omen was given. She had to consider her position. It meant—or did it?—that she had to be at war with the heavenly powers! . . . She clenched her hands. . .

In passing by Tietjens in his chair the general boomed out the words:

"I got your chit of this morning, Tietjens I must say. . ."

Tietjens lumbered out of his chair and stood at attention, his leg-of-mutton hands stiffly on the seams of his breeches.

"It's pretty strong," the general said, "marking a charge-sheet sent down from *my* department: *Case explained*. We don't lay charges without due thought. And Lance-Corporal Berry is a particularly reliable N.C.O. I have difficulty enough to get them. Particularly after the late riots. It takes courage, I can tell you."

"If," Tietjens said, "you would see fit, sir, to instruct the G.M.P. not to call Colonial troops damned conscripts, the trouble would be over. . . We're instructed to use special discretion, as officers, in dealing with troops from the Dominions. They are said to be very susceptible of insult. . ."

The general suddenly became a boiling pot from which fragments of sentences came away: *damned* insolence; court of inquiry; damned conscripts they were too. He calmed enough to say:

"They *are* conscripts, your men, aren't they? They give me more trouble. . . I should have thought that you would have wanted. . ."

Tietjens said:

"No, sir. I have not a man in my unit, as far as it's Canadian or British Columbian, that is not voluntarily enlisted. . ."

The general exploded to the effect that he was bringing the whole matter before the G.O.C.I.C.'s department. Campion could deal with it how he wished: it was beyond himself. He began to bluster away from them; stopped; directed a frigid bow to Sylvia who was not looking at him; shrugged his shoulders and stormed off.

It was difficult for Sylvia to get hold again of her thoughts in the smoking-room, for the evening was entirely pervaded with military effects that seemed to her the pranks of schoolboys. Indeed, after Cowley, who had by now quite a good skinful of liquor, had said to Tietjens:

"By Jove, I would not like to be you and a little bit on if old Blazes caught sight of you tonight," she said to Tietjens with real wonder:

"You don't mean to say that a gaga old fool like that could have any possible influence over you. . . *You!*"

Tietjens said:

"Well, it's a troublesome business, all this. . ."

She said that it so appeared to be, for before he could finish his sentence an orderly was at his elbow extending, along with a pencil, a number of dilapidated papers. Tietjens looked rapidly through them, signing one after the other and saying intermittently:

"It's a trying time." "We're massing troops up the line as fast as we can go." "And with an endlessly changing personnel. . ." He gave a snort of exasperation and said to Cowley: "That horrible little Pitkins has got a job as bombing instructor. He can't march the draft. . . Who the deuce am I to detail? Who the deuce is there? . . . You know all the little. . ." He stopped because the orderly could hear. A smart boy. Almost the only smart boy left him.

Cowley barged out of his seat and said he would telephone the mess to see who was there. . . Tietjens said to the boy:

"Sergeant-Major Morgan made out these returns of religions in the draft?"

The boy answered: "No, sir, I did. They're all right." He pulled a slip of paper out of his tunic pocket and said shyly:

"If you would not mind signing this, sir. . . I can get a lift on an A.S.C. trolley that's going to Boulogne tomorrow at six. . ."

Tietjens said:

"No, you can't have leave. I can't spare you. What's it for?"

The boy said almost inaudibly that he wanted to get married.

Tietjens, still signing, said: "Don't. . . Ask your married pals what it's like!"

The boy, scarlet in his khaki, rubbed the sole of one foot on the instep of the other. He said that saving madam's presence it was urgent. It was expected any day now. She was a real good gel. Tietjens signed the boy's slip and handed it to him without looking up. The boy stood with his eyes on the ground. A diversion came from the telephone, which was at the far end of the room. Cowley had not been able to get on to the camp because an urgent message with regard to German espionage was coming through to the sleeping general.

Cowley began to shout: "For goodness' sake hold the line. . . For goodness' sake hold the line. . . I'm *not* the general. . . I'm not the general." Tietjens told the orderly to awaken the sleeping warrior. A violent scene at the mouth of the quiescent instrument took place. The general roared to know who was the officer speaking. . . Captain Bubbleyjocks. . . Captain Cuddlestocks. . . what in hell's name! And who was he speaking for? . . . Who? Himself? . . . Urgent was it? . . . Didn't he know the proper procedure was by writing? . . . Urgent damnation! . . . Did he not know where he was? . . . In the First Army by the Cassell Canal. . . Well then. . . But the spy was in L. of C. territory, across the canal. . . The French civilian authorities were very concerned. . . They were, damn them! . . . And damn the officer. And damn the French *maire*. And damn the horse the supposed spy rode upon. . . And when the officer was damned let him write to First Army Headquarters about it and attach the horse and the bandoliers as an exhibit. . .

There was a great deal more of it. Tietjens, reading his papers still, intermittently explained the story as it came in fragments over the telephone in the general's repetitions. . . Apparently the French civilian authorities of a place called Warendonck had been alarmed by a solitary horseman in English uniform who had been wandering desultorily about their neighbourhood for several days, seeming to want to cross the canal bridges, but finding them guarded. . . There was an immense artillery dump in the neighbourhood, said to be the largest in the world, and the Germans dropped bombs as thick as peas all over those parts in the hopes of hitting it. . . Apparently the officer speaking was in charge of the canal bridgehead guards; but, as he was in First Army country, it was obviously an act of the utmost impropriety to awaken a general in charge of the spy-catching apparatus on the other side of the canal. . . The general, returning past them to an arm-chair farther from the telephone, emphasized this point of view with great vigour.

The orderly had returned; Cowley went once more to the telephone, having consumed another liqueur brandy. Tietjens finished his papers and went through them rapidly again. He said to the boy: "Got anything saved up?" The boy said: "A fiver and a few bob." Tietjens said: "How many bob?" The boy: "Seven, sir." Tietjens, fumbling clumsily in an inner pocket and a little pocket beneath his belt, held out one leg-of-mutton fist and said: "There! That will double it. Ten pounds fourteen! But it's very improvident of you. See that you save up a deuced lot more against the next one. Accouchements are confoundedly expensive things, as you'll learn, and ring money doesn't stretch for ever! . . ." He called out to the retreating boy: "Here, orderly, come back. . ." He added: "Don't let it get all over camp. . . I can't afford to subsidize all the seven-months children in the battalion. . . I'll recommend you for paid lance-corporal when you return from leave if you go on as well as you have done." He called the boy back again to ask him why Captain McKechnie had not signed the papers. The boy stuttered and stammered that Captain McKechnie was. . . He was. . .

Tietjens muttered: "Good God!" beneath his breath. He said:

"The captain has had another nervous breakdown. . . The orderly accepted the phrase with gratitude. That was it. A nervous breakdown. They say he had been very queer at mess. About divorce. Or the captain's uncle. A barrow-night! Tietjens said: "Yes, yes." He half rose in his chair and looked at Sylvia. She exclaimed painfully:

"You can't go. I insist that you can't go." He sank down again and muttered wearily that it was very worrying. He had been put in charge of this officer by General Campion. He ought not to have left the camp at all perhaps. But McKechnie had seemed better. A great deal of the calmness of her insolence had left her. She had expected to have the whole night in which luxuriously to torment the lump opposite her. To torment and to allure him. She said:

"You have settlements to come to now and here that will affect your whole life. Our whole lives! You propose to abandon them because a miserable little nephew of your miserable little friend. . ." She added in French: "Even as it is you cannot pay attention to these serious matters, because of these childish pre-occupations of yours. That is to be intolerably insulting to me!" She was breathless.

Tietjens asked the orderly where Captain McKechnie was now. The orderly said he had left the camp. The colonel of the depot had sent a couple of officers as a search-party. Tietjens told the orderly to go and find a taxi. He could have a ride himself up to camp. The orderly said taxis would not be running on account of the air-raid. Could he order the G.M.P. to requisition one on urgent military service? The exhilarated air-gun pooped off thereupon three times from the garden. For the next hour it sent off every two or three minutes. Tietjens said: "Yes! Yes!" to the orderly. The noises of the air raid became more formidable. A blue express letter of French civilian make was handed to Tietjens. It was from the duchess to inform him that coal for the use of greenhouses was forbidden by the French Government. She did not need to say that she relied on his honour to ensure her receiving her coal through the British military authorities, and she asked for an immediate reply. Tietjens expressed real annoyance while he read this. Distracted by the noise, Sylvia cried out that the letter must be from Valentine Wannop in Rouen. Did not the girl intend to let him have an hour in which to settle the whole business of his life? Tietjens moved to the chair next to hers. He handed her the duchess's letter.

He began a long, slow, serious explanation with a long, slow, serious apology. He said he regretted very much that when she should have taken the trouble to come so far in order to do him the honour to consult him about a matter which she would have been perfectly at liberty to settle for herself, the extremely serious military position should render him so liable to interruption. As far as he was concerned Groby was entirely at her disposal with all that it contained. And of course a sufficient income for the upkeep.

She exclaimed in an access of sudden and complete despair:

"That means that you do not intend to live there." He said that that must settle itself later. The war would no doubt last a good deal longer. While it lasted there could be no question of his coming back. She said that that meant that he intended to get killed. She warned him that, if he got killed, she would cut down the great cedar at the south-west corner of Groby. It kept all the light out of the principal drawing-room and the bedrooms above it. . . He winced: he certainly winced at that. She regretted that she had said it. It was along other lines that she desired to make him wince.

He said that, apart from his having no intention of getting himself killed, the matter was absolutely out of his hands. He had to go where he was ordered to go and do what he was told to do.

She exclaimed:

"You! *You!* Isn't it ignoble. That you should be at the beck and call of these ignoramuses. You!"

He went on explaining seriously that he was in no great danger—in no danger at all unless he was sent back to his battalion. And he was not likely to be sent back to his battalion unless he disgraced himself or showed himself negligent where he was. That was unlikely. Besides his category was so low that he was not eligible for his battalion, which, of course, was in the line. She ought to understand that everyone that she saw employed there was physically unfit for the line. She said:

"That's why they're such an awful lot. . . It is not to this place that one should come to look for a presentable man. . . Diogenes with his lantern was nothing to it."

He said:

"There's that way of looking at it. . . It is quite true that most of. . . let's say *your* friends. . . were killed off during the early days, or if they're still going they're in more active employments." What she called presentableness was very largely a matter of physical fitness. . . The horse, for instance, that he rode was rather a crock. . . But though it was German and not thoroughbred it contrived to be up to his weight. . . Her friends, more or less, of before the war were professional soldiers or of the type. Well, they were gone: dead or snowed under. But on the other hand, this vast town full of crocks did keep the thing going, if it could be made to go. It was not they that hindered the show: if it was hindered, that was done by her much less presentable friends, the ministry who, if they were professionals at all, were professional boodlers.

She exclaimed with bitterness:

"Then why didn't you stay at home to check them, if they *are* boodlers?" She added that the only people at home who kept social matters going at all with any life were precisely the more successful political professionals. When you were with them you would not know there was any war. And wasn't that what was wanted? Was the *whole* of life to be given up to ignoble horseplay? . . . She spoke with increased rancour because of the increasing thump and rumble of the air-raid. . . Of course the politicians were ignoble beings that, before the war, you would not have thought of having in your house. . . But whose fault was that, if not that of the better classes, who had gone away leaving England a dreary wilderness of fellows without consciences or traditions or manners? And she added some details of the habits at a country house of a member of the Government whom she disliked. "And," she finished up, "it's your fault. Why aren't you Lord Chancellor, or Chancellor of the Exchequer, instead of whoever is, for I am sure I don't know? You could have been, with your abilities and your interests. Then things would have been efficiently and honestly conducted. If your brother Mark, with not a tithe of your abilities, can be a permanent head of a department, what could you not have risen to with your gifts, and your influence. . . and your integrity?" And she ended up: "Oh, Christopher!" on almost a sob.

Ex-Sergeant-Major Cowley, who had come back from the telephone, and during an interval in the thunderings, had heard some of Sylvia's light cast on the habits of members of the home Government, so that his jaw had really hung down, now, in another interval, exclaimed:

"Hear, hear! Madam! . . . There is nothing the captain might not have risen to. . . He is doing the work of a brigadier now on the pay of an acting captain. . . And the treatment he gets is scandalous. . . Well, the treatment we all get is scandalous, tricked and defrauded as we are all at every turn. . . And look at this new start with the draft. . ." They had ordered the draft to be ready and countermanded it, and ordered it to be ready and countermanded it, until no one knew whether he stood on is 'ed or is 'eels. . . It was to have gone off last night: when they'd 'ad it marched down to the station they 'ad it marched back and told them all it would not be wanted for six weeks. . . Now it was to be got ready to go before daylight tomorrow morning in motor-lorries to the rail Ondekoeter way, the rail here 'aving been sabotaged! . . . Before daylight so that the enemy aeroplanes should not see it on the road. . . Wasn't that a thing to break the "arts of men and horderly rooms? It was outrageous. Did they suppose the 'Uns did things like that?

He broke off to say with husky enthusiasm of affection to Tietjens: "Look 'ere, old. . . I mean, sir. . . There's no way of getting hold of an officer to march the draft. Them as are eligible gets to 'ear of what drafts is going and they've all bolted into their burries. Not a man of 'em will be back in camp before five tomorrow morning. Not when they 'ears there's a draft to go at four of mornings like this. . . Now. . ." His voice became husky with emotion as he offered to take the draft hisself to oblige Captain Tietjens. And the captain knew he could get a draft off pretty near as good as himself: or very near. As for the draft-conducting major he lived in that hotel and he, Cowley, 'ad seen 'im. No four in the morning for 'im. He was going to motor to Ondekoeter Station about seven. So there was no sense in getting the draft off before five, and it was still dark then: too dark for the 'Un planes to see what was moving. He'd be glad if the captain would be up at the camp by five to take a final look and to sign any papers that only the commanding officer could sign. But he knew the captain had had no sleep the night before because of his, Cowley's, infirmity, mostly, so he couldn't do less than give up a day and a half of his leave to taking the draft. Besides, he was going home for the duration and he would not mind getting a look at the old places they'd seen in "fourteen, for the last time as a Cook's tourist. . .

Tietjens, who was looking noticeably white, said:

"Do you remember 0 Nine Morgan at Noircourt?"

Cowley said:

"No. . . Was 'e there? In your company, I suppose? . . . The man you mean that was killed yesterday. Died in your arms owing to my oversight. I ought to have been there." He said to Sylvia with the gloating idea N.C.O.'s had that wives liked to hear of their husband's near escapes: "Killed within a foot of the captain, 'e was. An 'orrible shock it must 'ave been for the captain." A horrible mess. . . The captain held him in his arms while he died. . . As if he'd been a baby. Wonderful tender, the captain was! Well, you're apt to be when it's one of your own men. . . No rank then! "Do you know the only time the King must salute a private soldier and the private takes no notice? . . . When 'e's dead. . ."

Both Sylvia and Tietjens were silent—and silvery white in the greenish light from the lamp. Tietjens indeed had shut his eyes. The old N.C.O. went on rejoicing to have the floor to himself. He had got on his feet preparatory to going up to camp, and he swayed a little. . .

"No," he said and he waved his cigar gloriously. "I don't remember 0 Nine Morgan at Noircourt. . . But I remember. . ."

Tietjens, with his eyes still shut, said:

"I only thought he might have been a man. . ."

"No," the old fellow went on imperiously, "I don't remember 'im. . . But, Lord, I remember what happened to *you!*" He looked down gloriously upon Sylvia: "The captain caught is foot in. . . You'd never believe what 'e caught is foot in! Never! . . . A pretty quiet affair it was, with a bit of moonlight. . . Nothing much in the way of artillery. . . Perhaps we surprised the 'Uns proper, perhaps they were wanting to give up their front-line trenches for a purpose. . . There was next to no one in 'em. . . I know it made me nervous. . . My heart was fair in my boots, because there was so little doing! . . . It was when there was little doing that the 'Uns could be expected to do their worst. . . Of course there was some machine-gunning. . . There was one in particular away to the right of us. . . And the moon, it was shining in the early morning. Wonderful peaceful. And a little mist. . . And frozen hard. . . Hard as you wouldn't believe. . . Enough to make the shells dangerous."

Sylvia said:

"It's not always mud, then?" and Tietjens, to her: "He'll stop if you don't like it." She said monotonously: "No. . . I want to hear."

Cowley drew himself up for his considerable effect:

"Mud!" he said. Not then. . . Not by half. . . I tell you, ma'am, we trod on the frozen faces of dead Germans as we doubled. . . A terrible lot of Germans we'd killed a day or so before. . . That was no doubt the reason they give up the trenches so easy: difficult to attack from, they was. . . Anyhow, they left the dead for us to bury, knowing probably they were going, with a better 'eart! . . . But it fair put the wind up me anyhow to think of what their counter-attack was going to be. . . The counter-attack is always ten times as bad as the preliminary resistance. They "as you with the rear of their trenches—the parados, we call it—as your front to boot. So I was precious glad when the moppers-up and supports come and went through us. . . Laughing, they was. . . Wiltshires. . . My missus comes from that country. . . Mrs. Cowley, I mean. . . So I'd seen the captain go down earlier on and I'd said: 'There's another of the best stopped one. . .'" He dropped his voice a little: he was one of the noted yarners of the regiment: "Caught is foot, 'e 'ad, between two 'ands. . . Sticking up out of the frozen ground. . . As it might be in prayer. . . Like this!" He elevated his two hands, the cigar between the fingers, the wrists close together and the fingers slightly curled inwards: "Sticking up in the moonlight. . . Poor devil!"

Tietjens said:

"I thought perhaps it was 0 Nine Morgan I saw that night. . . Naturally I looked dead. . . I hadn't a breath in my body. . . And I saw a Tommy put his rifle to his pal's upper arm and fire. . . As I lay on the ground. . ."

Cowley said:

"Ah, you saw that. . . I heard the men talking of it. . . But they naturally did not say who and where!"

Tietjens said with a negligence that did not ring true:

"The wounded man's name was Stilicho. . . A queer name. . . I suppose it's Cornish. . . It was B Company in front of us."

"You didn't bring 'em to a court martial?" Cowley asked. Tietjens said: No. He could not be quite certain. Though he was certain. But he had been worrying about a private matter. He had been worrying about it while he lay on the ground and that rather obscured his sense of what he saw. Besides, he said faintly, an officer must use his judgement. He had judged it better in this case not to have seen the. . . His voice had nearly faded away: it was clear to Sylvia that he was coming to a climax of some mental torture. Suddenly he exclaimed to Cowley:

"Supposing I let him off one life to get him killed two years after. My God! That would be too beastly!"

Cowley snuffled in Tietjens' ear something that Sylvia did not catch—consolatory and affectionate. That intimacy was more than she could bear. She adopted her most negligent tone to ask:

"I suppose the one man had been trifling with the other's girl. Or wife!"

Cowley exploded: "God bless you, no! They'd agreed upon it between them. To get one of them sent 'ome and the other, at any rate, out of *that* 'ell, leading him back to the dressing-station." She said:

"You mean to say that a man would do *that*, to get out of it? . . ."

Cowley said:

"God bless you, ma'am, with the '*ell* the Tommies "as of it. . . For it's in the line that the differences between the Other Ranks' life and the officers' comes in. . . I tell you, ma'am, old soldier as I am, and I've been in seven wars one with another. . . there were times in this war when I could have shrieked, holding my right hand down. . ."

He paused and said: "It was my idea. . . And it's been a good many others", that if I 'eld my "and up over the parapet with perhaps my hat on it, in two minutes there would be a German sharpshooter's bullet through it. And then me for Blighty, as the soldiers say. . . And if that could happen to me, a regimental sergeant-major, with twenty-three years in the service. . .

The bright orderly came in, said he had found a taxi, and melted into the dimness.

"A man," the sergeant-major said, "would take the risk of being shot for wounding his pal. . . They get to love their pals, passing the love of women. . ." Sylvia exclaimed: "Oh!" as if at a pang of toothache. "They do, ma'am," he said, "it's downright touching. . ."

He was by now very unsteady as he stood, but his voice was quite clear. That was the way it took him. He said to Tietjens:

"It's queer, what you say about home worries taking up your mind. . . I remember in the Afghan campaign, when we were in the devil of a hot corner, I got a letter from my wife, Mrs. Cowley, to say that our Winnie had the measles. . . And there was only one difference between me and Mrs. Cowley: I said that a child must have flannel next its skin, and she said flannelette was good enough. Wiltshire doesn't hold by wool as Lincolnshire does. Long fleeces the Lincolnshire sheep have. . . And. . . dodging the Afghan bullets all day among the boulders as we was, all I could think of. . . For you know, ma'am, being a mother yourself, that the great thing with measles is to keep a child warm. . . I kep' saying to myself—'arf crying I was—'If she only keeps wool next Winnie's skin! If she only keeps wool next Winnie's skin!' . . . But you know that, being a mother yourself. I've seen your son's photo on the captain's dressing-table. Michael, "is name is. . . So you see, the captain doesn't forget you and 'im."

Sylvia said in a clear voice:

"Perhaps you would not go on!"

Distracted as she was by the anti-air-gun in the garden, though it was on the other side of the hotel and permitted you to get in a sentence or two before splitting your head with a couple of irregular explosions, she was still more distracted by a sudden vision—a remembrance of Christopher's face when their boy had had a temperature of 105° with the measles, up at his sister's house in Yorkshire. He had taken the responsibility, which the village doctor would not face, of himself placing the child in a bath full of split ice. . . She saw him bending, expressionless in the strong lamp-light, with the child in his clumsy arms over the glittering, rubbled surface of the bath. . . He was just as expressionless then as now. . . He reminded her now of how he had been then: some strain in the lines of the face perhaps that she could not analyse. . . Rather as if he had a cold in the head—a little suffocating, with suppressing his emotions, of course: his eyes looking at nothing. You would not have said that he even saw the child—heir to Groby and all that! . . . Something had said to her, just in between two crashes of the gun: "It's his own child. He went as you might say down to hell to bring it back to life. . ." She knew it was Father Consett saying that. She knew it was true: Christopher had been down to hell to bring the child back. . . Fancy facing its pain in that dreadful bath! . . . The thermometer had dropped, running down under their eyes. . . Christopher had said: "A good heart, he's got! A good plucked one!" and then held his breath, watching the thin filament of bright mercury drop to normal. . . She said now, between her teeth: "The child is his property as much as the damned estate. . . Well, I've got them both. . ."

But it wasn't at this juncture that she wanted him tortured over that. So, when the second gun had done its crash, she had said to the bibulous old man:

"I wish you would not go on!" And Christopher had been prompt to the rescue of the *convenances* with:

"Mrs. Tietjens does not see eye to eye with us in some matters!"

She said to herself: "Eye to eye! My God! . . ." The whole of this affair, the more she saw of it, overwhelmed her with a sense of hatred. . . And of depression! . . . She saw Christopher buried in this welter of fools, playing a schoolboy's game of make-believe. But of a make-believe that was infinitely formidable and infinitely sinister. . . The crashing of the gun and of all the instruments for making noise seemed to her so atrocious and odious because they were, for her, the silly pomp of a schoolboy-man's game. . . Campion, or some similar schoolboy, said: "Hullo! Some German airplanes about. . . That lets us out on the air-gun! Let's have some pops!" . . . As they fire guns in the park on the King's birthday. It was sheer insolence to have a gun in the garden of an hotel where people of quality might be sleeping or wishing to converse!

At home she had been able to sustain the conviction that it was such a game. . . Anywhere: at the house of a minister of the Crown, at dinner, she had only to say: "Do let us leave off talking of these odious things. . ." And immediately there would be ten or a dozen voices, the minister's included, to agree with Mrs. Tietjens of Groby that they had altogether too much of it. . .

But here! . . . She seemed to be in the very belly of the ugly affair. . . It moved and moved, under your eyes dissolving, yet always there. As if you should try to follow one diamond of pattern in the coil of an immense snake that was in irrevocable motion. . . It gave her a sense of despair: the engrossment of Tietjens, in common with the engrossment of this disreputable toper. She had never seen Tietjens put his head together with any soul before: he was the lonely buffalo. . . Now 1 Anyone: any fatuous staff-officer, whom at home he would never so much as have spoken to: any trustworthy beer-sodden sergeant, any street urchin dressed up as orderly. . . They had only to appear and all his mind went into a close-headed conference over some ignoble point in the child's game: the laundry, the chiropody, the religions, the bastards. . . of millions of the indistinguishable. . . Or their deaths as well! But, in heaven's name what hypocrisy, or what inconceivable chicken-heartedness was this? They promoted this beanfeast of carnage for their own ends: they caused the deaths of men in inconceivable holocausts of pain and terror. Then they had crises of agony over the death of one single man. For it was plain to her that Tietjens was in the middle of a full nervous breakdown. Over one man's death! She had never seen him so suffer; she had never seen him so appeal for sympathy: him, a cold fiend of reticence! Yet he was now in an agony! Now! . . . And she began to have a sense of the infinitely spreading welter of pain, going away to an eternal horizon of night. . . 'Ell for the Other Ranks! Apparently it was hell for the officers as well.

The real compassion in the voice of that snuffling, half-drunken old man had given her a sense of that enormous wickedness. . . These horrors, these infinities of pain, this atrocious condition of the world had been brought about in order that men should indulge themselves in orgies of promiscuity. . . That in the end was at the bottom of male honour, of male virtue, observance of treaties, upholding of the flag. . . An immense warlock's carnival of appetites, lusts, ebrieties. . . And once set in motion there was no stopping it. . . This state of things would never cease. . . Because once they had tasted of the joy—the blood—of this game, who would let it end? . . . These men talked of these things that occupied them there with the lust of men telling dirty stories in smoking-rooms. . . That was the only parallel!

There was no stopping it, any more than there was any stopping the by now all but intoxicated ex-sergeant major. He was off! With, as might be expected, advice to a young couple with differences of opinion! The wine had made him bold!

In the depth of her pictures of these horrors, snatches of his wisdom penetrated to her intelligence. . . Queer snatches. . . She was getting it certainly in the neck! . . . Someone, to add to the noise, had started some mechanical musical instrument in an adjacent hall.

"Corn an' lasses
 Served by Ras'us!"

a throaty voice proclaimed,

"I'd be tickled to death to know that I could go
 And stay right there. . .

The ex-sergeant-major was adding to her knowledge the odd detail that when he, Sergeant-Major Cowley, went to the wars—seven of them—his missus, Mrs. Cowley, spent the first three days and nights unpicking and re-hemstitching every sheet and pillow-slip in the 'ouse. To keep 'erself f'm thinking. . . This was apparently meant as a reproof or an exhortation to her, Sylvia Tietjens. . . Well, he was all right! Of the same class as Father Consett, and with the same sort of wisdom.

The gramophone bowled: a new note of rumbling added itself to the exterior tumult and continued through six mitigated thumps of the gun in the garden. . . In the next interval, Cowley was in the midst of a valedictory address to her. He was asking her to remember that the captain had had a sleepless night the night before.

There occurred to her irreverent mind a sentence of one of the Duchess of Marlborough's letters to Queen Anne. The duchess had visited the general during one of his campaigns in Flanders. "My Lord," she wrote, "did me the honour three times in his boots!" . . . The sort of thing she would remember. . . She would—she would—have tried it on the sergeant-major, just to see Tietjens' face, for the sergeant-major would not have understood. . . And who cared if he did! . . . He was bibulously skirting round the same idea. . .

But the tumult increased to an incredible volume: even the thrillings of the near-by gramophone of two hundred horse-power, or whatever it was, became mere shimmerings of a gold thread in a drab fabric of sound. She screamed blasphemies that she was hardly aware of knowing. She had to scream against the noise: she was no more responsible for the blasphemy than if she had lost her identity under an anaesthetic. She had lost her identity. . . She was one of this crowd!

The general woke in his chair and gazed malevolently at their group as if they alone were responsible for the noise. It dropped. Dead! You only knew it, because you caught the tail end of a belated woman's scream from the hall and the general shouting: "For God's sake don't start that damned gramophone again!" In the blessed silence, after preliminary wheezes and guitar noises, an astonishing voice burst out:

"Less than the dust. . .
Before thy char. . ."

And then, stopping after a murmur of voices, began:
"Pale hands I loved. . ."

The general sprang from his chair and rushed to the hall. . . He came back crestfallenly.

"It's some damned civilian big-wig. . . A novelist, they say. . . I can't stop *him*. . ." He added with disgust: "The hall's full of young beasts and harlots. . . *Dancing!*" . . . The melody had indeed, after a buzz, changed to a languorous and interrupted variation of a waltz. "Dancing in the dark!" the general said with enhanced disgust. . . "And the Germans may be here at any moment. . . If they knew what I know! . . ."

Sylvia called across to him:
"Wouldn't it be fun to see the blue uniform with the silver buttons again and some decently set-up men? . . ."

The general shouted:
"*I'd* be glad to see them. . . I'm sick to death of these. . ."

Tietjens took up something he had been saying to Cowley: what it was Sylvia did not hear, but Cowley answered, still droning on with an idea Sylvia thought they had got past:

"I remember when I was sergeant in Quetta, I detailed a man—called Herring—for watering the company horses, after he begged off it because he had a fear of horses. . . A horse got him down in the river and drowned 'im. . . Fell with him and put its foot on his face. . . A fair sight he was. . . It wasn't any good my saying anything about military exigencies. . . Fair put me off my feed, it did. . . Cost me a fortune in Epsom salts. . ."

Sylvia was about to scream out that if Tietjens did not like men being killed it ought to sober him in his war-lust, but Cowley continued meditatively:

'Epsom salts they say is the cure for it. . . For seeing your dead. . . And of course you should keep off women for a fortnight. . . I know I did. Kept seeing Herring's face with the hoof-mark. And. . . there was a piece: a decent bit of goods in what we called the Government Compound. . .

He suddenly exclaimed:

"Saving your. . . Ma'am, I'm. . ." He stuck the stump of the cigar into his teeth and began assuring Tietjens that he could be trusted with the draft next morning, if only Tietjens would put him into the taxi.

He went away, leaning on Tietjens' arm, his legs at an angle of sixty degrees with the carpet. . .

"He can't. . ." Sylvia said to herself, "he can't, not. . . If he's a gentleman. . . After all that old fellow's hints. . . He'd be a damn coward if he kept off. . . For a fortnight. . . And who else is there not a public. . ." She said: "0 God! . . ."

The old general, lying in his chair, turned his face aside to say:

"I wouldn't, madam, not if I were you, talk about the blue uniform with silver buttons here. . . *We*, of course, understand. . ."

She said: "You see. . . even that extinct volcano. . . He's undressing me with his eyes full of blood veins. . . Then why can't *he*? . . ."

She said aloud:

"Oh, but even you, general, said you were sick of your companions!"

She said to herself:

"Hang it! . . . I will have the courage of my convictions. . . No man shall say I am a coward. . ."

She said:

"Isn't it saying the same thing as you, general, to say that I'd rather be made love to by a well-set-up man in blue and silver—or anything else!—than by most of the people one sees here! . . ."

The general said:

"Of course, if you put it that way, madam. . ." She said:

"What other way should a woman put it?" . . . She reached to the table and filled herself a lot of brandy. The old general was leering towards her:

"Bless me," he said, "a lady who takes liquor like that. . ."

She said:

"You're a Papist, aren't you? With the name of O'Hara and the touch of the brogue you have. . . And the devil you no doubt are with. . . You know what. . . Well, then. . . It's with a special intention! . . . As you say your Hail Marks. . ."

With the liquor burning inside her she saw Tietjens loom in the dim light.

The general, to her bitter amusement, said to him: "Your friend was more than a bit on. . . Not the society surely for madam!"

Tietjens said:

"I never expected to have the pleasure of dining with Mrs. Tietjens tonight. . . That officer was celebrating his commission and I could not put him off. . ." The general said: "Oh, ah! Of course not. . . I dare say. . ." and settled himself again in his chair. . .

Tietjens was overwhelming her with his great bulk. She had still lost her breath. . . He stooped over and said: it was the luck of the half-drunk; he said:

"They're dancing in the lounge. . ."

She coiled herself passionately into her wickerwork. It had dull blue cushions. She said:

"Not with anyone else. . . I don't want any introductions. . ." Fiercely! . . . He said:

"There's no one there that I could introduce you to. . ."

She said:

"Not if it's a charity!"

He said:

"I thought it might be rather dull. . . It's six months since I danced. . ." She felt beauty flowing over all her limbs. She had a gown of gold tissue. Her matchless hair was coiled over her ears. . . She was humming Venusberg music: she knew music if she knew nothing else. . .

She said: "You call the compounds where you keep the W.A.A.C.'s Venusbergs, don't you? Isn't it queer that Venus should be your own? . . . Think of poor Elisabeth!"

The room where they were dancing was very dark. . . It was queer to be in his arms. . . She had known better dancers. . . He had looked ill. . . Perhaps he was. . . Oh, poor Valentine-Elisabeth. . . What a funny position! . . . The good gramophone played. . . *Destiny*! . . . You see, father! . . . In his arms! . . . Of course, dancing is not really. . . But so near the real thing! So near! "Good luck to the special intention! . . ." She had almost kissed him on the lips. . . All but! *Effleurer*, the French call it. . . But she was not as humble. . . He had pressed her tighter. . . All these months without. . . My lord did me honour. . . Good for Malbrouck *s'en va-t-en guerre*. . . He *knew* she had almost kissed him on the lips. . . And that his lips had almost responded. . . The civilian, the novelist, had turned out the last light. . . Tietjens said, "Hadn't we better talk? . . ." She said: "In my room, then! I'm dog-tired. . . I haven't slept for six nights: . . . In spite of drugs. . ." He said: "Yes. Of course! Where else? . . ." Astonishingly. . . Her gown of gold tissue was like the colobium sindonis the King wore at the coronation. . . As they mounted the stairs she thought what a fat tenor Tannhäuser always was! . . . The Venusberg music was dinning in her ears. . . She said: "Sixty-six inexpressibles! I'm as sober as a judge. . . I need to be!"

PART III

I

A shadow—the shadow of the General Officer Commanding in Chief—falling across the bar of light that the sunlight threw in at his open door seemed providentially to awaken Christopher Tietjens, who would have thought it extremely disagreeable to be found asleep by that officer. Very thin, graceful and gay with his scarlet gilt oak-leaves, and ribbons, of which he had many, the general was stepping attractively over the sill of the door, talking backwards over his shoulder, to someone outside. So, in the old days, Gods had descended! It was, no doubt, really the voices from without that had awakened Tietjens, but he preferred to think the matter a slight intervention of Providence, because he felt in need of a sign of some sort! Immediately upon awakening he was not perfectly certain of where he was, but he had sense enough to answer with coherence the first question that the general put to him and to stand stiffly on his legs. The general had said:

"Will you be good enough to inform me, Captain Tietjens, why you have no fire-extinguishers in your unit? You are aware of the extremely disastrous consequences that would follow a conflagration in your lines?"

Tietjens said stiffly:

"It seems impossible to obtain them, sir."

The general said:

"How is this? You have indented for them in the proper quarter? Perhaps you do not know what the proper quarter is?"

Tietjens said:

"If this were a British unit, sir, the proper quarter would be the Royal Engineers." When he had sent his indent in for them to the Royal Engineers they informed him that this being a unit of troops from the Dominions, the quarter to which to apply was the Ordnance. On applying to the Ordnance, he was informed that no provision was made of fire-extinguishers for troops from the Dominions under Imperial officers, and that the proper course was to obtain them from a civilian firm in Great Britain, charging them against barrack damages. . . He had applied to several firms of manufacturers, who all replied that they were forbidden to sell these articles to anyone but to the War Office direct. . . "I am still applying to civilian firms," he finished.

The officer accompanying the general was Colonel Levin, to whom, over his shoulder, the general said: "Make a note of that, Levin, will you? and get the matter looked into." He said again to Tietjens:

"In walking across your parade-ground I noticed that your officer in charge of your physical training knew conspicuously nothing about it. You had better put him on to cleaning out your drains. He was unreasonably dirty."

Tietjens said:

"The sergeant-instructor, sir, is quite competent. The officer is an R.A.S.C. officer. I have at the moment hardly any infantry officers in the unit. But officers have to be on these parades—by A.C.I. They give no orders."

The general said dryly:

"I am aware from the officer's uniform of what arm he belonged to. I am not saying you do not do your best with the material at your command." From Campion on parade this was an extraordinary graciousness. Behind the general's back Levin was making signs with his eyes which he meaningly closed and opened. The general, however, remained extraordinarily dry in manner, his face having its perfectly expressionless air of studied politeness which allowed no muscle of its polished-cherry surface to move. The extreme politeness of the extremely great to the supremely unimportant!

He glanced round the hut markedly. It was Tietjens' own office and contained nothing but the blanket-covered tables and, hanging from a strut, an immense calendar on which days were roughly crossed out in red ink and blue pencil. He said:

"Go and get your belt. You will go round your cookhouses with me in a quarter of an hour. You can tell your sergeant-cook. What sort of cooking arrangements have you?"

Tietjens said:

"Very good cook-houses, sir."

The general said:

"You're extremely lucky, then. Extremely lucky! . . . Half the units like yours in this camp haven't anything but company cookers and field ovens in the open. . ." He pointed with his crop at the open door. He repeated with extreme distinctness "Go and get your belt!" Tietjens wavered a very little on his feet. He said:

"You are aware, sir, that I am under arrest."

Campion imported a threat into his voice:

"I gave you," he said, "an order. To perform a duty!"

The terrific force of the command from above to below took Tietjens staggering through the door. He heard the general's voice say: "I'm perfectly aware he's not drunk." When he had gone four paces Colonel Levin was beside him.

Levin was supporting him by the elbow. He whispered:

"The general wishes me to go with you if you are feeling unwell. You understand you are released from arrest!" He exclaimed with a sort of rapture: "You're doing splendidly. . . It's amazing. Everything I've ever told him about you. . . Yours is the only draft that got off this morning. . .

Tietjens grunted:

"Of course I understand that if I'm given an order to perform a duty, it means I am released from arrest." He had next to no voice. He managed to say that he would prefer to go alone. He said: " . . . He's forced my hand. . . The last thing I want is to be released from arrest. . .

Levin said breathlessly:

"You *can't* refuse. . . You can't upset him. . . Why, you *can't*. . . Besides, an officer cannot demand a court martial."

"You look," Tietjens said, "like a slightly faded bunch of wallflowers. . . I'm sure I beg your pardon. . . It came into my head!" The colonel drooped intangibly, his moustache a little ragged, his eyes a little rimmed, his shaving a little ridged. He exclaimed:

"Damn it! . . . Do you suppose I don't *care* what happens to you? . . . O'Hara came storming into my quarters at half-past three. . . I'm not going to tell you what he said. . ." Tietjens said gruffly:

"No, don't! I've all I can stand for the moment. . ."

Levin exclaimed desperately:

"I want you to understand. . . It's impossible to believe anything against. . ."

Tietjens faced him, his teeth showing like a badger's. He said:

"Whom? . . . Against whom? Curse you!"

Levin said pallidly:

"Against. . . Against. . . either of you. . .

"Then leave it at that!" Tietjens said. "He staggered a little until he reached the main lines. Then he marched. It was purgatory. They peeped at him from the corners of huts and withdrew. . . But they always did peep at him from the corners of huts and withdraw! That is the habit of the Other Ranks on perceiving officers. The fellow called McKechnie also looked out of a hut door. He too withdrew. . . There was no mistaking that! He had the news. . . On the other hand, McKechnie too was under a cloud. It might be his, Tietjens', duty, to strafe McKechnie to hell for having left camp last night. So he might be avoiding him. . . There was no knowing. . . He lurched infinitesimally to the right. The road was rough. His legs felt like detached and swollen objects that he dragged after him. He must master his legs. He mastered his legs. A batman carrying a cup of tea ran against him. Tietjens said: Tut that down and fetch me the sergeant-cook at the double. Tell him the general's going round the cook-houses in a quarter of an hour." The batman ran, spilling the tea in the sunlight.

In his hut, which was dim and profusely decorated with the doctor's ideals of female beauty in every known form of pictorial reproduction, so that it might have been lined with peach-blossom, Tietjens had the greatest difficulty in getting into his belt. He had at first forgotten to remove his hat, then he put his head through the wrong opening; his fingers on the buckles operated like sausages. He inspected himself in the doctor's cracked shaving-glass; he was exceptionally well shaved.

He had shaved that morning at six-thirty: five minutes after the draft had got off. Naturally, the lorries had been an hour late. It was providential that he had shaved with extra care. An insolently calm man was looking at him, the face divided in two by the crack in the glass: a naturally white-complexioned double-half of a face: a patch of high colour on each cheekbone; the pepper-and-salt hair ruffled, the white streaks extremely silver. He had gone very silver lately. But he swore he did not look worn. Not careworn. McKechnie said from behind his back:

"By Jove, what's this all about? The general's been strafing me to hell for not having my table tidy!"

Tietjens, still looking in the glass, said:

"You should keep your table tidy. It's the only strafe the battalion's had."

The general, then, must have been in the orderly room of which he had put McKechnie in charge. McKechnie went on, breathlessly:

"They say you knocked the general. . .

Tietjens said:

"Don't you know enough to discount what they say in this town?" He said to himself: "That was all right!" He had spoken with a cool edge on a contemptuous voice.

He said to the sergeant-cook who was panting—another heavy, grey-moustached, very senior N.C.O.:

"The general's going round the cook-houses. . . You be damn certain there's no dirty cook's clothing in the lockers!" He was fairly sure that otherwise his cook-houses would be all right. He had gone round them himself the morning of the day before yesterday. Or was it yesterday? . . .

It was the day after he had been up all night because the draft had been countermanded. . . It didn't matter. He said:

"I wouldn't serve out white clothing to the cooks. . . I bet you've got some hidden away, though it's against orders."

The sergeant looked away into the distance, smiled all-knowingly over his walrus moustache.

"The general likes to see 'em in white," he said, "and he won't know the white clothing has been countermanded." Tietjens said:

"The snag is that the beastly cooks always will tuck some piece of beastly dirty clothing away in a locker rather than take the trouble to take it round to their quarters when they've changed."

Levin said with great distinctness:

"The general has sent me to you with this, Tietjens. Take a sniff of it if you're feeling dicky. You've been up all night on end two nights running." He extended in the palm of his hand a bottle of smelling-salts in a silver section of tubing. He said the general suffered from vertigo now and then. Really he himself carried that restorative for the benefit of Miss de Bailly.

Tietjens asked himself why the devil the sight of that smelling-salts container reminded him of the brass handle of the bedroom door moving almost imperceptibly. . . and incredibly. It was, of course, because Sylvia had on her illuminated dressing-table, reflected by the glass, just such another smooth, silver segment of tubing. . . Was everything he saw going to remind him of the minute movement of that handle?

"You can do what you please," the sergeant-cook said, "but there will always be one piece of clothing in a locker of a G.O.C.I.C.'s inspection. And the general always walks straight up to that locker and has it opened. I've seen General Campion do it three times."

"If there's any found this time, the man it belongs to goes for a D.C.M.," Tietjens said. "See that there's a clean diet-sheet on the messing board."

"The generals really like to find dirty clothing," the sergeant-cook said; "it gives them something to talk about if they don't know anything else about cook-houses. . . I'll put up my own diet-sheet, sir. . . I suppose you can keep the general back for twenty minutes or so? It's all I ask."

Levin said towards his rolling, departing back:

"That's a damn smart man. Fancy being as confident as that about an inspection. . . Ugh! . . ." and Levin shuddered in remembrance of inspections through which in his time he had passed.

"He's a damn smart man!" Tietjens said. He added to McKechnie:

"You might take a look at dinners in case the general takes it into his head to go round them."

McKechnie said darkly:

"Look here, Tietjens, are you in command of this unit or am I?"

Levin exclaimed sharply, for him:

"What's that? What the. . ."

Tietjens said:

"Captain McKechnie complains that he is the senior officer and should command this unit."

Levin exclaimed:

"Of all the. . ." He addressed McKechnie with vigour: "My man, the command of these units is an appointment at disposition of headquarters. Don't let there be any mistake about that!"

McKechnie said doggedly:

"Captain Tietjens asked me to take the battalion this morning. I understood he was under. . .

"You," Levin said, "are attached to this unit for discipline and rations. You damn well understand that if some uncle or other of yours were not, to the general's knowledge, a protégé of Captain Tietjens', you'd be in a lunatic asylum at this moment. . ."

McKechnie's face worked convulsively, he swallowed as men are said to swallow who suffer from hydrophobia. He lifted his fist and cried out:

"My un. . ."

Levin said:

"If you say another word you go under medical care the moment it's said. I've the order in my pocket. Now, fall out. At the double!"

McKechnie wavered on the way to the door. Levin added:

"You can take your choice of going up the line tonight. Or a court of inquiry for obtaining divorce leave and then not getting a divorce. Or the other thing. And you can thank Captain Tietjens for the clemency the general has shown you!"

The hut now reeling a little, Tietjens put the opened smelling bottle to his nostrils. At the sharp pang of the odour the hut came to attention. He said:

"We can't keep the general waiting."

"He told me," Levin said, "to give you ten minutes. He's sitting in your hut. He's tired. This affair has worried him dreadfully. O'Hara is the first C.O. he ever served under. A useful man, too, at his job."

Tietjens leaned against his dressing-table of meat-cases. "You told that fellow McKechnie off, all right," he said. "I did not know you had it in you. . .

"Oh," Levin said, "it's just being with *him*. . . I get his manner and it does all right. . . Of course I don't often hear him have to strafe anybody in that manner. There's nobody really to stand up to him. Naturally. . . But just this morning I was in his cabinet doing private secretary, and he was talking to Pe. . . Talking while he shaved. And he said exactly that: You can take your choice of going up the line tonight or a court martial. . . So naturally I said as near the same as I could to your little friend. . ."

Tietjens said:

"We'd better go now."

In the winter sunlight Levin tucked his arm under Tietjens', leaning towards him gaily and not hurrying. The display was insufferable to Tietjens, but he recognized that it was indispensable. The bright day seemed full of things with hard edges—a rather cruel definiteness. . . Liver! . . .

The little depot adjutant passed them going very fast, as if before a wind. Levin just waved his hand in acknowledgment of his salute and went on, being enraptured in Tietjens' conversation. He said:

"You and. . . and Mrs. Tietjens are dining at the general's tonight. To meet the G.O.C.I.C. Western Division. And General O'Hara. . . We understand that you have definitely separated from Mrs. Tietjens. . ."

Tietjens forced his left arm to violence to restrain it from tearing itself from the colonel's grasp.

His mind had become a coffin-headed, leather-jawed charger, like Schomburg. Sitting on his mind was like sitting on Schomburg at a dull water-jump. His lips said: "Bub-bub-bub-bub!" He could not feel his hands. He said:

"I recognize the necessity. If the general sees it in that way. I saw it in another way myself." His voice was intensely weary. "No doubt," he said, "the general knows best!"

Levin's face exhibited real enthusiasm. He said:

"You decent fellow! You awfully decent fellow! We're all in the same boat. . . Now, will you tell me? For *him*. Was O'Hara drunk last night or wasn't he?"

Tietjens said:

"I think he was not drunk when he burst into the room with Major Perowne. . . I've been thinking about it! I think he became drunk. . . When I first requested and then ordered him to leave the room he leant against the doorpost. . . He was certainly then—in disorder! I then told him that I should order him under arrest, if he didn't go. . ."

Levin said:

"Mm! Mm! Mm!"

Tietjens said:

"It was my obvious duty. . . I assure you that I was perfectly collected. . . I beg to assure you that I was perfectly collected. . ."

Levin said: "I am not questioning the correctness. . . But. . . we are all one family. . . I admit the atrocious. . . the unbearable nature. . . But you understand that O'Hara had the right to enter your room. . . As P.M.! . . ."

Tietjens said:

"I am not questioning that it was his right. I was assuring you that I was perfectly collected because the general had honoured me by asking my opinion on the condition of General O'Hara. . .

They had by now walked far beyond the line leading to Tietjens' office and, close together, were looking down upon the great tapestry of the French landscape.

"*He*," Levin said, "is anxious for your opinion. It really amounts to as to whether O'Hara drinks too much to continue in his job! . . . And he says he will take your word. . . You could not have a greater testimonial. . ."

"He could not," Tietjens said studiedly, "do anything less. Knowing me."

Levin said:

"Good heavens, old man, you rub it in!" He added quickly: "He wishes me to dispose of this side of the matter. He will take my word and yours. You will forgive. . ."

The mind of Tietjens had completely failed: the Seine below looked like an S on fire in an opal. He said: "Eh?" And then: "Oh, yes! I forgive. . . It's painful. . . You probably don't know what you are doing."

He broke off suddenly:

"By God! . . . Were the Canadian Railway Service to go with my draft? They were detailed to mend the line here today. Also to go. . . I kept them back. . . Both orders were dated the same day and hour. I could not get on to headquarters either from the hotel or from here. . ."

Levin said:

"Yes, that's all right. He'll be immensely pleased. He's going to speak to you about that!" Tietjens gave an immense sigh of relief.

"I remembered that my orders were conflicting just before. . . It was a terrible shock to remember. . . If I sent them up in the lorries, the repairs to the railway might be delayed. . . If I didn't, you might get strafed to hell. . . It was an intolerable worry. . ."

Levin said:

"You remembered it just as you saw the handle of your door moving. . ."

Tietjens said from a sort of a mist:

"Yes. You know how beastly it is when you suddenly remember you have forgotten something in orders. As if the pit of your stomach had. . ."

Levin said:

"All I ever thought about if I'd forgotten anything was what would be a good excuse to put up to the adjutant. . . When I was a regimental officer. . ."

Suddenly Tietjens said insistently:

"How did you know that? . . . About the door handle? Sylvia couldn't have seen it. . ." He added: "And she could not have known what I was thinking. . . She had her back to the door. . . And to me. . . Looking at me in the glass. . . She was not even aware of what had happened. . . So she could not have seen the handle move!"

Levin hesitated:

"I. . ." he said. "Perhaps I ought not to have said that. . . You've told us. . . That is to say, you've told. . ." He was pale in the sunlight. He said: "Old man. . . Perhaps you don't know. . . Didn't you perhaps ever, in your childhood?"

Tietjens said:

"Well. . . What is it?"

"That you talk. . . when you're sleeping!" Levin said.

Astonishingly, Tietjens said:

"What of that? . . . It's nothing to write home about! With the overwork I've had and the sleeplessness. . ."

Levin said, with a pathetic appeal to Tietjens' omniscience:

"But doesn't it mean. . . We used to say when we were boys. . . that if you talk in your sleep. . . you're. . . in fact a bit dotty?"

Tietjens said without passion:

"Not necessarily. It means that one has been under mental pressure, but all mental pressure does not drive you over the edge. Not by any means. . . Besides, what does it matter?"

Levin said:

"You mean you don't care. . . Good God!" He remained looking at the view, drooping, in intense dejection. He said: "This *beastly* war! This *beastly* war! . . . Look at all that view. . ."

Tietjens said:

"It's an encouraging spectacle, really. The beastliness of human nature is always pretty normal. We lie and betray and are wanting in imagination and deceive ourselves, always, at about the same rate. In peace and in war! But, somewhere in that view there are enormous bodies of men. . . If you got a still more extended range of view over this whole front you'd have still more enormous bodies of men. . . Seven to ten million. . . All moving towards places towards which they desperately don't want to go. Desperately! Every one of them is desperately afraid. But they go on. An immense blind will forces them in the effort to consummate the one decent action that humanity has to its credit in the whole of recorded history. The one we are engaged in. That effort is the one certain creditable fact in all their lives. . . But the *other* lives of all those men are dirty, potty and discreditable little affairs. . . Like yours. . . Like mine. . ."

Levin exclaimed:

"Just heavens! *What* a pessimist you are!"

Tietjens said: "Can't you see that that is optimism?" "But," Levin said, "we're being beaten out of the field. . . You don't know how desperate things are."

Tietjens said:

"Oh, I know pretty well. As soon as this weather really breaks we're probably done."

"We can't," Levin said, "possibly hold them. Not possibly."

"But success or failure," Tietjens said, "have nothing to do with the credit of a story. And a consideration of the virtues of humanity does not omit the other side. If we lose they win. If success is necessary to your idea of virtue—*virtus*—they then provide the success instead of ourselves. But the thing is to be able to stick to the integrity of your character, whatever earthquake sets the house tumbling over your head. . . That, thank God, we're doing. . ."

Levin said:

"I don't know. . . If you knew what is going on at home. . ."

Tietjens said:

"Oh, I know. . . I know that ground as I know the palm of my hand. I could invent that life if I knew nothing at all about the facts."

Levin said:

"I believe you could." He added: "Of course you could. . . And yet the only use we can make of you is to martyrize you because two drunken brutes break into your wife's bedroom. . ."

Tietjens said:

"You betray your non-Anglo-Saxon origin by being so vocal. . . And by your illuminative exaggerations!"

Levin suddenly exclaimed:

"What the devil were we talking about?"

Tietjens said grimly:

"I am here at the disposal of the competent military authority—You!—that is inquiring into my antecedents. I am ready to go on belching platitudes till you stop me." Levin answered:

"For goodness' sake help me. This is horribly painful. *He*—the general—has given me the job of finding out what happened last night. He won't face it himself. He's attached to you both."

Tietjens said:

"It's asking too much to ask me to help you. . . What did I say in my sleep? What has Mrs. Tietjens told the general?"

"The general," Levin said, "has not seen Mrs. Tietjens. He could not trust himself. He knew she would twist him round her little finger."

Tietjens said:

"He's beginning to learn. He was sixty last July, but he's beginning."

"So that," Levin said, "what we do know we learnt in the way I have told you. And from O'Hara of course. The general would not let Pe. . . , the other fellow, speak a word, while he was shaving. He just said: 'I won't hear you. I won't hear you. You can take your choice of going up the line as soon as there are trains running or being broke on my personal application to the King in Council.'"

"I didn't know," Tietjens said, "that he could talk as straight as that."

"He's dreadfully hard hit," Levin answered; "if you and Mrs. Tietjens separate—and still more if there's anything real against either of you—

it's going to shatter all his illusions. And. . ." He paused: "Do you know Major Thurston? A gunner? Attached to our anti-aircraft crowd? . . . The general is very thick with him. . ."

Tietjens said:

"He's one of the Thurston's of Lobden Moorside. . . I don't know him personally. . ."

Levin said:

"He's upset the general a good deal. . . With something he told him. . ."

Tietjens said:

"Good God!" And then: "He can't have told the general anything against me. . . Then it must be against. . ."

Levin said:

"Do you want the general always to be told things against you in contradistinction to things about. . . another person?"

Tietjens said:

"We shall be keeping the fellows in my cook-house a confoundedly long time waiting for inspections. . . I'm in your hands as regards the general. . ."

Levin said:

"The general's in your hut: thankful to goodness to be alone. He never is. He said he was going to write a private memorandum for the Secretary of State, and I could keep you any time I liked as long as I got everything out of you. . ."

Tietjens said:

"Did what Major Thurston allege take place. . . Thurston has lived most of his life in France. . . But you had better not tell me. . ."

Levin said:

"He's our anti-aircraft liaison officer with the French civilian authorities. Those sort of fellows generally have lived in France a good deal. A very decentish, quiet man. He plays chess with the general and they talk over the chess. . . But the general is going to talk about what he said to you himself. . ."

Tietjens said:

"Good God! . . . He going to talk as well as you. . . You'd say the coils were closing in. . ."

Levin said:

"We can't go on like this. . . It's my own fault for not being more direct. But this can't last all day. We could neither of us stand it. . . I'm pretty nearly done. . ."

Tietjens said:

"Where *did* your father come from, really? Not from Frankfurt? . . ."

Levin said:

"Constantinople. . . His father was financial agent to the Sultan; my father was his son by an Armenian presented to him by the Selamlik along with the Order of the Medjidje, first class."

"It accounts for your very decent manner, and for your common sense. If you had been English I should have broken your neck before now."

Levin said:

"Thank you! I hope I always behave like an English gentleman. But I am going to be brutally direct now. . . He went on: "The really queer thing is that you should always address Miss Wannop in the language of the Victorian *Correct Letter-Writer*. You must excuse my mentioning the name: it shortens things. You said 'Miss Wannop' every two or three half-minutes. It convinced the general more than any possible assertions that your relations were perfectly. . ."

Tietjens, his eyes shut, said:

"I talked to Miss Wannop in my sleep. . ."

Levin, who was shaking a little, said:

"It was very queer. . . Almost ghostlike. . . There you sat, your arms on the table. Talking away. You appeared to be writing a letter to her. And the sunlight streaming in at the hut. I was going to wake you, but he stopped me. He took the view that he was on detective work, and that he might as well detect. He had got it into his mind that you were a Socialist."

"He would," Tietjens commented. "Didn't I tell you he was beginning to learn things? . . ."

Levin exclaimed:

"But you aren't a So. . ."

Tietjens said:

"Of course, if your father came from Constantinople and his mother was a Georgian, it accounts for your attractiveness. You *are* a most handsome fellow. And intelligent. . . If the general has put you on to inquire whether I am a Socialist I will answer your questions."

Levitt said:

"No. . . That's one of the questions he's reserving for himself to ask. It appears that if you answer that you are a Socialist he intends to cut you out of his will. . ."

Tietjens said:

"His will! . . . Oh, yes, of course, he might very well leave me something. But doesn't that supply rather a motive for me to say that I *am*? I don't want this money."

Levin positively jumped a step backwards. Money, and particularly money that came by way of inheritance, being one of the sacred things of life for him, he exclaimed:

"I don't see that you *can* joke about such a subject!"

Tietjens answered good-humouredly:

"Well, you don't expect me to play up to the old gentleman in order to get his poor old shekels." He added: "Hadn't we better get it over?"

Levin said:

"You've got hold of yourself?"

Tietjens answered:

"Pretty well. . . You'll excuse my having been emotional so far. You aren't English, so it won't have embarrassed you."

Levin exclaimed in an outraged manner:

"Hang it, I'm English to the backbone! What's the matter with me?"

Tietjens said:

"Nothing. . . Nothing in the world. That's just what makes you un-English. We're all. . . well, it doesn't matter what's wrong with *us*. . . What did you gather about my relations with Miss Wannop?"

The question was unemotionally put and Levin was still so concerned as to his origins that he did not at first grasp what Tietjens had said. He began to protest that he had been educated at Winchester and Magdalen. Then he exclaimed, "*Oh!*" And took time for reflection.

"If," he said finally, "the general had not let out that she was young and attractive. . . at least, I suppose attractive. . . I should have thought that you regarded her as an old maid. . . You know, of course, that it came to me as a shock, the thought that there was anyone. . . That you had allowed yourself. . . Anyhow. . . I suppose that I'm simple. . ."

Tietjens said:

"What did the general gather?"

"He. . ." Levin said, "he stood over you with his head held to one side, looking rather cunning. . . like a magpie listening at a hole it's dropped a nut into. . . First he looked disappointed: then quite glad. A simple kind of gladness. Just glad, you know. . . When we got outside the hut he said 'I suppose in *vino veritas*,' and then he asked me the Latin for 'sleep' . . . But I had forgotten it too. . ."

Tietjens said:

"What did I say?"

"It's. . ." Levin hesitated, "extraordinarily difficult to say what you *did* say. . . I don't profess to remember long speeches to the letter. . . Naturally it was a good deal broken up. . . I tell you, you were talking to a young lady about matters you don't generally talk to young ladies about. . . And obviously you were trying to let your. . . Mrs. Tietjens, down easily. . . You were trying to explain also why you had definitely decided to separate from Mrs. Tietjens. . . And you took it that the young lady might be troubled. . . at the separation. . ."

Tietjens said carelessly:

"This is rather painful. Perhaps you would let me tell you exactly what *did* happen last night. . .

Levin said:

"If you only would!" He added rather diffidently: "If you would not mind remembering that I am a military court of inquiry. It makes it easier for me to report to the general if you say things dully and in the order they happened."

Tietjens said:

"Thank you. . ." and after a short interval, "I retired to rest with my wife last night at. . . I cannot say the hour exactly. Say half-past one. I reached this camp at half-past four, taking rather over half an hour to walk. What happened, as I am about to relate, took place therefore before four."

"The hour," Levin said, "is not material. We know the incident occurred in the small hours. General O'Hara made his complaint to me at three-thirty-five. He probably took five minutes to reach my quarters."

Tietjens asked:

"The exact charge was. . ."

"The complaints," Levin answered, "were very numerous indeed. . . I could not catch them all. The succinct charge was at first being drunk and striking a superior officer, then merely that of conduct prejudicial in that you struck. . . There is also a subsidiary charge of conduct prejudicial in that you improperly marked a charge-sheet in your orderly room. . . I did not catch what all that was about. . . You appear to have had a quarrel with him about his red caps. . ."

"That," Tietjens said, "is what it is really all about." He asked: "The officer I was said to have struck was. . . ?" Levin said:

"Perowne. . ." dryly.

Tietjens said:

"You are sure it was not himself. I am prepared to plead guilty to striking General O'Hara."

"It is not," Levin said, "a question of pleading guilty. There is no charge to that effect against you, and you are perfectly aware that you are not under arrest. . . An order to perform any duty after you have been placed under arrest in itself releases you and dissolves the arrest."

Tietjens said coolly:

"I am perfectly aware of that. And that that was General Campion's intention in ordering me to accompany him round my cook-houses. . . But I doubt. . . I put it to you for your serious attention whether that is the best way to hush this matter up. . . I think it would be more expedient that I should plead guilty to a charge of striking General O'Hara. And naturally to being drunk. An officer does not strike a general when he is sober. That would be a quite inconspicuous affair. Subordinate officers are broken every day for being drunk."

Levin had said "Wait a minute," twice. He now exclaimed with a certain horror:

"Your mania for sacrificing yourself makes you lose all. . . all sense of proportion. You forget that General Campion is a gentleman. Things cannot be done in a hole-and-corner manner in this command. . ."

Tietjens said:

"They're done unbearably. . . It would be nothing to me to be broke for being drunk, but raking up all this is hell."

Levin said:

"The general is anxious to know exactly what has happened. You will kindly accept an order to relate exactly what happened."

Tietjens said:

"That is what is perfectly damnable. . ." He remained silent for nearly a minute, Levin slapping his leggings with his riding-crop in a nervously passionate rhythm. Tietjens stiffened himself and began:

"General O'Hara came to my wife's room and burst in the door. I was there. I took him to be drunk. But from what he exclaimed I have since imagined that he was not so much drunk as misled. There was another man lying in the corridor where I had thrown him. General O'Hara exclaimed that this was Major Perowne. I had not realized that this was Major Perowne. I do not know Major Perowne very well and he was not in uniform. I had imagined him to be a French waiter coming to call me to the telephone. I had seen only his face round the door: he was looking round the door. My wife was in a state. . . bordering on nudity. I had put my hand under his chin and thrown him through the doorway. I am physically very strong and I exercised all my strength. I am aware of that. I was excited, but not more excited than the circumstances seemed to call for. . ."

Levin exclaimed:

"But. . . At three in the morning! The telephone!"

"I was ringing up my headquarters and yours. All through the night. The O.I.C. draft, Lieutenant Cowley, was also ringing me up. I was anxious to know what was to be done about the Canadian railway men. I had three times been called to the telephone since I had been in Mrs. Tietjens' room, and once an orderly had come down from the camp. I was also conducting a very difficult conversation with my wife as to the disposal of my family's estates, which are large, so that the details were complicated. I occupied the room next door to Mrs. Tietjens and till that moment, the communicating door between the rooms being open, I had heard when a waiter or an orderly had knocked at my own door in the corridor. The night porter of the hotel was a dark, untidy, surly sort of fellow. . . Not unlike Perowne."

Levin said:

"Is it necessary to go into all this? We. . ."

Tietjens said:

"If I am to make a statement it seems necessary. I would prefer you to question me. . ."

Levin said:

"Please go on. . . We accept the statement that Major Perowne was not in uniform. He states that he was in his pyjamas and dressing-gown. Looking for the bathroom."

Tietjens said: "Ah!" and stood reflecting. He said:

"May I hear the. . . purport of Major Perowne's statement?"

"He states," Levin said, "what I have just said. He was looking for the bathroom. He had not slept in the hotel before. He opened a door and looked round it, and was immediately thrown with great violence down into the passage with his head against the wall. He says that this dazed him so that, not really appreciating what had happened, he shouted various accusations against the person who had assaulted him. . . General O'Hara then came out of his room. . ."

Tietjens said:

"What accusations did Major Perowne shout?"

"He doesn't. . ." Levin hesitated, "'eh! . . . elaborate them in his statement."

Tietjens said:

"It is, I imagine, material that I should know what they are. . ."

Levin said:

"I don't know that. . . If you'll forgive me. . . Major Perowne came to see me, reaching me half an hour after General O'Hara. He was very. . . extremely nervous and concerned. I am bound to say. . . for Mrs. Tietjens. And also very concerned to spare yourself! . . . It appears that he had shouted out just anything. . . As it might be 'Thieves!' or 'Fire!' . . . But when General O'Hara came out he told him, being out of himself, that he had been invited to your wife's room, and that. . . Oh, excuse me. . . I'm under great obligations to you. . . the very greatest. . . that you had attempted to blackmail him!"

Tietjens said:

"Well! . . ."

"You understand," Levin said, and he was pleading, "that that is what he said to General O'Hara in the corridor. He even confessed it was madness. . . He did not maintain the accusation to me. . ."

Tietjens said:

"Not that Mrs. Tietjens had given him leave? . . ."

Levin said with tears in his eyes:

"I'll not go on with this. . . I will rather resign my commission than go on tormenting you. . ."

"You can't resign your commission," Tietjens said.

"I can resign my appointment," Levin answered. He went on sniffling: "This beastly war! . . . This beastly war! . . ."

Tietjens said:

"If what is distressing you is having to tell me that you believe Major Perowne came with my wife's permission I know it's true. It's also true that my wife expected me to be there. She wanted some fun: not adultery. But I am also aware—as Major Thurston appears to have told General Campion—that Mrs. Tietjens was with Major Perowne. In France. At a place called Yssingueux-les-Pervenches. . ."

"That wasn't the name," Levin blubbered. "It was Saint. . . Saint. . . Saint something. In the Cevennes. . ."

Tietjens said:

"Don't, there! . . . Don't distress yourself. . ."

"But I'm. . ." Levin went on, "under great obligations to you. . ."

"I'd better," Tietjens said, "finish this matter myself."

Levin said:

"It will break the general's heart. He believes so absolutely in Mrs. Tietjens. Who wouldn't? . . . How the devil could you guess what Major Thurston told him?"

"He's the sort of brown, trustworthy man who always does know that sort of thing," Tietjens answered. "As for the general's belief in Mrs. Tietjens, he's perfectly justified. . . Only there will be no more parades. Sooner or later it has to come to that for us all. . ." He added with a little bitterness: "Only not for you. Being a Turk or a Jew you are a simple, Oriental, monogamous, faithful soul. . ." He added again: "I hope to goodness the sergeant-cook has the sense not to keep the men's dinners back for the general's inspection. . . But of course he will not. . ."

Levin said:

"What in the world would that matter?" fiercely. "He keeps men waiting as much as three hours. On parade."

"Of course," Tietjens said, "if that is what Major Perowne told General O'Hara it removes a good deal of my suspicions of the latter's sobriety. Try to get the position. General O'Hara positively burst in the little sneck of the door that I had put down and came in shouting: 'Where is the —— blackmailer?' And it was a full three minutes before I could get rid of him. I had had the presence of mind to switch off the light and he persisted in asking for another look at Mrs. Tietjens. You see, if you consider it, he is a very heavy sleeper. He is suddenly awakened after, no doubt, not a few pegs. He hears Major Perowne shouting about blackmail and thieves. . . I dare say this town has its quota of blackmailers. O'Hara might well be anxious to catch one in the act. He hates me, anyhow, because of his Red Caps. I'm a shabby-looking chap he doesn't know much about. Perowne passes for being a millionaire. I daresay he is: he's said to be very stingy. That would be how he got hold of the idea of blackmail and hypnotized the general with it. . ."

He went on again:

"But I wasn't to know that. . . I had shut the door on Perowne and didn't even know he was Perowne. I really thought he was the night porter coming to call me to the telephone. I only saw a roaring satyr. I mean that was what I thought O'Hara was. . . And I assure you I kept my head. . . When he persisted in leaning against the doorpost and asking for another look at Mrs. Tietjens, he kept on saying: 'The woman' and 'The hussy.' Not 'Mrs. Tietjens.' . . . I thought then that there was something queer. I said: 'This is my wife's room,' several times. He said something to the effect of how could he know she was my wife, and. . . that she had made eyes at himself in the lounge, so it might have been himself as well as Perowne.. I dare say he had got it into his head that I had imported some tart to blackmail someone. . . But you know. . . I grew exhausted after a time. . . I saw outside in the corridor one of the little subalterns he has on his staff, and I said: 'If you do not take General O'Hara away I shall order you to put him under arrest for drunkenness.' That seemed to drive the general crazy. I had gone closer to him, being determined to push him out of the door, and he decidedly smelt of whisky. Strongly. . . But I dare say he was thinking himself outraged, really. And perhaps also coming to his senses. As there was nothing else for it I pushed him gently out of the room. In going he shouted that I was to consider myself under arrest. I so considered myself. . . That is to say that, as soon as I had settled certain details with Mrs. Tietjens, I walked up to the camp, which I took to be my quarters, though I am actually under the M.O.'s orders to reside in this hotel owing to the state of my lungs. I saw the draft off, that not necessitating my giving any orders. I went to my sleeping quarters, it being then about six-thirty, and towards seven awakened McKechnie, whom I asked to take my adjutant's and battalion parade and orderly-room. I had breakfast in my hut, and then went into my private office to await developments. I think I have now told you everything material. . ."

II

Gﬞ eneral Lord Edward Campion, G.C.B., K.C.M.G. (military), D.S.O., etc., sat, radiating glory and composing a confidential memorandum to the Secretary of State for War, on a bully-beef case, leaning forward over a military blanket that covered a deal table. He was for the moment in high good humour on the surface, though his subordinate minds were puzzled and depressed. At the end of each sentence that he wrote—and he wrote with increasing satisfaction!—a mind that he was not using said: "What the devil am I going to do with that fellow?" Or: "How the devil is that girl's name to be kept out of this mess?"

Having been asked to write a confidential memorandum for the information of the home authorities as to what, in his opinion, was the cause of the French railway strike, he had hit on the ingenious device of reporting what was the opinion of the greater part of the forces under his command. This was a dangerous line to take, for he might well come into conflict with the home Government. But he was pretty certain that any inquiries that the home Government could cause to be made amongst the local civilian population would confirm what he was writing—which he was careful to state was not to be taken as a communication of his own opinion. In addition, he did not care what the Government did to him.

He was satisfied with his military career. In the early part of the war, after materially helping mobilisation, he had served with great distinction in the East, in command mostly of mounted infantry. He had subsequently so distinguished himself in the organising and transporting of troops coming and going overseas that, on the part of the lines of communication where he now commanded becoming of great importance, he knew that he had seemed the only general that could be given that command. It had become of enormous importance—these were open secrets!—because, owing to divided opinions in the Cabinet, it might at any moment be decided to move the bulk of H.M. Forces to somewhere in the East. The idea underlying this—as General Campion saw it—had at least some relation to the necessities of the British Empire, and strategy embracing world politics as well as military movements—a fact which is often forgotten. There was this much to be said for it: the preponderance of British Imperial interests might be advanced as lying in the Middle and Far Eaststo the east, that is to say, of Constantinople. This might be denied, but it was a feasible proposition. The present operations on the Western front, arduous, and even creditable, as they might have been until relatively lately, were very remote from our Far-Eastern possessions and mitigated from, rather than added to, our prestige. In addition, the unfortunate display in front of Constantinople in the beginning of the war had almost eliminated our prestige with the Mohammedan races. Thus a demonstration in enormous force in any region between European Turkey and the north-western frontiers of India might point out to Mohammedans, Hindus, and other Eastern races, what overwhelming forces Great Britain, were she so minded, could put into the field. It is true that that would mean the certain loss of the war on the Western front, with corresponding loss of prestige in the West. But the wiping out of the French republic would convey little to the Eastern races, whereas we could no doubt make terms with the enemy nations, as a price for abandoning our allies, that might well leave the Empire, not only intact, but actually increased in colonial extent, since it was unlikely that the enemy empires would wish to be burdened with colonies for some time.

General Campion was not overpoweringly sentimental over the idea of the abandonment of our allies. They had won his respect as fighting organizations, and that, to the professional soldier, is a great deal; but still he was a professional soldier, and the prospect of widening the bounds of the British Empire could not be contemptuously dismissed at the price of rather sentimental dishonour. Such bargains had been struck before during wars involving many nations, and doubtless such bargains would be struck again. In addition, votes might be gained by the Government from the small but relatively noisy and menacing part of the British population that favoured the enemy nations.

But when it came to tactics—which it should be remembered concerns itself with the movement of troops actually in contact with enemy forces—General Campion had no doubt that that plan was the conception of the brain of a madman. The dishonour of such a proceeding must of course be considered—and its impracticability was hopeless. The dreadful nature of what would be our debacle did we attempt to evacuate the Western front might well be unknown to, or might be deliberately ignored by, the civilian mind. But the general could almost see the horrors as a picture—and, professional soldier as he was, his mind shuddered at the picture. They had by now in the country enormous bodies of troops who had hitherto not come into contact with the enemy forces. Did they attempt to withdraw these in the first place the native population would at once turn from a friendly into a bitterly hostile factor, and moving troops through hostile country is to the nth power a more lengthy matter than moving them through territory where the native populations lend a helping hand, or are at least not obstructive. They had in addition this enormous force to ration, and they would doubtless have to supply them with ammunition on the almost certain breaking through of the enemy forces. It would be impossible to do this without the use of the local railways—and the use of these would at once be prohibited. If, on the other hand, they attempted to begin the evacuation by shortening the front, the operation would be very difficult with troops who, by now, were almost solely men trained only in trench warfare, with officers totally unused to that keeping up of communications between units which is the life and breath of a retreating army. Training, in fact, in that element had been almost abandoned in the training camps where instruction was almost limited to bomb-throwing, the use of machine-guns, and other departments which had been forced on the War Office by eloquent civilians—to the almost complete neglect of the rifle. Thus at the mere hint of a retreat the enemy forces must break through and come upon the vast, unorganised, or semi-organised bodies of troops in the rear. . .

The temptation for the professional soldier was to regard such a state of things with equanimity. Generals have not infrequently enormously distinguished themselves by holding up retreats from the rear when vanguard commanders have disastrously failed. But General Campion resisted the temptation of even hoping that this chance of distinguishing himself might offer itself. He could not contemplate with equanimity the slaughter of great bodies of men under his command, and not even a successful retreating action of that description could be carried out without horrible slaughter. And he would have little hope of conducting necessarily delicate and very hurried movements with an army that, except for its rough training in trench warfare, was practically civilian in texture. So that although, naturally, he had made his plans for such an eventuality, having indeed in his private quarters four enormous paper-covered blackboards upon which he had changed daily the names of units according as they passed from his hands or came into them and became available, he prayed specifically every night before retiring to bed that the task might not be cast upon his shoulders. He prized very much his universal popularity in his command, and he could not bear to think of how the eyes of the Army would regard him as he put upon them a strain so appalling and such unbearable sufferings. He had, moreover, put that aspect of the matter very strongly in a memorandum that he had prepared in answer to a request from the home Government for a scheme by which an evacuation might be effected. But he considered that the civilian element in the Government was so entirely indifferent to the sufferings of the men engaged in these operations, and was so completely ignorant of what are military exigencies, that the words he had devoted to that department of the subject were merely wasted. . .

So everything pushed him into writing confidentially to the Secretary of State for War a communication that he knew must be singularly distasteful to a number of the gentlemen who would peruse it. He chuckled indeed as he wrote, the open door behind him and the sunlight pouring in on his radiant figure. He said:

"Sit down, Tietjens. Levin, I shall not want you for ten minutes," without raising his head, and went on writing. It annoyed him that, from the corner of his eye, he could see that Tietjens was still standing, and he said rather irritably: "Sit down, sit down. . ."

He wrote:

"It is pretty generally held here by the native population that the present very serious derangement of traffic, if not actively promoted, is at least winked at by the Government of this country. It is, that is to say, intended to give us a taste of what would happen if I took any measures here for returning any large body of men to the home country or elsewhere, and it is said also to be a demonstration in favour of a single command—a measure which is here regarded by a great weight of instructed opinion as indispensable to the speedy and successful conclusion of hostilities. . ."

The general paused over that sentence. It came very near the quick. For himself he was absolutely in favour of a single command, and in his opinion, too, it was indispensable to any sort of conclusion of hostilities at all. The whole of military history, in so far as it concerned allied operations of any sort—from the campaigns of Xerxes and operations during the wars of the Greeks and Romans, to the campaigns of Marlborough and Napoleon and the Prussian operations of 1866 and 1870—pointed to the conclusion that a relatively small force acting homogeneously was, to the nth power again, more effective than vastly superior forces of allies acting only imperfectly in accord or not in accord at all. Modern development in arms had made no shade at all of difference to strategy and had made differences merely of time and numbers to tactics. Today, as in the days of the Greek Wars of the Allies, success depended on apt timing of the arrival of forces at given points, and it made no difference whether your lethal weapons acted from a distance of thirty miles or were held and operated by hand; whether you dealt death from above or below the surface of the ground, through the air by dropped missiles or by mephitic and torturing vapours. What won combats, campaigns, and, in the end, wars, was the brain which timed the arrival of forces at given points—and that must be one brain which could command their presence at these points, not a half-dozen authorities requesting each other to perform operations which might or might not fall in with the ideas or the prejudices of any one or other of the half-dozen. . .

Levin came in noiselessly, slid a memorandum slip on to the blanket beside the paper on which the general was writing. The general read: *T. agrees completely, sir, with your diagnosis of the facts, except that he is much more ready to accept General O'H.'s acts as reasonable. He places himself entirely in your hands.*

The general heaved an immense sigh of relief. The sunlight streaming in became very bright. He had had a real sinking at the heart when Tietjens had boggled for a second over putting on his belt. An officer may not demand or insist on a court martial. But he, Campion, could not in decency have refused Tietjens his court martial if he stood out for it. He had a right to clear his character publicly. It would have been impossible to refuse him. Then the fat would have been in the fire. For, knowing O'Hara through pretty nearly twenty-five years—or it must be thirty!—of service Campion was pretty certain that O'Hara had made a drunken beast of himself. Yet he was very attached to O'Hara—one of the old type of rough-diamond generals who swore your head off, but were damn capable men! . . . It was a tremendous relief.

He said sharply:

"Sit down, can't you, Tietjens! You irritate me by standing there!" He said to himself: "An obstinate fellow. . . Why, he's gone!" and his mind and eyes being occupied by the sentence he had last written, the sense of irritation remained with him. He re-read the closing clause: " . . . a single command—a measure which is here regarded by a great weight of instructed opinion as indispensable to the speedy and successful termination of hostilities. . ."

He looked at this, whistling beneath his breath. It was pretty thick. He was not asked for his opinion as to the single command: yet he decidedly wanted to get it in and was pretty well prepared to stand the consequences. The consequences might be something pretty bad: he might be sent home. That was quite possible. That, even, was better than what was happening to poor Puffles, who was being starved of men. He had been at Sandhurst with Puffles, and they had got their commissions on the same day to the same regiment. A damn good soldier, but too hot-tempered. He was making an extraordinarily good thing of it in spite of his shortage of men, which was the talk of the army. But it must be damn agonizing for him, and a very improper strain on his men. One day—as soon as the weather broke—the enemy *must* break through. Then he, Puffles, would be sent home. That was what the fellows at Westminster and in Downing Street wanted. Puffles had been a great deal too free with his tongue. They would not send him home before he had a disaster because, unless he were in disgrace, he would be a thorn in their sides: whereas if he were disgraced no one much would listen to him. It was smart practice. . . *Sharp* practice!

He tossed the sheet on which he had been writing across the table and said to Tietjens:

"Look at that, will you?" In the centre of the hut Tietjens was sitting bulkily on a bully-beef case that had been brought in ceremoniously by a runner. "He *does* look beastly shabby," the general said. "There are three. . . four grease stains on his tunic. He ought to get his hair cut!" He added: "It's a perfectly damnable business. No one but this fellow would have got into it. He's a firebrand. That's what he is. A regular firebrand!"

Tietjens' troubles had really shaken the general not a little. He was left up in the air. He had lived the greater part of his life with his sister, Lady Claudine Sandbach, and the greater part of the remainder of his life at Groby, at any rate after he came home from India and during the reign of Tietjens' father. He had idolized Tietjens' mother, who was a saint! What indeed there had been of the idyllic in his life had really all passed at Groby, if he came to think of it. India was not so bad, but one had to be young to enjoy that. . .

Indeed, only the day before yesterday he had been thinking that if this letter that he was thinking out did result in his being sent back, he should propose to stand for the half of the Cleveland

Parliamentary Division in which Groby stood. What with the Groby influence and his nephew's in the country districts, though Castlemaine had not much land left up there, and with Sandbach's interest in the ironworking districts, he would have an admirable chance of getting in. Then he would make himself a thorn in the side of certain persons.

He had thought of quartering himself on Groby. It would have been easy to get Tietjens out of the army and they could all—he, Tietjens and Sylvia—live together. It would have been his ideal of a home and of an occupation. . .

For, of course, he was getting old for soldiering: unless he got a fighting army there was not much more to it as a career for a man of sixty. If he *did* get an army he was pretty certain of a peerage and hefty political work could still be done in the Lords. He would have a good claim on India and that meant dying a Field-Marshal.

On the other hand, the only command that was at all likely to be going—except for deaths, and the health rate amongst army commanders was pretty high!—was poor Puffles'. And that would be no pleasant command—with men all hammered to pieces. He decided to put the whole thing to Tietjens. Tietjens, like a meal-sack, was looking at him over the draft of the letter that he had just finished reading. The general said:

"Well?"

Tietjens said:

"It's splendid, sir, to see you putting the matter so strongly. It must be put strongly, or we're lost."

The general said:

"You think that?"

Tietjens said:

"I'm sure of it, sir. . . But unless you are prepared to throw up your command and take to politics. . ."

The general exclaimed:

"You're a most extraordinary fellow. . . That was exactly what I was thinking about: this very minute."

"It's not so extraordinary," Tietjens said. "A really active general thinking as you do is very badly needed in the House. As your brother-in-law is to have a peerage whenever he asks for it, West Cleveland will be vacant at any moment, and with his influence and Lord Castlemaine's your nephew's not got much land, but the name is immensely respected in the country districts. . . And, of course, using Groby for your headquarters. . ."

The general said:

"That's pretty well botched, isn't it?"

Tietjens said without moving a muscle:

"Why, no, sir. Sylvia is to have Groby and you would naturally make it your headquarters. . . You've still got your hunters there. . ."

The general said:

"Sylvia is really to have Groby. . . Good God!"

Tietjens said:

"So it was no great conjuring trick, sir, to see that you might not mind. . ."

The general said:

"Upon my soul. I'd as soon give up my chance of heaven. . . no, not heaven, but India, as give up Groby."

"You've got," Tietjens said, "an admirable chance of India. . . The point is: which way? If they give you the sixteenth section. . ."

"I hate," the general said, "to think of waiting for poor Puffles' shoes. I was at Sandhurst with him. . ."

"It's a question, sir," Tietjens said, "of which is the best way. For the country and yourself. I suppose if one were a general one would like to have commanded an army on the Western front. . ."

The general said:

"I don't know. . . It's the logical end of a career. . . But I don't feel that my career is ending. . . I'm as sound as a roach. And in ten years' time what difference will it make?"

"One would like," Tietjens said, "to see you doing it. . ."

The general said:

"No one will know whether I commanded a fighting army or this damned Whiteley's outfitting store. . ."

Tietjens said:

"I know that, sir. . . But the sixteenth section will desperately need a good man if General Perry is sent home. And particularly a general who has the confidence of all ranks. . . It will be a wonderful position. You will have every man that's now on the Western front at your back after the war. It's a certain peerage. . . It's certainly a sounder proposition than that of a free-lance—which is what you'd be—in the House of Commons."

The general said:

"Then what am I to do with my letter? It's a damn good letter. I don't like wasting letters."

Tietjens said:

"You want it to show through that you back the single command for all you are worth, yet you don't want them to put their finger on your definitely saying so yourself?"

The general said:

" . . . That's it. That's just what I do want. . ." He added: "I suppose you take my view of the whole matter. The Government's pretence of evacuating the Western front in favour of the Middle East is probably only a put-up job to frighten our Allies into giving up the single command. Just as this railway strike is a counter-demonstration by way of showing what would happen to us if we did begin to evacuate. . ."

Tietjens said:

"It looks like that. . . I'm not, of course, in the confidence of the Cabinet. I'm not even in contact with them as I used to be. . . But I should put it that the section of the Cabinet that is in favour of the Eastern expedition is very small. It's said to be a one-man party—with hangerson—but arguing him out of it has caused all this delay. That's how I see it."

The general exclaimed:

"But, good God! . . . How is such a thing possible? That man must walk along his corridors with the blood of a million—I mean it, of a million—men round his head. He could not stand up under it. . . That fellow is prolonging the war indefinitely by delaying us now. And men being killed all the time! . . . I can't. . ." He stood up and paced, stamping up and down the hut. . . "At Bonderstrom," he said, "I had half a company wiped out under me. . . By my own fault, I admit. I had wrong information. . ." He stopped and said: "Good God! . . . Good God! . . . I can see it now. . . And it's unbearable! After eighteen years. I was a brigadier then. It was your own regiment—the Glamorganshires. . . They were crowded into a little nullah and shelled to extinction. . . I could see it going on and we could not get on to the Boer guns with ours to stop 'em. . . That's hell," he said, "that's the real hell. . . I never inspected the Glamorganshires after that for the whole war. I could not bear the thought of facing their eyes. . . Buller was the same. . . Buller was worse than I. . . He never held up his head again after. . ."

Tietjens said:

"If you would not mind, sir, not going on. . .

The general stamped to a halt in his stride. He said: "Eh? . . . What's that? What's the matter with you?"

Tietjens said:

"I had a man killed on me last night. In this very hut; where I'm sitting is the exact spot. It makes me. . . It's a sort of. . . Complex, they call it now. . ."

The general exclaimed:

"Good God! I beg your pardon, my dear boy. . . I ought not to have. . . I have never behaved like that before another soul in the world. . . Not to Buller. . . Not to Gatacre, and they were my closest friends. . . Even after Spion Kop I never. . ." He broke off and said: "I've such an absolute belief in your trustworthiness, I *know* you won't betray what you've seen. . . What I've just said. . ." He paused and tried to adopt the air of the listening magpie. He said: "I was called Butcher Campion in South Africa, just as Gatacre was called Backacher. I don't want to be called anything else because I've made an ass of myself before you. . . No, damn it all, not an ass. I was immensely attached to your sainted mother." He said: "It's the proudest tribute any commander of men can have. . . To be called Butcher and have your men follow you in spite of it. It shows confidence, and it gives you, as commander, confidence! . . . One has to be prepared to lose men in hundreds at the right minute in order to avoid losing them in tens of thousands at the wrong! . . ." He said: "Successful military operations consist not in taking or retaining positions, but in taking or retaining them with a minimum sacrifice of effectives. . . I wish to God you civilians would get that into your heads. The men have it. They know that I will use them ruthlessly—but that I will not waste one life. . ." He exclaimed: "Damn it, if I had ever thought I should have such troubles, in your father's days. . . !" He said: "Let's get back to what we were talking about. . . My memorandum to the Secretary. . ." He burst out: "My God! . . . *What* can that fellow think when he reads Shakespeare's *When all those heads, legs, arms, joined together on the Last Day shall. . .* How does it run? Henry V's address to his soldiers. . . *Every subject's body is the king's. . . but every subject's soul is his own. . . And there is no king, be his cause ever so just. . .* My God! My God! . . . *as can try it out with all unspotted soldiers. . .* Have you ever thought of that?"

Alarm overcame Tietjens. The general was certainly in disorder. But over what? There was not time to think. Campion was certainly dreadfully overworked. . . He exclaimed:

"Sir, hadn't you better? . . ." He said: "If we could get back to your memorandum. . . I am quite prepared to write a report to the effect of your sentence as to the French civilian population's attitude. That would throw the onus on me. . ."

The general said agitatedly:

"No! No! . . . You've got quite enough on your back as it is. Your confidential report states that you are suspected of having too great common interests with the French. That's what makes the whole position so impossible. . . I'll get Thurston to write something. He's a good man, Thurston. Reliable. . ." Tietjens shuddered a little. The general went on astonishingly:

"But at my back I always hear
Time's winged chariot hurrying near:
And yonder all before me lie
Deserts of vast eternity!" . . .

"That's a general's life in this accursed war. . . You think all generals are illiterate fools. But I have spent a great deal of time in reading, though I never read anything written later than the seventeenth century."

Tietjens said:

"I know, sir. . . You made me read Clarendon's *History of the Great Rebellion* when I was twelve."

The general said:

"In case we. . . I shouldn't like. . . In short. . ." He swallowed: it was singular to see him swallow. He was lamentably thin when you looked at the man and not the uniform.

Tietjens thought:

"What's he nervous about? He's been nervous all the morning."

The general said:

"I am trying to say—it's not much in my line—that in case we never met again, I do not wish you to think me an ignoramus."

Tietjens thought:

"He's not ill. . . and he can't think me so ill that I'm likely to die. . . A fellow like that doesn't really know how to express himself. He's trying to be kind and he doesn't know how to. . ."

The general had paused. He began to say:

"But there are finer things in Marvell than that. . ."

Tietjens thought:

"He's trying to gain time. . . Why on earth should he? . . . What is this all about?" His mind slipped a notch. The general was looking at his finger-nails on the blanket. He said:

"There's, for instance:

"The grave's a fine and secret place
But none I think do there embrace. . .

At those words it came to Tietjens suddenly to think of Sylvia, with the merest film of clothing on her long, shining limbs. . . She was working a powder-puff under her armpits in a brilliant illumination from two electric lights, one on each side of her dressing table. She was looking at him in the glass with the corners of her lips just moving. A little curled. . . He said to himself:

"One is going to that fine and secret place. . . Why not have?" She had emanated a perfume founded on sandalwood. As she worked her swansdown powder-puff over those intimate regions he could hear her humming. Maliciously! It was then that he had observed the handle of the door moving minutely. She had incredible arms, stretched out amongst a wilderness of besilvered cosmetics. Extraordinarily lascivious! Yet clean! Her gilded sheath gown was about her hips on the chair. . .

Well! she had pulled the strings of one too many shower-baths!

Shining; radiating glory but still shrivelled so that he reminded Tietjens of an old apple inside a damascened helmet; the general had seated himself once more on the bully-beef case before the blanketed table. He fingered his very large, golden fountain-pen. He said:

"Captain Tietjens, I should be glad of your careful attention!"

Tietjens said:

"Sir!" His heart stopped.

The general said that that afternoon Tietjens would receive a movement order. He said stiffly that he must not regard this new movement order as a disgrace. It was promotion. He, Major-General Campion, was requesting the colonel commanding the depot to inscribe the highest possible testimonial in his, Tietjens', small-book. He, Tietjens, had exhibited the most extraordinary talent for finding solutions for difficult problems—The colonel was to write that!—In addition he, General Campion, was requesting his friend, General Perry, commanding the sixteenth section. . .

Tietjens thought:

"Good God. I am being sent up the line. He's sending me to Perry's Army. . . That's certain death!"

. . . To give Tietjens the appointment of second in command of the VIth Battalion of his regiment!

Tietjens said, but he did not know where the words came from:

"Colonel Partridge will not like that. He's praying for McKechnie to come back!"

To himself he said:

"I shall fight this monstrous treatment of myself to my last breath."

The general suddenly called out:

"There you are. . . There is another of your infernal worries. . ."

He put a strong check on himself, and, dryly, like the very great speaking to the very unimportant, asked:

"What's your medical category."

Tietjens said:

"Permanent base, sir. My chest's rotten!"

The general said:

"I should forget that, if I were you. . . The second in command of a battalion has nothing to do but sit about in arm-chairs waiting for the colonel to be killed." He added: "It's the best I can do for you. . . I've thought it out very carefully. It's the best I can do for you."

Tietjens said:

"I shall, of course, forget my category, sir. . ."

Of course he would never fight any treatment of himself!

There it was then: the natural catastrophe! As when, under thunder, a dam breaks. His mind was battling with the waters. What would it pick out as the main terror? The mud: the noise: dread always at the back of the mind? Or the worry! The worry! Your eyebrows always had a slight tension on them. . . Like eye-strain!

The general had begun, soberly:

"You will recognize that there is nothing else that I can do."

His answering:

"I recognize, naturally, sir, that there is nothing else that you can do. . ." seemed rather to irritate the general. He wanted opposition: he *wanted* Tietjens to argue the matter. He was the Roman father counselling suicide to his son: but he wanted Tietjens to expostulate. So that he, General Campion, might absolutely prove that he, Tietjens, was a disgraceful individual. . . It could not be done. The general said:

"You will understand that I can't—no commander could!—have such things happening in my command. . ."

"I must accept that, if you say it, sir."

The general looked at him under his eyebrows. He said:

"I have already told you that this is promotion. I have been much impressed by the way you have handled this command. You are, of course, no soldier, but you will make an admirable officer for the militia, that is all that our troops now are. . ." He said: "I will emphasize what I am saying. . . No officer could—without being militarily in the wrong—have a private life that is as incomprehensible and embarrassing as yours. . ."

Tietjens said:

"He's hit it! . . ."

The general said:

"An officer's private life and his life on parade are as strategy to tactics. . . I don't want, if I can avoid it, to go into your private affairs. It's extremely embarrassing. . . But let me put it to you that. . . I wish to be delicate. But you are a man of the world! . . . Your wife is an extremely beautiful woman. . . There has been a scandal. . . I admit not of your making. . . But if, on the top of that, I appeared to show favouritism to you. . ."

Tietjens said:

"You need not go on, sir. . . I understand. . ." He tried to remember what the brooding and odious McKechnie had said. . . only two nights ago. . . He couldn't remember. . . It was certainly a suggestion that Sylvia was the general's mistress. It had then, he remembered, seemed fantastic. . . Well, what else *could* they think? He said to himself: "It absolutely blocks out my staying here!" He said aloud: "Of course, it's my own fault. If a man so handles his womenfolk that they get out of hand, he has only himself to blame."

The general was going on. He pointed out that one of his predecessors had lost that very command on account of scandals about women. He had turned the place into a damned harem! . . .

He burst out, looking at Tietjens with a peculiar goggle-eyed intentness:

"If you think I'd care about losing my command over Sylvia or any other damned Society woman. . ." He said: "I beg your pardon. . ." and continued reasonably:

"It's the men that have to be considered. They think—and they've every right to think it if they wish to—that a man who's a wrong 'un over women isn't the man they can trust their lives in the hands of. . ." He added: "And they're probably right. . . A man who's a real wrong 'un. . . I don't mean who sets up a gal in a tea-shop. . . But one who sells his wife, or. . . At any rate, in our army. . . The French may be different! . . . Well, a man like that usually has a yellow streak when it comes to fighting. . . Mind, I'm not saying always. . . Usually. . . There was a fellow called. . ."

He went off into an anecdote. . .

Tietjens recognized the pathos of his trying to get away from the agonizing present moment, back to an India where it was all real soldiering and good leather and parades that had been parades. But he did not feel called upon to follow. He could not follow. He was going up the line. . .

He occupied himself with his mind. What was it going to do? He cast back along his military history: what had his mind done in similar moments before? . . . But there had never been a similar moment! There had been the sinister or repulsive business of going up, getting over, standing to—even of the casualty clearing-station! . . . But he had always been physically keener, he had never been so depressed or overwhelmed.

He said to the general:

"I recognize that I cannot stop in this command. I regret it, for I have enjoyed having this unit. . . But does it necessarily mean the VIth Battalion?"

He wondered what was his own motive at the moment. Why had he asked the general that? . . . The thing presented itself as pictures: getting down bulkily from a high French train, at dawn. The light picked out for you the white of large hunks of bread—half-loaves— being handed out to troops themselves invisible. . . The ovals of light on the hats of English troops: they were mostly West Countrymen. They did not seem to want the bread much. . . A long ridge of light above a wooded bank: then suddenly, pervasively, a sound! . . . For all the world as, sheltering from rain in a cottager's wash-house on the moors, you hear the cottager's clothes boiling in a copper. . . Bubble. . . bubble. . . bubbubbub. . . bubble. . . Not terribly loud—but terribly demanding attention! . . . The Great Strafe! . . .

The general had said:

"If I could think of anything else to do with you, I'd do it. . . But all the extraordinary rows you've got into. . . They block me everywhere. . .

Do you realize that I have requested General O'Hara to suspend his functions until now? . . ."

It was amazing to Tietjens how the general mistrusted his subordinates—as well as how he trusted them! . . . It was probably that that made him so successful an officer. Be worked for by men that you trust: but distrust them all the time—along certain lines of frailty: liquor, women, money! . . . Well, he had a long knowledge of men!

He said:

"I admit, sir, that I misjudged General O'Hara. I have said as much to Colonel Levin and explained why."

The general said with a gloating irony:

"A damn pretty pass to come to. . . You put a general officer under arrest. . . Then you say you had misjudged him! . . . I am not saying you were not performing a duty. . ." He went on to recount the classical case of a subaltern, cited in King's Regulations, temp. William IV, who was court-martialled and broken for not putting under arrest his colonel who came drunk on to parade. . . He was exhibiting his sensuous delight in misplaced erudition.

Tietjens heard himself say with great slowness:

"I absolutely deny, sir, that I put General O'Hara under arrest! I have gone into the matter very minutely with Colonel Levin."

The general burst out:

"By God! I had taken that woman to be a saint. . . I swear she is a saint. . .

Tietjens said:

"There is no accusation against Mrs. Tietjens, sir!"

The general said:

"By God, there is!"

Tietjens said:

"I am prepared to take all the blame, sir."

The general said:

"You shan't. . . I am determined to get to the bottom of all this. . . You have treated your wife damn badly. . . You admit to that. . ."

Tietjens said:

"With great want of consideration, sir. . ."

The general said:

"You have been living practically on terms of separation from her for a number of years? You don't deny that that was on account of your own misbehaviour. For how many years?"

Tietjens said:

"I don't know, sir. . . Six or seven!"

The general said sharply:

"Think, then. . . It began when you admitted to me that you had been sold up because you kept a girl in a tobacco-shop? That was at Rye in 1912 . . ."

Tietjens said:

"We have not been on terms since 1912, sir."

The general said:

"But why? . . . She's a most beautiful woman. She's adorable. What could you want better? . . . She's the mother of your child. . ."

Tietjens said:

"Is it necessary to go into all this, sir? . . . Our differences were caused by. . . by differences of temperament. She, as you say, is a beautiful and reckless woman. . . Reckless in an admirable way. I, on the other hand. . ."

The general exclaimed:

"Yes! that's just it. . . What the hell are you? . . . You're not a soldier. You've got the makings of a damn good soldier. You amaze me at times. Yet you're a disaster; you are a disaster to every one who has to do with you. You are as conceited as a hog; you are as obstinate as a bullock. . . You drive me mad. . . And you have ruined the life of that beautiful woman. . . For I maintain she once had the disposition of a saint. . . Now: I'm waiting for your explanation!"

Tietjens said:

"In civilian life, sir, I was a statistician. Second secretary to the Department of Statistics. . ."

The general exclaimed convictingly:

"And they've thrown you out of that! Because of the mysterious rows you made. . ."

Tietjens said:

"Because, sir, I was in favour of the single command. . ."

The general began a long wrangle: "But why were you? What the hell had it got to do with you?" Couldn't Tietjens have given the Department the statistics they wanted—even if it meant faking them? What was discipline for if subordinates were to act on their consciences? The home Government had wanted statistics faked in order to dish the Allies. . . Well. . . Was Tietjens French or English? Every *damn* thing Tietjens did. . . Every damn thing, made it more impossible to do anything for him! With his attainments he ought to be attached to the staff of the French Commander-in-Chief. But that was forbidden in his, Tietjens', confidential report. There was an underlined note in it to that effect. Where else, then, in Heaven's name, could Tietjens be sent to? He looked at Tietjens with intent blue eyes:

"Where else, in God's name. . . I am not using the Almighty's name blasphemously. . . *can* you be sent to? I *know* it's probably death to send you up the line—in your condition of health. And to poor Perry's Army. The Germans will be through it the minute the weather breaks."

He began again: "You understand: I'm not the War Office. I can't send any officer anywhere. I can't send you to Malta or India. Or to other commands in France. I can send you home—in disgrace. I can send you to your own battalion. On promotion! . . . Do you understand my situation? . . . I have no alternative."

Tietjens said:

"Not altogether, sir."

The general swallowed and wavered from side to side. He said:

"For God's sake, try to. . . I am genuinely concerned for you. I won't—I'm damned if I will!—let it appear that you're disgraced. . . If you were McKechnie himself I wouldn't! The only really good jobs I've got to give away are on my own staff. I can't have you there. Because of the men. At the same time. . ."

He paused and said with a ponderous shyness:

"I believe there's a God. . . I believe that, though wrong may flourish, right will triumph in the end! . . . If a man is innocent, his innocence will one day appear. . . In a humble way I want to. . . help Providence. . . I want some one to be able one day to say: '*General Campion, who knew the ins and outs of the affair*. . .' promoted you! In the middle of it. . ." He said: "It isn't much. But it's not nepotism. I would do as much for any man in your position."

Tietjens said:

"It's at least the act of a Christian gentleman!"

A certain lack-lustre joy appeared in the general's eyes. He said:

"I'm not used to this sort of situation. . . I hope I've always tried to help my junior officers. . . But a case like this. . ." He said:

"Damn it. . . The general commanding the 9th French Army is an intimate friend of mine. . . But in face of your confidential report—I *can't* ask him to ask for you. That's blocked!"

Tietjens said:

"I do not propose, sir, at any rate in your eyes, to pass as putting the interests of any power before those of my own country. If you examine my confidential report you will find that the unfavourable insertions are initialled G. D. . . They are the initials of a Major Drake. . ."

The general said bewilderingly:

"Drake. . . Drake. . . I've heard the name."

Tietjens said:

"It doesn't matter, sir. . . Major Drake's a gentleman who doesn't like me. . ."

The general said:

"There are so many. You don't try to make yourself popular, I must say!"

Tietjens said to himself:

"The old fellow feels it! . . . But he can hardly expect me to tell him that Sylvia thinks Drake was the father of my own son, and desires my ruin!" But of course the old man *would* feel it. He, Tietjens, and his wife, Sylvia, were as near a son and daughter as the old man had. The obvious answer to make to the old man's query as to where he, Tietjens, ought to be sent was to remind him that his brother Mark had had an order put through to the effect that Tietjens was to be put in command of divisional transport. . . *Could* he remind the old man of that? Was it a thing one could do?

Yet the idea of commanding divisional transport was like a vision of Paradise to Tietjens. For two reasons: it was relatively safe, being concerned with a lot of horses. . . and the knowledge that he had that employment would put Valentine Wannop's mind at rest.

Paradise! . . . But could one wangle out of a hard into a soft job? Some other poor devil very likely wanted it. On the other hand—think of Valentine Wannop! He imagined her torture of mind, wandering about London, thinking of him in the very worst spot of a doomed army. She would get to hear of that. Sylvia would tell her! He would bet Sylvia would ring her up and tell her. Imagine, then, writing to Mark to say that he was with the transport! Mark would pass it on to the girl within half a minute. Why. . . he, Tietjens, would wire. He imagined himself scribbling the wire while the general talked and giving it to an orderly the moment the talk was over. . . But *could* he put the idea into the old man's head! Is it done? . . . Would, say. . . say, an Anglican saint do it?

And then. . . Was he up to the job? What about the accursed obsession of 0 Nine Morgan that intermittently jumped on him?

All the while he had been riding Schomburg the day before, 0 Nine Morgan had seemed to be just before the coffin-headed brute's off-shoulder. The animal must fall! . . . He had had the passionate impulse to pull up the horse. And all the time a dreadful depression! A weight! In the hotel last night he had nearly fainted over the thought that Morgan might have been the man whose life he had spared at Noircourt. . . It was getting to be a serious matter! It might mean that there was a crack in his, Tietjens', brain. A lesion! If that was to go on. . . . 0 Nine Morgan, dirty as he always was, and with the mystified eyes of the subject races on his face, rising up before his horse's off-shoulder! But alive, not with half his head cut away. . . If that was to go on he would not be fit to deal with transport, which meant a great deal of riding.

But he would chance that. . . Besides, some damn fool of a literary civilian had been writing passionate letters to the papers insisting that all horses and mules must be abolished in the army. . . Because of their pestilence-spreading dung! . . . It might be decreed by A.C.I. that no more horses were to be used! . . . Imagine taking battalion supplies down by night with motor lorries, which was what that genius desired to see done! . . .

He remembered once or twice—it must have been in September, '16—having had the job of taking battalion transport down from Locre to B.H.Q., which were in the château of Kemmell village. . . You muffled every bit of metal you could think of: bits, trace-chains, axles. . . and yet, whilst you hardly breathed, in the thick darkness some damn thing would always chink and jolt; beef tins made a noise of old iron. . . And *bang*, after a long whine, would come the German shell, registered exactly on to the corner of the road where it went down by the shoulder of the hill: where the placards were ordering you not to go more than two men together. . . Imagine doing it with lorries, that could be heard five miles away! . . . The battalion would go pretty short of rations! . . . The same antichevaline genius had emitted the sentiment that he had rather the Allies lost the war than that cavalry should distinguish themselves in any engagement! . . . A wonderful passion for the extermination of dung. . . ! Or perhaps this hatred of the horse was social. . . Because the cavalry wear long moustaches dripping with Macassar oil and breakfast off caviare, chocolate and Pommery Greno they must be abolished! . . . Something like that. . . He exclaimed: "By God! How my mind wanders! How long will it go on?" He said: "I am at the end of my tether." He had missed what the general had said for some time.

The general said:

"Well. Has he?"

Tietjens said:

"I didn't catch, sir!"

"Are you deaf?" the general asked. "I'm sure I speak plain enough. You've just said there are no horses attached to this camp. I asked you if there is not a horse for the colonel commanding the depot. . . A German horse, I understand!"

Tietjens said to himself:

"Great heavens! I've been talking to him. What in the world about?" It was as if his mind were falling off a hillside. He said:

"Yes, sir. . . Schomburg. But as that's a German prisoner, captured on the Marne, it is not on our strength. It is the private property of the colonel. I ride it myself. . ."

The general exclaimed dryly:

"You *would*. . ." He added more dryly still: "Are you aware that there is a hell of a strafe put in against you by a R.A.S.C. second-lieutenant called Hotchkiss? . . ."

Tietjens said quickly:

"If it's over Schomburg, sir. . . it's a washout. Lieutenant Hotchkiss has no more right to give orders about him than as to where I shall sleep. . . And I would rather die than subject any horse for which I am responsible to the damnable torture Hotchkiss and that swine Lord Beichan want to inflict on service horses. . ."

The general said maleficently:

"It looks as if you damn well will die on that account!"

He added: "You're perfectly right to object to wrong treatment of horses. But in this case your objection blocks the only other job open to you." He quietened himself a little. "You are probably not aware," he went on, "that your brother Mark. . ."

Tietjens said:

"Yes, I am aware. . ."

The general said: "Do you know that the 19th Division to which your brother wants you sent is attached to Fourth Army now—and it's Fourth Army horses that Hotchkiss is to play with? . . . How could I send you there to be under his orders?"

Tietjens said:

"That's perfectly correct, sir. There is nothing else that you can do. . ." He was finished. There was now nothing left but to find out how his mind was going to take it. He wished they could go to his cook-houses!

The general said:

"What was I saying? . . . I'm dreadfully tired. . . No one could stand this. . ." He drew from inside his tunic a lapis-lazuli coloured, small be-coroneted note-case and selected from it a folded paper that he first looked at and then slipped between his belt and his tunic. He said: "On top of all the responsibility I have to bear!" He asked: "Has it occurred to you that, if I'm of any service to the country, your taking up my energy—*sapping* my energy over your affairs!—is aiding your country's enemies? . . . I can only afford four hours sleep as it is. . . I've got some questions to ask you. . . He referred to the slip of paper from his belt, folded it again and again slipped it into his belt.

Tietjens' mind missed a notch again. . . It *was* the fear of the mud that was going to obsess him. Yet, curiously, he had never been under heavy fire in mud. . . You would think that that would not have obsessed him. But in his ear he had just heard uttered in a whisper of intense weariness, the words: *Es ist nicht zu ertragen; es ist das dasz uns verloren hat*. . . words in German, of utter despair, meaning: It is unbearable: it is that that has ruined us. . . The mud! . . . He had heard those words, standing amidst volcano craters of mud, amongst ravines, monstrosities of slime, cliffs and distances, all of slime. . . He had been going, for curiosity or instruction, from Verdun where he had been attached to the French—on a holiday afternoon when nothing was doing, with a guide, to visit one of the outlying forts. . . Deaumont? . . . No, Douaumont. . . Taken from the enemy about a week before. . . When would that be? He had lost all sense of chronology. . . In November. . . A beginning of some November. . . With a miracle of sunshine: not a cloud: the mud towering up shut you in intimately with a sky that ached for limpidity. . . And the slime had moved. . . following a French bombardier who was strolling along eating nuts, disreputably, his shoulders rolling. . . *Déserteurs*. . . The moving slime was German deserters. . . You could not see them: the leader of them—an officer!—had his glasses so thick with mud that you could not see the colour of his eyes, and his half-dozen decorations were like the beginnings of swallows' nests, his beard like stalactites. . . Of the other men you could only see the eyes—extraordinarily vivid: mostly blue like the sky! . . . Deserters! Led by an officer! Of the

Hamburg Regiment! As if an officer of the Buffs had gone over! . . . It was incredible. . . And that was what the officer had said as he passed: not shamefacedly, but without any humanity left in him. . . *Done!* . . . Those moving saurians compacted of slime kept on passing him afterwards, all the afternoon. . . And he could not help picturing their immediate antecedents for two months. . . In advanced pill-boxes. . . No, they didn't have pill-boxes then. . . In advanced pockets of mud, in dreadful solitude amongst those ravines. . . suspended in eternity, at the last day of the world. And it had horribly shocked him to hear again the German language, a rather soft voice, a little suety. . . Like an obscene whisper. . . The voice obviously of the damned: hell could hold nothing curious for those poor beasts. . . His French guide had said sardonically: *On dirait l'Inferno de Dante*! . . . Well, those Germans were getting back on him. They were now to become an obsession! A complex, they said nowadays. . . The general said coolly:

"I presume you refuse to answer?"

That shook him cruelly.

He said desperately:

"I had to end what I took to be an unbearable position for both parties. In the interests of my son!" Why in the world had he said that? . . . He was going to be sick. It came back to him that the general had been talking of his separation from Sylvia. Last night that had happened. He said: "I may have been right: I may have been wrong. . ."

The general said icily:

"If you don't choose to go into it. . ."

Tietjens said:

"I would prefer not to. . ."

The general said:

"There is no end to this. . . But there are questions it's my duty to ask. . . If you do not wish to go into your marital relations, I cannot force you. . . But, damn it, are you sane? Are you responsible? Do you intend to get Miss Wannop to live with you before the war is over? Is she, perhaps, here, in the town, now? Is that your reason for separating from Sylvia? Now, of all times in the world!"

Tietjens said:

"No, sir. I ask you to believe that I have absolutely no relations with that young lady. None! I have no intention of having any. None! . . ."

The general said:

"I believe that!"

"Circumstances last night," Tietjens said, "convinced me suddenly, there on the spot, that I had been wronging my wife. . . I had been putting a strain on the lady that was unwarrantable. It humiliates me to have to say it! I had taken a certain course for the sake of the future of our child. But it was an atrociously wrong course. We ought to have separated years ago. It has led to the lady's pulling the strings of all these shower-baths. . ."

The general said:

"Pulling the. . ."

Tietjens said:

"It expresses it, sir. . . Last night was nothing but pulling the string of a shower-bath. Perfectly justifiable. I maintain that it was perfectly justifiable."

The general said:

"Then why have you given her Groby? . . . You're not a little soft, are you? . . . You don't imagine you've. . . say, got a mission? Or that you're another person? . . . That you have to. . . to forgive. . ." He took off his pretty hat and wiped his forehead with a tiny cambric handkerchief. He said: "Your poor mother was a little. . ."

He said suddenly:

"Tonight when you are coming to my dinner. . . I hope you'll be decent. Why do you so neglect your personal appearance? Your tunic is a disgusting spectacle. . ."

Tietjens said:

"I had a better tunic, sir. . . but it has been ruined by the blood of the man who was killed here last night. . ."

The general said:

"You don't say you have only two tunics? . . . Have you no mess clothes?"

Tietjens said:

"Yes, sir, I've my blue things. I shall be all right for tonight. . . But almost everything else I possessed was stolen from my kit when I was in hospital. . . Even Sylvia's two pair of sheets. . ."

"But hang it all," the general exclaimed, "you don't mean to say you've spaflled all your father left you?"

Tietjens said:

"I thought fit to refuse what my father left me owing to the way it was left. . ."

The general said:

"But, good God! . . . Read that!" He tossed the small sheet of paper at which he had been looking across the table. It fell face downwards. Tietjens read, in the minute handwriting of the general's:

"Colonel's horse: Sheets: Jesus Christ: Wannop girl: Socialism?"

The general said irritably:

"The other side. . . the other side. . ."

The other side of the paper displayed the words in large capitals: WORKERS OF THE WORLD, a wood-cut of a sickle and some other objects. Then high treason for a page.

The general said:

"Have you ever seen anything like that before? Do you know what it is?"

Tietjens answered:

"Yes, sir. I sent that to you. To your Intelligence. . ." The general thumped both his fists violently on the army blanket:

"You. . ." he said. "It's incomprehensible. . . It's incredible. . ."

Tietjens said:

"No, sir. . . You sent out an order asking commanders of units to ascertain what attempts were being made by Socialists to undermine the discipline of their other ranks. . . I naturally asked my sergeant-major, and he produced this sheet, which one of the men had given to him as a curiosity. It had been handed to the man in the street in London. You can see my initials on the top of the sheet!"

The general said:

"You. . . you'll excuse me, but you're not a Socialist yourself?"

Tietjens said:

"I knew you were working round to that, sir. But I've no politics that did not disappear in the eighteenth century. You, sir, prefer the seventeenth!"

"Another shower-bath, I suppose," the general said.

"Of course," Tietjens said, "if it's Sylvia that called me a Socialist, it's not astonishing. I'm a Tory of such an extinct type that she might take me for anything. The last megatherium. She's absolutely to be excused. . ."

The general was not listening. He said:

"What was wrong with the way your father left his money to you?"

"My father," Tietjens said—the general saw his jaw stiffen— "committed suicide because a fellow called Ruggles told him that I was. . . what the French called *maquereau*. . . I can't think of the

English word. My father's suicide was not an act that can be condoned. A gentleman does not commit suicide when he has descendants. It might influence my boy's life very disastrously. . ."

The general said:

"I can't. . . I *can't* get to the bottom of all this. . . What in the world did Ruggles want to go and tell your father that for? . . . What are you going to do for a living after the war? They won't take you back into your office, will they?"

Tietjens said:

"No, sir. The Department will not take me back. Every one who has served in this war will be a marked man for a long time after it is over. That's proper enough. *We're* having our fun now."

The general said:

"You say the wildest things."

Tietjens answered:

"You generally find the things I say come true, sir. Could we get this over? Ruggles told my father what he did because it is not a good thing to belong to the seventeenth or eighteenth centuries in the twentieth. Or really, because it is not good to have taken one's public-school's ethical system seriously. I am really, sir, the English public schoolboy. That's an eighteenth-century product. What with the love of truth that—God help me!—they rammed into me at Clifton and the belief Arnold forced upon Rugby that the vilest of sins—the vilest of all sins—is to peach to the head master! That's me, sir. Other men get over their schooling. I never have. I remain adolescent. These things are obsessions with me. Complexes, sir!"

The general said:

"All this seems to be very wild. . . What's this about peaching to a head master?"

Tietjens said:

"For a swan song, it's not wild, sir. You're asking for a swan song. I am to go up into the line so that the morals of the troops in your command may not be contaminated by the contemplation of my marital infelicities."

The general said:

"You don't want to go back to England, do you?" Tietjens exclaimed:

"Certainly not! Very certainly not! I can never go home. I have to go underground somewhere. If I went back to England there would be nothing for me but going underground by suicide."

The general said:

"You see all that? I can give you testimonials. . ."

Tietjens asked:

"Who couldn't see that it's impossible?"

The general said:

"But. . . suicide! You won't do that. As you said: think of your son."

Tietjens said:

"No, sir. I shan't do that. But you see how bad for one's descendants suicide is. That is why I do not forgive my father. Before he did it I should never have contemplated the idea. Now I have contemplated it. That's a weakening of the moral fibre. It's contemplating a fallacy as a possibility. For suicide is no remedy for a twisted situation of a psychological kind. It is for bankruptcy. Or for military disaster. For the man of action, not for the thinker. Creditors' meetings wipe the one out. Military operations sweep on. But my problem will remain the same whether I'm here or not. For it's insoluble. It's the whole problem of the relations of the sexes."

The general said:

"Good God! . . ."

Tietjens said:

"No, sir, I've not gone off my chump. That's my problem! . . . But I'm a fool to talk so much. . . It's because I don't know what to say."

The general sat staring at the tablecloth: his face was suffused with blood. He had the appearance of a man in monstrous ill-humour. He said:

"You had better say what you want to say. What the devil do you mean? . . . What's this all about? . . ."

Tietjens said:

"I'm enormously sorry, sir. It's difficult to make myself plain."

The general said:

"Neither of us do. What is language for? What the *hell* is language for? We go round and round. I suppose I'm an old fool who cannot understand your modern ways. . . But you're not modern. I'll do you *that* justice. . . That beastly little McKechnie is modern. . . I shall ram him into your divisional-transport job, so that he won't incommode you in your battalion. . . Do you understand what the little beast did? He got leave to go and get a divorce. And then did not get a divorce. *That's* modernism. He said he had scruples. I understand that he and his wife and. . . some dirty other fellow. . . slept three in a bed. That's modern scruples. . ."

Tietjens said:

"No sir, it's not really. . . But what is a man to do if his wife is unfaithful to him?"

The general said as if it were an insult:

"Divorce the harlot! Or live with her! . . ." Only a beast he went on, would expect a woman to live all her life alone in a cockloft! She's bound to die. Or go on the streets. . . What sort of a fellow wouldn't see that? Was there any sort of beast who'd expect a woman to live. . . with a man beside her. . . Why, she'd. . . she'd be bound to. . . He'd have to take the consequences of whatever happened. The general repeated: "Whatever happened! If she pulled all the strings of all the shower-baths in the world!"

Tietjens said:

"Still, sir. . . there are. . . there used to be. . . in families of. . . position. . . a certain. . ." He stopped.

The general said:

"Well. . ."

Tietjens said:

"On the part of the man. . . a certain. . . Call it. . . parade!"

The general said:

"Then there had better be no more parades. . ." He said: "Damn it! . . . Besides us, all women are saints. . . Think of what child-bearing is. I know the world. . . Who would stand that? . . . You? . . . I. . . I'd rather be the last poor devil in Perry' lines!"

He looked at Tietjens with a sort of injurious cunning: "Why *don't* you divorce?" he asked.

Panic came over Tietjens. He knew it would be his last panic of that interview. No brain could stand more. Fragments of scenes of fighting, voices, names, went before his eyes and ears. Elaborate problems. . . The whole map of the embattled world ran out in front of him—as large as a field. An embossed map in greenish *papier mâché*—a ten-acre field of embossed *papier mâché*: with the blood of O Nine Morgan blurring luminously over it. Years before. . . How many months? . . . Nineteen, to be exact, he had sat on some tobacco plants on the Mont de Kats. . . No, the Montagne Noire. In Belgium. . . What had he been doing? . . . Trying to get the lie of the land. . . No. . . Waiting to point out positions to some fat home general who had never come. The Belgian proprietor of the tobacco plants had arrived, and had screamed his head off over the damaged plants. . .

But, up there you saw the whole war. . . Infinite miles away, over the sullied land that the enemy forces held: into Germany proper. Presumably you could breathe in Germany proper. . . Over your right shoulder you could see a stump of a tooth. The Cloth Hall at Ypres: at an angle of 50° below. . . Dark lines behind it. . . The German trenches before Wytschaete!

That was before the great mines had blown Wytschaete to hell. . .

But—every half-minute by his wrist-watch—white puffs of cotton-wool existed on the dark lines—the German trenches before Wytschaete. Our artillery practice. . . Good shooting. Jolly good shooting!

Miles and miles away to the left. . . beneath the haze of light that, on a clouded day, the sea threw off, a shaft of sunlight fell, and was reflected in a grey blue. . . It was the glass roofs of a great airplane shelter!

A great plane, the largest he had then seen, was moving over, behind his back, with four little planes as an escort. . . Over the vast slag-heaps by Bethune. . . High, purplish-blue heaps, like the steam domes of engines or the breasts of women. . . Bluish purple. More blue than purple. . . Like all Franco-Belgian Gobelins tapestry. . . And all quiet. . . Under the vast pall of quiet cloud! . . .

There were shells dropping in Poperinghe. . . Five miles out, under his nose. . . The shells dropped. White vapour rose and ran away in plumes. . . What sort of shells? . . . There were twenty different kinds of shells. . .

The Huns were shelling Poperinghe! A senseless cruelty. It was five miles behind the lines! Prussian brutality. . . There were two girls who kept a tea-shop in Poperinghe. . . High coloured. . . General Plumer had liked them. . . a fine old general. . . The shells had killed them both. . . Any man might have slept with either of them with pleasure and profit. . . Six thousand of H.M. officers must have thought the same about those high-coloured girls. Good girls! . . . But the Hun shells got them. . . What sort of fate was that? . . . To be desired by six thousand men and smashed into little gobbets of flesh by Hun shells?

It appeared to be mere Prussianism—the senseless cruelty of the Hun!—to shell Poperinghe. An innocent town with a tea-shop five miles behind Ypres. . . Little noiseless plumes of smoke rising under the quiet blanketing of the pale maroon skies, with the haze from the aeroplane shelters, and the great aeroplanes over the Bethune slag-heaps. . . What a dreadful name—Bethune. . .

Probably, however, the Germans had heard that we were massing men in Poperinghe. It was reasonable to shell a town where men were being assembled. . . Or we might have been shelling one of their towns with an Army H.Q. in it. So they shelled Poperinghe in the silent grey day. . . That was according to the rules of the service. . . General Campion, accepting with equanimity what German airplanes did to the hospitals, camps, stables, brothels, theatres, boulevards, chocolate stalls and hotels of his town, would have been vastly outraged if Hun planes had dropped bombs on his private lodgings. . . The rules of war! . . . You spare, mutually, each other's headquarters and blow to pieces girls that are desired by six thousand men apiece. . .

That had been nineteen months before! . . . Now, having lost so much emotion, he saw the embattled world as a map. . . An embossed map of greenish *papier mâché*. The blood of 0 Nine Morgan was blurring luminously over it. At the extreme horizon was territory labelled *White Ruthenians*! Who the devil were those poor wretches?

He exclaimed to himself: "By heavens! Is this epilepsy?" He prayed: "Blessed saints, get me spared that!" He exclaimed: "No, it isn't! . . . I've complete control of my mind. My uppermost mind." He said to the general:

"I can't divorce, sir. I've no grounds."

The general said:

"Don't lie. You know what Thurston knows. Do you mean that you have been guilty of contributory misconduct? . . . Whatever it is? And can't divorce! I don't believe it."

Tietjens said to himself:

"Why the devil am I so anxious to shield the whore? It's not reasonable. It is an obsession!"

White Ruthenians are miserable people to the south of Lithuania. You don't know whether they incline to the Germans or to the Poles. The Germans don't even know. . . The Germans were beginning to take their people out of the line where we were weak: they were going to give them proper infantry training. That gave him, Tietjens, a chance. They would not come over strong for at least two months. It meant, though, a great offensive in the spring. Those fellows had sense. In the poor, beastly trenches the Tommies knew nothing but how to chuck bombs. Both sides did that. But the Germans were going to cure it! Stood chucking bombs at each other from forty yards. The rifle was obsolete! Ha! ha! Obsolete! . . . The civilian psychology!

The general said:

"No, I don't believe it. I knew you did not keep any girl in any tobacco-shop. I remember every word you said at Rye in 1912. I wasn't sure then. I am now. You tried to let me think it. You had shut up your house because of your wife's misbehaviour. You let me believe you had been sold up. You weren't sold up at all."

. . . *Why* should it be the civilian psychology to chuckle with delight, uproariously, when the imbecile idea was promulgated that the rifle was obsolete? *Why* should public opinion force on the War Office a training-camp course that completely cut out any thorough instruction in the rifle and communication drill? It was queer. . . It was of course disastrous. Queer. Not altogether mean. Pathetic, too. . .

"Love of truth!" the general said. "Doesn't that include a hatred for white lies? No; I suppose it doesn't, or your servants could not say you were not at home. . ."

. . . Pathetic! Tietjens said to himself. Naturally the civilian population wanted soldiers to be made to look like fools: and to be done in. They wanted the war won by men who would at the end be either humiliated or dead. Or both. Except, naturally, their own cousins or fiancées' relatives. That was what it came to. That was what it meant when important gentlemen said that they had rather the war were lost than that cavalry should gain any distinction in it! . . . But it was partly the simple, pathetic illusion of the day that great things could only be done by new inventions. You extinguished the Horse, invented something very simple and became God! That is the real pathetic fallacy. You fill a flower-pot with gunpowder and chuck it in the other fellow's face, and heigh presto! the war is won. All the soldiers fall down dead! And You: you who forced the idea on the reluctant military, are the Man that Won the War. You deserve all the women in the world. And. . . you get them! Once the cavalry are out of the way! . . .

The general was using the words:

"Head master!" It brought Tietjens completely back. He said collectedly:

"Really, sir, why this strafe of yours is so terribly long is that it embraces the whole of life."

The general said:

"You're not going to drag a red herring across the trail. . . I say you regarded me as a head master in 1912. Now I am your commanding officer—which is the same thing. You must not peach to me. That's what you call the Arnold of Rugby touch. . . But who was it said: *Magna est veritas et prev. . . Prev* something!"

Tietjens said:

"I don't remember, sir."

The general said:

"What was the secret grief your mother had? In 1912? She died of it. She wrote to me just before her death and said she had great troubles. And begged me to look after you, very specially! Why did she do that?" He paused and meditated. He asked: "How do you define Anglican sainthood? The other fellows have canonizations, all shipshape like Sandhurst examinations. But us Anglicans. . . I've heard fifty persons say your mother was a saint. She was. But why?"

Tietjens said:

"It's the quality of harmony, sir. The quality of being in harmony with your own soul. God having given you your own soul you are then in harmony with heaven."

The general said:

"Ah, that's beyond me. . . I suppose you will refuse any money I leave you in my will?"

Tietjens said:

"Why, no, sir."

The general said:

"But you refused your father's money. Because he believed things against you. What's the difference?"

Tietjens said:

"One's friends ought to believe that one is a gentleman. Automatically. That is what makes one and them in harmony. Probably your friends are your friends because they look at situations automatically as you look at them. . . Mr. Ruggles knew that I was hard up. He envisaged the situation. If he were hard up, what would he do? Make a living out of the immoral earnings of women. . . That translated into the Government circles in which he lives means selling your wife or mistress. Naturally he believed that I was the sort of fellow to sell my wife. So that's what he told my father. The point is, my father should not have believed him."

"But I. . ." the general said.

Tietjens said:

"You never believed anything against me, sir."

The general said:

"I know I've damn well worried myself to death over you. . ."

Tietjens was sentimental at rest, still with wet eyes. He was walking near Salisbury in a grove, regarding long pastures and ploughlands running to dark, high elms from which, embowered. . . Embowered was the word!—peeped the spire of George Herbert's church. . . One ought to be a seventeenth-century parson at the time of the renaissance of Anglican saintliness. . . who wrote, perhaps poems. No, not poems. Prose. The statelier vehicle!

That was home-sickness! . . . He himself was never to go home!

The general said:

"Look here. . . Your father. . . I'm concerned about your father. . . Didn't Sylvia perhaps tell him some of the things that distressed him?"

Tietjens said distinctly:

"No, sir. That responsibility cannot be put on to Sylvia. My father chose to believe things that were said against me by a perfect—or a nearly perfect—stranger. . ." He added: "As a matter of fact, Sylvia and my father were not on any sort of terms. I don't believe they exchanged two words for the last five years of my father's life."

The general's eyes were fixed with an extreme hardness on Tietjens'. He watched Tietjens' face, beginning with the edges round the nostrils, go chalk white. He said: "He knows he's given his wife away! . . . Good God!" With his face colourless, Tietjens' eyes of porcelain-blue stuck out extraordinarily. The general thought: "What an ugly fellow! His face is all crooked!" They remained looking at each other.

In the silence the voices of men talking over the game of House came as a murmur to them. A rudimentary card game monstrously in favour of the dealer. When you heard voices going on like that you knew they were playing House. . . So they had had their dinners.

The general said:

"It isn't Sunday, is it?"

Tietjens said:

"No, sir; Thursday, the seventeenth, I think, of January. . ."

The general said:

"Stupid of me. . ."

The men's voices had reminded him of church bells on a Sunday. And of his youth. . . He was sitting beside Mrs. Tietjens' hammock under the great cedar at the corner of the stone house at Groby. The wind being from the east-north-east the bells of Middlesbrough came to them faintly. Mrs. Tietjens was thirty; he himself thirty; Tietjens—the father—thirty-five or so. A most powerful quiet man. A wonderful landowner. Like his predecessor for generations. It was not from him that this fellow got his. . . his. . . his what? . . . Was it mysticism? . . . Another word! He himself home on leave from India: his head full of polo. Talking for hours about points in ponies with Tietjens' father, who was a wonderful hand with a horse.

But this fellow was much more wonderful! . . . Well, he got that from the sire, not the dam! . . . He and Tietjens continued to look at each other. It was as if they were hypnotized. The men's voices went on in a mournful cadence. The general supposed that he too must be pale. He said to himself: "This fellow's mother died of a broken heart in 1912. The father committed suicide five years after. He had not spoken to the son's wife for four or five years! That takes us back to 1912 . . . Then, when I strafed him in Rye, the wife was in France with Perowne."

He looked down at the blanket on the table. He intended again to look up at Tietjens' eyes with ostentatious care. That was his technique with men. He was a successful general because he knew men. He knew that all men will go to hell over three things: alcohol, money. . . and sex.

This fellow apparently hadn't. Better for him if he had! He thought: "It's all gone. . . mother! father! Groby! This fellow's down and out. It's a bit thick."

He thought:

"But he's right to do as he is doing."

He prepared to look at Tietjens. . . He stretched out a sudden, ineffectual hand. Sitting on his beef-case, his hands on his knees, Tietjens had lurched. A sudden lurch—as an old house lurches when it is hit by a H.E. shell. It stopped at that. Then he righted himself. He continued to stare direct at the general. The general looked carefully back. He said—very carefully too:

"In case I decide to contest West Cleveland, it is your wish that I should make Groby my headquarters?"

Tietjens said:

"I beg, sir, that you will!"

It was as if they both heaved an enormous sigh of relief. The general said:

"Then I need not keep you. . ."

Tietjens stood on his feet, wanly, but with his heels together.

The general also rose, settling his belt. He said:

" . . . You can fall out."

Tietjens said:

"My cook-houses, sir. . . Sergeant-Cook Case will be very disappointed. . . He told me that you couldn't find anything wrong if I gave him ten minutes to prepare. . ."

The general said:

"Case. . . Case. . . Case was in the drums when we were at Delhi. He ought to be at least Quartermaster by now. . . But he had a woman he called his sister. . ."

Tietjens said:

"He still sends money to his sister."

The general said:

" . . . He went absent over her when he was colour-sergeant and was reduced to the ranks. . . Twenty years ago that must be! . . . Yes, I'll see your dinners!"

In the cook-houses, brilliantly accompanied by Colonel Levin, the cook-house spotless with limed walls and mirrors that were the tops of camp-cookers, the general, Tietjens at his side, walked between goggle-eyed men in white who stood to attention holding ladles. Their eyes bulged, but the corners of their lips curved because they liked the general and his beautifully unconcerned companions. The cook-house was like a cathedral's nave, aisles being divided off by the pipes of stoves. The floor was of coke-brize shining under french polish and turpentine.

The building paused, as when a godhead descends. In breathless focusing of eyes the godhead, frail and shining, walked with short steps up to a high-priest who had a walrus moustache and, with seven medals on his Sunday tunic, gazed away into eternity. The general tapped the sergeant's Good Conduct ribbon with the heel of his crop. All stretched ears heard him say:

"How's your sister, Case? . . ."

Gazing away, the sergeant said:

"I'm thinking of making her Mrs. Case. . ."

Slightly leaving him, in the direction of high, varnished pitch-pine panels, the general said:

"I'll recommend you for a Quartermaster's commission any day you wish. . . Do you remember Sir Garnet inspecting field kitchens at Quetta?"

All the white tubular beings with global eyes resembled the pierrots of a child's Christmas nightmare. The general said: "Stand at ease, men. . . Stand easy!" They moved as white objects move in a childish dream. It was all childish. Their eyes rolled.

Sergeant Case gazed away into infinite distance.

"My sister would not like it, sir," he said. "I'm better off as a first-class warrant officer!"

With his light step the shining general went swiftly to the varnished panels in the eastern aisle of the cathedral. The white figure beside them became instantly tubular, motionless and global-eyed. On the panels were painted: Tea! Sugar! Salt! Curry Pdr! Flour! Pepper!

The general tapped with the heel of his crop on the locker-panel labelled Pepper: the top, right-hand locker-panel. He said to the tubular, global-eyed white figure beside it: "Open that, will you, my man? . . ."

To Tietjens this was like the sudden bursting out of the regimental quick-step, as after a funeral with military honours the band and drums march away, back to barracks.

THE END

A Note About the Author

Ford Madox Ford (1873–1939) was an English novelist, poet, and editor. Born in Wimbledon, Ford was the son of Pre-Raphaelite artist Catherine Madox Brown and music critic Francis Hueffer. In 1894, he eloped with his girlfriend Elsie Martindale and eventually settled in Winchelsea, where they lived near Henry James and H. G. Wells. Ford left his wife and two daughters in 1909 for writer Isobel Violet Hunt, with whom he launched *The English Review*, an influential magazine that published such writers as Thomas Hardy, Joseph Conrad, Ezra Pound, and D. H. Lawrence. As Ford Madox Hueffer, he established himself with such novels as *The Inheritors* (1901) and *Romance* (1903), cowritten with Joseph Conrad, and *The Fifth Queen* (1906–1907), a trilogy of historical novels. During the Great War, however, he began using the penname Ford Madox Ford to avoid anti-German sentiment. *The Good Soldier* (1915), considered by many to be Ford's masterpiece, earned him a reputation as a leading novelist of his generation and continues to be named among the greatest novels of the twentieth century. Recognized as a pioneering modernist for his poem "Antwerp" (1915) and his tetralogy *Parade's End* (1924–1928), Ford was a friend of James Joyce, Ernest Hemingway, Gertrude Stein, and Jean Rhys. Despite his reputation and influence as an artist and publisher who promoted the early work of some of the greatest English and American writers of his time, Ford has been largely overshadowed by his contemporaries, some of whom took to disparaging him as their own reputations took flight.

A Note from the Publisher

Spanning many genres, from non-fiction essays to literature classics to children's books and lyric poetry, Mint Edition books showcase the master works of our time in a modern new package. The text is freshly typeset, is clean and easy to read, and features a new note about the author in each volume. Many books also include exclusive new introductory material. Every book boasts a striking new cover, which makes it as appropriate for collecting as it is for gift giving. Mint Edition books are only printed when a reader orders them, so natural resources are not wasted. We're proud that our books are never manufactured in excess and exist only in the exact quantity they need to be read and enjoyed. To learn more and view our library, go to minteditionbooks.com

bookfinity & 📖 MINT EDITIONS

Enjoy more of your favorite classics with Bookfinity,
a new search and discovery experience for readers.
With Bookfinity, you can discover more vintage
literature for your collection, find your Reader Type,
track books you've read or want to read,
and add reviews to your favorite books.
Visit www.bookfinity.com, and click on
Take the Quiz to get started.

Don't forget to follow us
@bookfinityofficial and @mint_editions